MURDER Pays a Call

NANCY J. COHEN

OGP
ORANGE
GROVE
PRESS

Chapter One

Keri hurried from the parking lot toward her downtown office in Sunny Grove, Florida. A quick glance at her watch told her she was already late for her phone appointment with Fiona Sullivan. She didn't like to keep clients waiting, especially not one of her top influencers. Fiona could make or break her business with one scathing remark.

Not that Fiona would ever sink her reputation. She made regular referrals to Keri's personal concierge agency and had been directly responsible for adding the city's elite to her customer list. Fiona was more than a valued customer, though. She was also a mentor and a dear friend.

Keri turned the corner onto Broad Street across from Central Park and took a breath of cool, November air. The sidewalk was just as crowded as her busy schedule. Tourists vied with locals for space during the pre-holiday crush. Located just north of Orlando, the historic town was a popular destination at any time of year.

She dodged a couple of women pushing strollers and a guy who was reading a newspaper without looking ahead. At the corner, a woman using a walker struggled to get into the chocolate shop. Keri rushed over to hold the door open for her.

Just a little further along, she reached her office. Stepping inside always gave her a swell of pride. She'd converted the place from a travel agency two years ago. Four desks, two of them currently occupied, faced the storefront windows. File cabinets and bookshelves lined the walls. It looked utilitarian, but she hadn't had time to soften the décor.

Nancy J. Cohen

"Hey, guys," she said, nodding to her employees at the two front desks. Her reserved spot was behind them, next to an unoccupied post. She'd hoped to add a fourth staff member in the new year, but with their proposed rent increase, that goal had been delayed.

Purdy glanced up and tapped his smartwatch. "You're late, Keryn." He nearly always used her proper name, not her nickname.

Keri grinned, aware he liked to chide her. It was his way of showing concern. "I know," she said in a breezy tone. "I just wanted to see that disapproving look on your face. Tell me again what time *you* arrive every morning."

His chin lifted. "I put in enough overtime that you owe me. It's only because I love you that I don't complain to the boss."

"I am the boss, mister. Now get back to work."

"Yes, ma'am." Purdy adjusted his eyeglasses and focused on his computer. The motion pulled his sport coat taut across his wide shoulders. The fabric's charcoal color matched his hair, which he kept as neat and trim as his personality.

He'd been a certified accountant in his previous job. Now Purdy served as their office manager, taking charge of the agency's bookkeeping and vendor contracts. Keri relied on his precision and attention to detail, although he'd confessed that had he been less rigid, it might have saved his marriage. Nonetheless, she appreciated his meticulous approach, as it relieved her of duties she'd rather not perform.

At the adjacent desk, Staz pursed her crimson lips. "Keri, did you call Fiona yet? I know you have an appointment with her." With her height and sultry dark eyes, Staz—whose real name was Anastasia—could have easily gotten a job as a model. Her name rhymed with pizazz, which Purdy said fit her fashionable style. Today she wore a short black skirt, knee-high boots, and a jade sweater. Large silver hoops peeked out from her chin-length black hair.

Despite her outward appearance, Staz's brainy side had led her to a degree in information technology. Keri relied on her technical skills to cover the virtual office jobs, website updates, and social media campaigns. She also served as their corporate party planner.

"I've been too busy," Keri replied. "I had to adjust the reservation for the butterfly group's breakfast on Tuesday. They added four more registrants, and the room only holds thirty. Fortunately, the manager said they could squeeze in a few more chairs."

Staz's brow creased beneath her blunt-cut bangs. "You should have notified me. I would have contacted them for you."

"I know, but it's already done. Did Fiona send over the signed copies of her contracts?" Keri's client was old-school and preferred not to transmit sensitive data via email.

"Yes. The packet is on your desk."

As Staz turned away, Keri sank into her chair and accessed Fiona's number on her cell phone.

Fiona picked up after two rings. "Keri, I thought you'd forgotten about me. Is everything all right?" She sounded more concerned than annoyed by the delay.

Keri's posture eased at her reaction. Fiona treated her more like a surrogate granddaughter than a hired assistant. Keri valued her sage advice and appreciated her as a role model. Nearly eighty, Fiona had more energy than most women half her age.

"Yes, I got held up finishing a task. Sorry I'm late."

"No worries. Let's get started." Fiona was a major benefactor for PHEADA—pronounced *FEE-dah*—a local nonprofit organization. The acronym stood for Preventing Heart Disease through the Arts. Saturday night's party was their kickoff event for the holiday season, and Keri's firm was managing the affair.

Fiona dipped right in. "Regarding the catering, I assume you ordered the California rolls. Ossie insisted on sushi, as most people seem to like it."

Keri winced. Oswald Pittman, president of PHEADA, liked to approve each item and could be a pain with his micromanagement. Then again, Fiona was the same way with details. They were a pair in that regard. Half of Keri's job was reassuring them that all was in order.

"Everything is on track with the food vendors," she said. "Tommy Woo will be bringing sushi as part of his menu. All the chefs are excited to participate. They've been very generous in donating their time this year."

"You've done a super job in organizing things and getting sponsors, dear. I can't sing your praises highly enough."

Keri's spirits lifted at her words. "We've been lucky to have so many participants."

"That's due to your efforts. Ossie said to remind you the artists' easels mustn't crowd the aisles."

"Don't worry. Everyone has been given a set of the rules."

"And you've reconfirmed with the string quartet?"

"They're all set to go. As for the florist, she'll start decorating as soon as the doors open."

"Good; it sounds as though you've got everything under control. Did you have a chance to read my fundraiser speech?"

"Yes, and it's inspirational. I still don't understand why Ossie won't take the spotlight, though."

"He said I'm in charge of the event, so it's my job. He'd rather work the crowd and charm the donors. You know he's more of a people person, while I'm the organizer type. He may nitpick the details, but he leaves it up to you and me to run the show."

I'd agree with you there. Ossie can be annoying, but he means well.

"He is talented at persuading people to donate money," Keri conceded. "PHEADA made a very generous donation to the heart association last year with the proceeds from the party."

"This is true. On a personal note, would you be able to take me shopping in the next few days? I'm wearing my sparkly blue top tomorrow night, but I'll need something new for my birthday party the following weekend."

Keri pictured Fiona's silver hair and vibrant green eyes. She preferred bright colors in her ensembles, and along with her penchant for tea, reminded Keri of Queen Elizabeth II.

"For you, I'll make the time," she said with genuine fondness.

"Speaking of your birthday, we need to review the details when I bring your groceries tomorrow. I've received your signed contracts and testimonials, by the way. I'll look them over to make sure we haven't missed anything." Fiona had copied the certificates of appreciation she'd received from town dignitaries and wanted Keri to read them at her milestone celebration.

"There's something else we need to talk about while I've got you," Fiona said, lowering her voice. "But it's not a discussion we can have on the phone."

Fiona sounded so serious that a moment of panic engulfed her. "What is it? You're not ill, are you?" She'd lost her mother three years ago. She couldn't bear the thought of losing Fiona, too. Then she'd truly feel alone.

"No, I'm fine," Fiona reassured her. "It's just that… I fear I've made a terrible mistake. I need to tell you about it in person. You're the only one I can trust."

"Now I'm concerned. What kind of mistake?" Had Fiona offended someone in her social circle? Made a rude comment to the wrong person? That would be unlike her.

"We'll discuss it tomorrow. Maybe I'm imagining things." Yet her fearful tone told Keri that whatever she felt might have merit.

"O-kay. Should I come earlier?"

"No, no. I know you have a gazillion things to do this time of year. I wish I could still drive, but I can't seem to find my way these days. I'm lucky to have you to help me."

Keri's heartstrings thrummed. If it were up to her, she wouldn't even charge Fiona, but then Purdy would berate her for being too soft. "We're lucky to have each other. Is there anything else I can get for you tomorrow, like your favorite chocolate croissant?"

Fiona laughed, but her voice lacked true mirth. "No, thanks. I have some apple strudel that we can eat with our tea. I'll look forward to seeing you at ten o'clock."

Keri rang off, curious as to what was on Fiona's mind. She'd find out soon enough.

Purdy swiveled in his chair to glare at her. "I didn't hear you mention the horticultural club. You know how much we need to snag their monthly meetings to boost our budget. That income could make up for the rent increase in January."

Keri sighed, knowing he was right. "I'll ask Fiona for a recommendation after the PHEADA party. The mayor will be there, along with his entourage tomorrow night, and I'm hoping to make some new connections at this event to bring in more revenue."

Staz glanced over her shoulder. "Do you want company? I was going to work on the necklace for my jewelry-making class, but I can come along if you need support."

Keri waved a hand. "I appreciate it, but I'll manage." She knew Staz loved her crafting classes, while Keri didn't have the patience to create art of any kind. She'd rather support the artists. But Staz had given her an idea. Maybe next year, they could include a wider variety of talents at PHEADA events to broaden the appeal.

Work consumed her for the better part of the day, though her mind kept wandering to Fiona's remarks. What had concerned her so much that she couldn't tell Keri on the phone?

Purdy stretched and spoke, intruding on her thoughts. "What are you gals doing tonight? I'm heading over to Boxi Park if either of you want to join me."

Keri shook her head. "No, thanks. I'm going to bed early. I've too much to do tomorrow."

Purdy might enjoy the Friday night scene at Boxi Park, but it was a far drive for her. He'd do well enough by himself, though. Short and stout, he wasn't the type you'd think would attract women, but each outing netted him new admirers. Keri suspected he turned on his wit and charm away from the office.

"It's tempting, but I'll still be here making phone calls," Staz said with a pout. "I got a request from a woman who makes holiday wreathes to see if we can find her a spot at a seasonal festival. It's almost impossible to get an opening at this late date."

Purdy snorted. "Good luck with that."

"Check with the churches if you can't find any space at town events," Keri suggested. "They all hold bazaars this time of year and might have spots available. You could try the farmer's markets, too."

Staz gave her a grateful nod. "I will, thanks. Before I forget, your friend Lora from the print shop emailed me the proofs for our Christmas cards. I hope it was okay that I gave my approval."

"Sure. That's one more thing off our list." Keri sifted through the clutter on her desktop, searching for the manila envelope Fiona had sent. She'd better review the vendor contracts for her party before their meeting tomorrow. Oh, there it was.

When she dumped the contents on her desk, a photo fell out from among the papers.

Whoa, what's this?

She lifted the picture. An attractive woman with wavy red hair and green eyes clung to the arm of an older gentleman in a tuxedo. He had a cigar stuck in his mouth, while the redhead wore a black cocktail dress with a star-shaped brooch and sparkly earrings.

Wait a minute. That woman looks like Fiona, only a younger version. A glance at the back showed no date stamp or other imprint.

"Look, this picture was inside Fiona's package," she told her staff. "I'm not sure if she meant to include it or not."

Purdy spun around and squinted at it. "Maybe she wants you to make a collage for her birthday. You can ask her tomorrow. She might have sent this as a reminder."

"She has been forgetful lately, so you could be right. A collage is a great idea." Keri snapped a picture of the image to keep on her phone and stuck the print in her purse. She'd return it to Fiona in the morning.

Another thought surfaced. Could this photo be related to what Fiona intended to tell her? If so, it made tomorrow's appointment even more imperative.

Chapter Two

Keri bounded from her car at ten o'clock on Saturday morning, anxious to see Fiona and get the scoop on what was bothering her. Having been to the farmer's market earlier, she collected her grocery bags from the backseat, locked the doors, and approached the two-story Mediterranean-style house bordering Lake Belfrey.

A couple of damp, plastic-wrapped newspapers lay on the lawn. Fiona usually brought them inside to read with her breakfast. Why were they still here?

She scooped up the *Orlando Sentinel* and *Sunny Grove Gazette*, shook them out and tucked them into one of her bags. As she approached the entrance, she noticed the front drapes remained closed. That was odd. Fiona liked to let in the sunlight as soon as dawn arrived. Maybe she'd overslept, although that rarely happened.

Could Fiona be sick? Despite her reassurance on the phone, something could be ailing her. Fear struck Keri as a vision of her mother's collapse and trip to the hospital arose in her mind. Mom had died of a massive stroke a few days later. Surely, nothing similar would happen now.

Her palms sweaty, Keri hastened up the porch steps and rang the doorbell.

Nobody answered. She twisted the knob and gave a sigh of relief when the door opened. Fiona must have unlocked it. Maybe she was upstairs getting dressed.

"Fiona, I'm here," Keri called from the foyer.

When her friend didn't respond, Keri set down the shopping bags along with her purse on a side table. Familiar with the house, she walked through the high-ceilinged living and dining rooms, which were furnished with expensive antiques. The smell of lemon polish lingered throughout.

Fiona wasn't in sight, nor did Keri find her in the kitchen. The place was quiet, without a kettle on the stove or a teapot in sight. The granite countertops were empty except for a toaster, a coffeemaker, and a ceramic utensil holder. Not even a crumb showed on the smooth surface.

Why wasn't Fiona there making tea? They always sat together and enjoyed refreshments during her visits. Fiona had even mentioned serving apple strudel on the phone.

She resumed her search with an increased sense of urgency. Fiona wasn't watching TV in the family room. The flat-screen television remained as silent as the rest of the house. She peered at the set of double sliding glass doors that led to a screened pool patio.

The vertical blinds were partially open. Outside, the aqua pool appeared clear, with nary a ripple. In the distance, the lake glistened, its calm surface the opposite of Keri's edgy nerves. She tested the doors, relieved to find them still locked. At least she didn't have to worry about Fiona falling into the pool.

Elderly people had falls all the time. Could Fiona have taken a tumble in the bathroom? Her heart thudded in her chest as she approached the stairs.

"Fiona, I'm coming up," she hollered. An eerie silence accompanied her up the carpeted steps. At the top landing, she paused to listen. She didn't hear any sounds of water running or pipes clanging, so Fiona wasn't in the shower. Nor did she hear movement from inside Fiona's bedroom.

Dread pricked her neck like sharp nettles as she approached the owner's suite. As she stepped across the threshold, her throat tightened.

Oh my God. She froze in her tracks.

Fiona lay on the queen-sized bed atop disheveled covers. A cotton nightgown clung to her thin frame. She wasn't moving.

Keri inhaled short gasps of air as her brain tried to catch up with reality. *Is she breathing? Go and check. Don't just stand there.*

She roused herself and moved forward to nudge Fiona's still form. "Fiona, wake up. It's me, Keri."

Fiona didn't move, not even a twitch. She lay as still as death, her eyes closed as though in slumber. Nor did her chest rise and fall like it should. Keri fumbled for a pulse. Nothing. She jerked her hand away at the clammy feel of Fiona's wrist.

It's too late. She's gone.

The loss hit her like an iron poker to her gut. How could she manage without Fiona's support? She'd always made her feel better when things troubled her. Now she'd never get the chance to return the favor.

Awareness flooded her as she took in the rest of the scene. Dresser drawers lay askew, their contents spilled across the carpet. A nightstand drawer rested on the floor along with a lamp and a pillow. Even the cushion from Fiona's favorite armchair had been tossed aside.

The implications chilled her blood. Somebody had been there and done this.

Just as that thought struck, she heard a faint rustling sound coming from the direction of Fiona's walk-in closet.

Her heart skipped a beat. She backed away, her pulse thrumming in her ears. With a pivot worthy of a dancer, she twirled on her heels and sped down the steps and out the exit.

Once outside, Keri yanked her cell phone from her pants pocket and punched in nine-one-one with trembling fingers. It took a couple of tries to get it right.

"Hello. Do you need police or medical?" said a woman's calm voice.

"Both of them. My friend is lying in her bed at home and not moving. I-I think she's dead. Her room has been ransacked, and I thought I heard a noise coming from her closet."

"What's the address, ma'am?"

Keri choked out the information.

"Is this the best number to reach you in case we get disconnected?"

"Yes, it is."

"The paramedics are on their way. Are you with the lady now?"

"No, I'm outside by the front porch."

"The team should be there shortly. If you're safe, I'm signing off unless you need me to stay on the line," the dispatcher said.

Keri glanced around but didn't see anyone lurking nearby. If there had been someone in the house, they hadn't followed her outside. She should be okay being in plain view of the street.

"Thanks, I'll be all right." She disconnected and had stashed her phone away when a wave of dizziness struck her. She sank to the steps and leaned over her knees. This all seemed surreal, like a nightmare from which she couldn't awaken. The image of Fiona's body pervaded her mind and clogged her throat.

Needing a distraction, she scanned the street. For a Saturday morning, the neighborhood seemed quiet. No joggers pounded the pavement for their morning run. No kids played outside. How could things appear so tranquil when Fiona lay dead inside her house?

She leapt up to pace the pavement. Soon flashing lights appeared in the distance, and a red truck with the fire department logo rumbled into view. The paramedic team spilled out and approached her with their gear in hand.

"My friend is upstairs in her bedroom. It's the first door on the right," Keri said with a sweeping gesture toward the house.

She shivered in the cool breeze that had stirred up. A beige and black police car arrived and squealed to a halt at the curb. Two uniformed officers emerged and approached her.

"Ma'am, are you the lady who phoned for help?" the older one asked.

"Yes, that's me." Her body shook, and she fought to maintain her composure.

"I'm Officer Turnbull. Can you tell us what happened?" After she told her story, he nodded. "We'll take a look. Please wait here." He motioned to his colleague, and they trooped toward the front door.

It was a short wait. When the pair came back outside, Officer Turnbull rejoined her while the other guy stayed on the front porch and spoke into his phone.

"We've notified Detective Saunders," Turnbull said. "He's on his way and will want a statement from you. Can I get your contact info, please?"

Keri complied. "My friend's name is Fiona Sullivan," she added as he wrote in his notepad.

"Would you happen to know her next of kin?"

"Fiona's nephew, Garvan Connor, lives in St. Augustine. I don't have his address."

"All right, thanks."

"Was there anyone inside? I thought I'd heard a noise coming from the closet."

"A hangar had fallen, so maybe that's what you heard. No one else was there."

He left to rejoin his partner, and Keri studied a crack in the driveway while considering what a detective might ask her. She hadn't observed many details inside Fiona's room. The mess on the floor indicated an intruder must have been present. A shudder wracked her as she imagined possible scenarios.

Stop. You don't know what really happened. Focus on the here and now.

She pushed aside her dark thoughts and leaned against her car until a sedan pulled up to the curb. A man in a navy suit emerged and conferred with Officer Turnbull, who nodded in her direction. Mr. Blue Suit headed her way with long, loping steps.

"I'm Detective Jeff Saunders. I understand you found the deceased?" he asked in a gravelly voice. His slightly hooked nose and beefy shoulders gave him the air of a prizefighter. He wore a necktie with colorful autumn leaves that belied his somber manner.

She nodded, swallowing past a lump in her throat. "I'm Keri Armstrong, a friend of hers."

"Can you explain what happened?" He peered at her with keen brown eyes. His graying temples put his age in the fortyish range.

Her words came out in a nervous rush. "I was bringing some groceries Fiona had ordered. When she didn't answer the doorbell, I went inside. She'd left the door unlocked for me."

"Was that unusual?"

"No, although she'd greet me in the foyer, if not at the door. I thought I'd find her in the kitchen, but she wasn't there." Her voice cracked at the memory. She'd miss their ritual of drinking tea brewed in Fiona's favorite English cottage teapot. She always offered honey and sugar, even though Keri didn't use sweetener.

"Go on," Saunders said, rousing her back to the present.

"I was afraid she might have fallen and needed help, so I went upstairs. I found her lying in bed and not moving. Her wrist was cool, and I couldn't find a pulse. Then I heard a noise and got scared, so I ran outside." Her throat closed, and she fell silent.

"I'm going to check things out. Please stay here until I return."

She dabbed at her eyes, needing a tissue. "I left my purse in the front hallway. Can I go in and get it?"

"No, I'll bring it to you. We don't want anyone to contaminate the scene."

"Too late for me. I've already touched things."

His lips pressed together but he refrained from commenting. After he turned away, Keri waited on the front path as neighbors congregated along the sidewalk.

Her brain remained blissfully blank until a white crime scene van pulled up to the curb. A couple of techs got out and trudged up the walkway, carrying their equipment. The medical examiner soon followed, while neighbors jostled each other for a view.

A woman across the street waved a sign. *Go Home, Criminals. My Eyes Are On You.*

What did that mean? None of the other neighbors were paying her any attention. In fact, most of them gave the lady a wide berth.

Detective Saunders hollered to Keri from the front stoop. "Is this your bag?" he asked, holding up her purse. At her nod, he rejoined her.

"Thanks." She took the bag from him, slung its crossbody strap over her shoulder and then dug for a tissue. "Do you see that woman across the street? Maybe she knows something."

Saunders waved a hand in dismissal. "That's Veronica Batten. Batty is more like it. We've had calls from her about spies and serial killers. I wouldn't consider her a reliable witness."

"All right. Am I free to go?"

"If you don't mind, I've a few more questions to ask you."

"Sure, no problem. I'm glad to help." Maybe she could worm some answers out of him while they talked. After the shock subsided, she'd want to know how Fiona had died.

"Let's go around to the patio. There's something I need to show you there." Saunders signaled for her to follow him.

Curious as to what he might reveal, Keri passed the technicians attaching crime scene tape to the front entry and trailed him across the dry grass toward the rear.

Saunders used a handkerchief to open the screened door. Inside the patio, he pointed to a solid white door that Keri knew led into the family room cabana bath. Florida pool homes often had bathrooms with outdoor access so people with wet swimsuits didn't trek through the house.

"What do you know about this damage?" Saunders said with a gesture.

Keri's mouth gaped as she took a closer look. The door appeared dented, and its lock was broken. She felt her innards melt as she realized what it meant.

"Is this how the intruder broke in?" she asked in a squeaky voice.

"That's my guess. They must have forced their way in through here and exited out the front door. If it was still nighttime, it would have been dark outside. They wouldn't expect to be seen fleeing the scene."

Her brain processed this theory. "That would explain the unlocked front door. Fiona couldn't have done it if she was already—" She choked on the word, unable to finish.

"Your fingerprints will be on the doorknob. You'll have to come down to the station to give us a set for comparison." He gazed quizzically at her, as though expecting her to protest.

Realization sank like a rock in her gut. He didn't believe she was involved in this incident, did he? Was that why he'd brought her back here, to observe her reaction?

"Sure, detective. I'll cooperate in any way necessary to learn what happened to Fiona." Her knees folded, and she sank onto a sling patio chair.

Saunders pulled one over to join her. A ray of sunlight shimmered off a gold band on his ring finger. She stayed quiet, staring at the lake. It gleamed in the rising sun, while birds twittered in nearby trees.

Her throat constricted at the thought of Fiona no longer enjoying this view. They'd often sat outside together to watch the clouds and sip their tea. Fiona would ask about her life and give wise advice. What would she do without her?

"Are you okay?" Saunders asked, his expression softening.

She sniffled. "Not really. I can't believe Fiona is gone."

"I'm sorry for your loss. Is it okay if we record this session?" At her nod of approval, Saunders set his phone to record and readied his notebook and pen. "Let's start with the easy questions. Please state your name, address, and phone number." He jotted her basic information down quickly and continued. "And what was your relationship to the deceased?"

"I own a personal concierge business called *A Friend in Need* Agency. We do a variety of jobs for busy professionals, working mothers, and the elderly, as well as planning corporate events. I did various tasks for Fiona that we personalized to her needs."

"What's the difference between a personal concierge and a personal assistant?"

Keri nodded, being familiar with this question. "The simplest explanation is that a personal assistant usually works for a single individual or company, while a personal concierge is an independent contractor with a number of clients. Naturally, there's some overlap between the two roles."

"What kinds of things did you do for Ms. Sullivan?"

"I helped her pay bills, drove her to doctor's appointments, picked up her meds, and took her shopping. Also, I arranged for her patronage at various cultural events, such as PHEADA's kickoff party being held tonight."

"What's Fee-Dah?"

Keri spelled it for him. "It's a nonprofit group that pairs local artists with fundraising events to benefit the heart association. I met Fiona at one of their walkathons when she was giving out awards."

"Tell me again why you came here today." Saunders gazed at her with an impassive expression, his pen poised over his notebook.

She'd already told him. Was he hoping to catch her with an inconsistency?

"I came by to drop off her groceries," she repeated, keeping her voice even. "We also needed to discuss the details for her eightieth birthday party. She'd hired me to plan the event, which is… was… next weekend."

Fiona had been so excited to celebrate her milestone. Now her friends would be gathered for her funeral instead. Maybe Keri should offer to help Garvan make the arrangements, since she would know who to notify.

A lawnmower erupted to life in the distance, making her realize someone would have to contact Fiona's lawn service, stop her newspaper delivery, and do myriad other tasks. But that would come later, after she was put to rest.

Detective Saunders regarded her from under his thick brows. "When did you last talk to Miss Sullivan?"

"Yesterday—Friday—we spoke on the phone. She was anxious that everything should go perfectly for tonight's event." Oh, no. Ossie was supposed to pick Fiona up later. Who would tell him not to bother?

She sighed, realizing she'd have to adjust her own plans due to Fiona's death. It was more than just a personal loss. They'd take a financial hit at the agency without her retainer fees.

"When you spoke, how did Miss Sullivan sound to you in terms of her mood?" Saunders asked, tilting his head.

"She was worried about something that she meant to tell me about today," Keri replied, berating herself for thinking about money at such a time.

"Oh? Regarding what?"

"She wouldn't explain over the phone." Regret beat upon her shoulders like a sodden blanket. She should have convinced Fiona to tell her then.

Static erupted on the detective's police radio, and he turned down the volume. "When did you last meet in person?"

Keri shifted restlessly, anxious for this interview to be over. "I drove her to a doctor's appointment on Thursday."

He wrote down the name of the physician. "How did she feel after this visit?"

"She was rather quiet, now that you mention it, although she did say the doctor gave her a clean bill of health. I took her directly home."

"Regarding her medications, when did she pick up her latest refill?"

"I got it for her on Tuesday. They were sleeping pills she took on occasion. The doctor renewed her other meds on Thursday."

"She could manage taking her own pills?"

Keri nodded. "She still had a fairly sharp mind. Well, she had been repeating herself more often, and once or twice she'd forgotten things I told her, but that's normal for someone her age."

"Did your tasks include financial management?"

"Fiona wasn't computer savvy and needed me to do her

online banking transactions. Sometimes she'd forget to pay a bill and then I'd have to remind her."

"Was she able to write checks herself?"

"Yes. I did not have access to her accounts otherwise, if that's what you're asking." She hoped he didn't think she had abused her position. There were plenty of unscrupulous people out there who took advantage of the elderly. But she merely wanted to help senior citizens enjoy their leisure time by simplifying their lives.

"When you were inside her room, did you notice anything missing?"

His change of subject took her aback. She shook her head. "I was too upset to look around." She banished the image of Fiona's frail body lying on the bed. She'd grieve later, when she was alone. "However, I do have an inventory of items in her house. I'd recorded most of her antiques and collectibles because I was helping her sell some of them on eBay."

He glowered at her as though she'd been withholding information. "I'd appreciate a copy when you have a chance."

"I can do that." Keri hesitated, then posed the question foremost on her mind. "How did she die, Detective?"

"The medical examiner will determine the cause of death. You'd mentioned her next of kin was a nephew named Garvan Connor. Did Miss Sullivan have any children?"

"No, she never married." Fiona had admitted to Keri that she'd fallen in love with a man years ago, but it hadn't worked out.

"Have you ever met the nephew?"

"We've run into each other at social events. He lives in St. Augustine with his wife Enid and their son, so he doesn't come into town that often."

"How was his relationship with his aunt?"

"It was strained. Fiona complained that he never invited her over for the holidays."

"Is Garvan her main beneficiary?"

"I have no idea. She didn't discuss her estate plans with me. Fiona was very fond of her best friend's daughter, Diane Foster," she explained, hoping she hadn't besmirched Garvan's character. "When Diane's mom died, Fiona became like a surrogate mother to her."

"Does she reside in the area?"

"Diane and her husband, Cal, live in Winter Garden with their two children. She'll be heartbroken over Fiona's death."

He wrote down their names and then closed his notebook. "Please let me know when you can stop by the station to leave your prints."

"Sure, no problem. I can probably do it tomorrow or Monday," she said, unable to avoid a shiver of distaste. She'd like to get that chore done as soon as possible.

"That will work." Saunders switched off his recorder, and they exchanged business cards. He accompanied her toward the street.

Keri's stomach somersaulted as she noticed an unmarked black van blocking the driveway. Two husky fellows pushed a gurney holding a draped form toward the vehicle.

Fiona... Tears pricked her eyes, and her lips quivered. She glanced away, willing herself to stay strong until she had some privacy.

The throng of neighbors had increased. They stood chatting amongst themselves while viewing the action. The lady across the street waved her sign, calling out to passersby who ignored her. Keri couldn't hear what she was saying.

"At least the newscasters haven't arrived yet," she said, hoping Fiona's death wouldn't be sensationalized by the press. This had turned into enough of a circus already.

He gave her a wry glance. "They have bigger fish to fry. By the way, I must advise you not to discuss this case with anyone."

"I don't spread gossip. If I did, I'd be out of business in a heartbeat."

"That may be true, but keep one thing in mind. You might have been the last person to speak to your friend. Maybe you know more than you realize."

Chapter Three

Keri parted from Detective Saunders and unlocked her Honda Civic parked in the driveway. Its cherry red color seemed too bright in the wake of a tragedy, but she hadn't wanted a silver or white car, like so many others in Florida.

Sagging against the driver's seat cushion, she waited until the body removal unit left before starting the engine. Finally, she put the car in gear and pulled onto the road with her brain on automatic. Her phone rang as she headed downtown.

"Hi, it's Lisa," said a familiar voice on the car's speaker system. "I've had a change in plans and need my plane reservations switched *immediately*. I'll have to leave later in the afternoon on Monday."

Keri winced at Lisa's shrill tone. She always wanted things done on the spot. "Sorry, but I'm driving right now. I'll call you back when I'm at the office." She rang off, lacking the energy to deal with mundane demands. Still, she had obligations to her clients and needed to focus.

She stopped to pick up Mr. Witherspoon's dry cleaning and Mrs. Brody's roll of stamps at the post office before their weekly visits. Then she headed to her office to take care of Lisa's reservation change.

Her workplace felt like a sanctuary when she entered. She halted at the sight of Purdy bent over his desk. Normally, her staff took weekends off.

"Hey, Purdy. What are you doing here?"

He glanced up. "Oh hi, Keryn. I had some things to finish that couldn't wait. Aren't you supposed to be at Fiona's house?"

"Well, yes, about that…" Trying to keep her voice steady, she told him the bad news.

His eyes rounded behind his wire-framed glasses. "Good God, I'm so sorry. That must have been a terrible shock."

Keri went to her desk, sank into her chair and set down her purse. She ran a shaky hand over her face. Her brain still felt numb. "It was horrible. I still can't believe she's gone."

"You don't look so good. Can I get you a drink of water?"

"That might help, thanks." She only now realized she'd skipped lunch. Who could think about food under the circumstances?

Purdy complied and then hovered by her desk. "It's a good thing you were due to visit this morning, or who knows when her… when she might have been discovered."

Words failed her in offering a response. She grabbed a tissue and let the tears flow.

Purdy stood facing her with the awkward expression men got when confronted with a weepy woman. "I'm sorry," he repeated. "I know how much you respected her."

"That's not all," she said between sniffles. "Don't tell anyone this, but somebody broke in through the back door and ransacked her bedroom."

"What? Are you saying it was a home invasion?"

"It appears that way. I heard a noise coming from the closet and ran outside." A shudder passed through her at the memory. She took a sip of water to steady her nerves.

"Thank goodness you're safe." He dropped back into his chair. "Fiona must have woken up during the robbery. How terrifying to find a stranger in your room."

"I know. Her pillow was on the floor. I could see how the thief might have tried to subdue her if she woke up and screamed. Then he probably threw the pillow aside after she went limp."

"What a nightmare. At least she was caught up on our retainer fees. Otherwise, we'd be in the hole this month." At Keri's horrified glance, he added, "I know that's not a nice thing to say, but it's my job to look after our bottom line."

"You're right, Purdy. But seriously?" Despite his callousness, it was lucky for her he had been anxious to escape the corporate culture when she was looking for a business manager. He'd readily accepted her lower salary offer and basic benefit package to join the agency.

"Is the PHEADA party still on for tonight?" he asked, bringing up another worry. They had a lot riding on this evening's event.

"It's their biggest fundraiser of the year, so I'd assume so."

"Wasn't Fiona supposed to give the pitch for donations?"

"Yes. I suppose that duty will fall to Ossie now."

"What if he reads her speech? It would be a fitting tribute to her."

She stared at him. "That's a great idea, Purdy. I'll ask Ossie about it. I need to notify him anyway about what's happened. He was supposed to give Fiona a ride tonight."

Unfortunately, her call got sent to voicemail, so she left a message.

"Hey, Ossie. It's Keri Armstrong. Please give me a call as soon as possible. I have some urgent news." She hoped he wouldn't take too long to get back to her.

"Staz or I could go in your place tonight if you need time to yourself," Purdy offered.

Her heart softened. She supposed he really did care, even if he didn't always show it the right way. "Thanks, but I'd rather not stay home alone. I'm afraid Fiona's death might cast a pall over the party, but I like your idea of doing a tribute to her. I could also bring the testimonials she gave me to read at her birthday. They're certificates of appreciation from town dignitaries praising her contributions."

Purdy snorted. "Not everyone might be impressed by her accolades. You might want to save them for her funeral instead."

"What do you mean?"

"I hadn't mentioned this to you before, since you thought so highly of her, but some people resented Fiona for being a busybody. They might even be relieved she's no longer around."

"That can't be true. Everyone liked her. She was very generous with her time and money."

"Perhaps so, but I've heard rumors that she expected something in return. She'd use people's personal issues to get her way."

"Maybe that was their excuse for accepting her patronage." Fiona must have heard plenty of gossip at society events, but Keri couldn't conceive of her using that knowledge to twist people's arms into doing favors for her.

Feeling the need to escape, she got up and fled to the restroom. Her fingers shook as she dabbed at her teary eyes. How dare Purdy insinuate Fiona might have made enemies?

Then again, should she dismiss his words so quickly? Unless Fiona had died from sheer fright, somebody had killed her. While it appeared to be a random robber, that might not be the only explanation.

Back at her desk, she addressed her colleague from the rear. "I do appreciate your support, Purdy, and I realize I've tended to put Fiona on a pedestal. Maybe I need to listen to what other people have to say about her."

He swiveled in his chair to regard her. "I didn't mean to be disrespectful. Fiona helped us in many ways. Do you mind if I notify Staz? She'll want to know."

"Go ahead."

He called their colleague and spoke in a low tone to fill her in. "Staz says she's terribly sorry and asks if she can do anything for you," he said to Keri.

"No, thanks. I'm good. But tell her I appreciate the offer."

They spoke for a few more minutes and then Purdy hung up.

"What are you working on that brought you into the office on a Saturday?" she asked.

He grimaced. "Thanksgiving is almost here, and I haven't ordered our business gifts yet for the holidays. I won't have time to do it on Monday."

"Why not?"

"I've an appointment with Diligent Cleaning Services. We've received complaints that their housekeepers are slacking off, and I want to discuss it with the owner. Staz may be late on Monday, too. She has a few errands to do before coming into the office."

"All right. I'll let you get back to work then."

"Don't worry. I won't ask for overtime," he said in a teasing tone. "You know I'd be here seven days a week if you didn't insist I take time off. I hope to get in a snooze at home before I go clubbing later. Kitty is bringing some of her friends along for happy hour."

Keri smiled despite her grief. "That should be fun." She dealt with Lisa Neville's reservation change and then did some mindless tasks to keep from thinking about Fiona, but her brain kept replaying scenes from that morning. Soon she gave up and called it a day. By then, Purdy had already left.

Just as she was getting ready to depart, Ossie returned her call.

"Have you heard the news about Fiona?" Keri asked immediately.

"No, I've been occupied all day. What's up?"

"She passed away last night. I know how much everyone in your organization appreciated her, and she held a special place in my heart, too. Things won't be the same without her."

"This is terrible. Just terrible. It's a blow to our entire community."

"Obviously, you won't have to pick her up tonight." Keri paused. "I assume that as president, you'll be doing the fundraiser speech this evening. I have a copy of Fiona's talk if you want to give it as a tribute to her. I also have copies of certificates of appreciation she'd received from town leaders. Many of those people will be present this evening if you want to read them. It would give you the perfect opportunity to ask for donations in her memory."

"That's a marvelous idea. Thank you for suggesting it."

Keri's heart swelled. It seemed only fitting that they should honor Fiona tonight. "I'll email you the speech," she said before disconnecting. She took care of that task and then grabbed her purse prior to leaving, remembering to stuff Fiona's printed testimonials inside. As she did so, she noticed the photo she'd meant to return to Fiona. Now she'd never know what her friend had wanted to do with it.

As she stood, a text message came through from her bestie, Lora.

What's going on? I heard Fiona Sullivan was found dead this morning.

It's true. I still find it hard to believe.

I'm so sorry. I know you valued your friendship with her.

Thanks. I'm at the office, and I need to go home and get ready for tonight's PHEADA party. I'll call you later to fill you in.

Ten minutes later, Keri zipped into the gated parking garage at her four-story condo building. It wasn't far, so she could walk to work, but she needed her car for client errands. Luckily, she didn't meet anyone in the elevator, which was a blessing.

Once inside her three-bedroom apartment, she flicked on the recessed lighting in the kitchen and set her purse down on the stone countertop. Her gaze swept the white cabinetry and stainless-steel appliances. Further along was a high-ceilinged living area with a dining table set and a comfy sofa arrangement. A sixty-inch, flat-screen TV hung on the opposite wall.

She headed into the bathroom to get comfortable, but a glance in the mirror gave her a fright. Her face looked wan and her hair dull. She'd better fix herself up before tonight's party.

She'd just removed her earrings when a scraping noise caught her attention. It seemed to be coming from the opposite end of the living room where the guest bedroom and home office were located. She took a few faltering steps in that direction. Could it be the same window that had rattled loose in the last storm?

"Hello, is anyone there?" she called. Her pulse accelerated as she crossed the carpet. The odd noise became definite thumps that turned her veins into ice. Was someone rummaging through her things?

If she were smart, she'd hightail it outside and call the cops. But what if it truly was the window banging loose? She wasn't eager to encounter the police for a second time that day.

Steeling her nerves, she stepped across the threshold. Her body sagged in relief as she saw it was Lora dragging a chair across the room.

"Lora! What are you doing here?" Keri cried as her racing pulse subsided.

Lora spun around with a startled glance. With a sheepish grin, she tore out a pair of earbuds from her ears.

"Hey, Keri. I didn't hear you come in." Lora wore a gauzy top with distressed jeans and was barefoot on the carpet. Corkscrew blond curls framed her heart-shaped face.

"How did you get in the door? And what is *that*?" Keri pointed to an open suitcase on top of the queen-size guest bed.

"I still have a key from when I helped you move, remember? And I texted you earlier."

"Yes, about *Fiona*. You didn't say a word about being at the condo." She placed the flashlight on the dresser, bewildered by the rapid turn of events.

"You ended the call before I could tell you. Rick and I broke up. I need a place to stay while I look for a place to rent."

"Oh, no. Not again." Lora had more breakups than a sidewalk had cracks. Normally, Keri wouldn't mind her company, but after her horrible day, she would have preferred to be alone.

"The jerk never keeps his word. He took my money for those college courses and lied to me about it. He didn't register for a single class. I'm through with him for good this time."

"I hope you mean it. It's not the first time he's been unreliable." Keri gestured to the bed. "You're welcome to stay until you get your feet on the ground again."

Lora's face brightened. "It'll only be a few days, and I won't be a bother. I promise."

Finding a new place at a decent price would probably take longer than Lora realized, but Keri couldn't refuse a friend in need when that was her motto. "Make yourself comfortable. I'm going to shower and get dressed for tonight's party."

"Can I come with you? I don't feel like staying here by myself."

"You'd need a ticket for admission, and we're sold out."

"You're the party planner, aren't you? Just tell the attendant at the door that I'm your assistant."

"That would work." And she had to admit Lora's company would be welcome. "Do you have something to wear?" she asked, glancing at her friend's clothes strewn across the bed.

"Not a problem. I packed a few fancy dresses." Lora flung her arms around Keri. "Thanks, Keri. You're the best. I knew I could count on you."

Keri patted her on the back. Lora always was a touchy-feely kind of person.

"Can you tell me what happened to Fiona?" Lora asked, pulling away. "It must have been awful."

"I'll give you the deets when we're in the car. How did you hear about it?"

"Pam called me. She got a tip from one of her press contacts."

"Naturally. She always hears things before we do." Pam, a journalist, had connections everywhere. The three of them had been roommates in college, along with Michelle, who lived in Sarasota. Pam covered society news for the community newspaper but yearned to do more serious pieces.

Lora trailed her into the kitchen, where Keri grabbed a drink of water.

"Can I make you something to eat? Knowing how you react when stressed, I'll bet you've skipped lunch." Lora opened the refrigerator door and peered inside. "Ugh, isn't there anything less sugary to drink? Lemonade is too sweet, and so is orange juice. And where's the food? There's nothing in here except hummus, yogurt, apples and grapes."

"I wasn't expecting company," Keri said with an exasperated sigh. Lora was *always* hungry. When they'd roomed together, her supplies had taken up most of the space in the fridge. "If you want a snack, look in the freezer. I'll wait until tonight's party. We need to leave by six-thirty."

She disappeared into the bathroom to soak in a hot shower. Her tears flowed under the spray of water, along with a river of fond memories.

Afterward, she dried her puffy eyes and blow-dried her hair. The routine tasks soothed her, and she lay down on her bed for a brief rest.

She must have dozed off because no time seemed to have gone by when Lora knocked on the door. "Keri, it's getting late. Are you almost done?"

"I'll be out soon," she hollered back, glancing at her clock with alarm and bounding out of bed. She needed to hustle to leave in time.

Since it was bound to be chilly outside, she chose a two-piece jacket dress in forest green with a chiffon skirt to wear along with emerald jewelry that enhanced her eyes. Unlike Lora, who could wear black well, Keri preferred richer colors to go with her creamy skin tone and dark brown hair.

Sure enough, Lora wore a black sheath dress with a silver heart necklace. Her hair was its usual mass of blond curls. She wore high heels that would have made Keri's feet sore for a week.

Once they were in the car and headed for the party, Keri thought about all the people she'd have to face there. Was she really in the mood to be sociable?

"You have that troubled look on your face," Lora observed. "What's wrong?"

"It'll be sad not to see Fiona tonight. She loved a good party. I don't know if I have the heart to mingle with her friends after what happened today."

"Do you want to talk about it now?"

Keri gave Lora an abbreviated version of what had transpired. She was careful not to mention any details that wouldn't be known to the public.

"Was hers the only house on the block that the burglars hit?" Lora asked.

Keri gave her a startled glance. "That's a good question. Detective Saunders didn't mention any other incidents in the neighborhood, but I could ask Pam to research the crime reports."

It might be significant if Fiona's house was the only one targeted. But then again, she was a wealthy patron of the arts known around town for her generosity. A clever thief could have tracked her movements.

"Let's hope you can relax and enjoy yourself tonight," Lora said, shifting in her seat. "It might be nice if someone from PHEADA says some kind words about her."

Keri offered her a small smile. "Ossie, their president, has agreed to read the speech she'd prepared. And I've brought some testimonials from people she's helped. I meant to read them at her birthday party, but now Ossie can share them. The artists will be disappointed by her absence. She always bought a painting—not that she had any wall space left."

"How did she get started collecting so much stuff? You've never said much about her background."

Keri braked at a red light. "Fiona owned an antique shop in New York City. She traveled extensively to buy special items from all over the world. From the contents of her house, it seemed as though she'd shipped her entire inventory to Florida when she relocated. Her place is cluttered to the hilt."

Fiona's treasures would belong to someone else now. Keri hoped her beneficiary would appreciate the pieces she'd lovingly collected.

"How can I help you at the party?" Lora asked as the light changed, and they moved ahead in a line of traffic.

Keri rolled her shoulders. Talking about Fiona raised her

stress level. "I'll be greeting people and thanking them for coming as well as touching base with the chefs. Then I'm hoping to make some new connections for our agency. You can circulate with me if you want. I can introduce you around."

When they arrived at the art museum, they headed for the venue's brightly lit entrance. Music from the string quartet Keri had hired wafted outside.

Her steps slowed as she detected a lilac scent that reminded her of Fiona's favorite perfume. The hairs on her arms lifted as she sensed a presence nearby. Perhaps Fiona was joining the party for one last time.

Or maybe she was stuck in limbo until Keri learned the truth about her death.

Purdy's remarks surfaced about how some people might be glad she was gone. This could be a good opportunity to sound out Fiona's friends regarding how they felt about her. A random thief was only one possibility. But what if someone had purposefully entered her house to do her harm?

If that was the case, Keri would do her best to root out the culprit. Fiona deserved justice, and Keri's sense of honor wouldn't accept anything less for her friend. It might be the final favor she could do for Fiona that would allow her to rest in peace.

Chapter Four

"This is fabulous," Lora said with a broad sweep of her arm as they entered the cavernous museum lobby. "You've done an amazing job."

Keri paused and surveyed the space with the critical eye of a party planner. Balloons and floral bouquets festooned the hall, providing splashes of autumn red, yellow and orange against the whitewashed walls. Guests mingled in clusters, browsed the paintings for sale by participating artists, or stood at cocktail tables scattered around the room. She felt an inner glow of satisfaction at a job well done.

The musicians played beside the marble staircase. Toward the rear, a row of food stations offered chef-made specialties, while waiters circulated offering bite-sized appetizers to the crowd. Fiona had insisted on pigs in blankets, saying they were her favorite. Since Ossie had his sushi station, she'd wanted her choice, no matter how plebeian.

In honor of Fiona, Keri snatched a pastry-covered frank from a passing server and bit into it, savoring the salty flavor. As she swallowed, her eyes misted at how Fiona would have loved this event. She'd be saying hello to her friends, her face aglow with pleasure. Now it was Keri's job to greet everyone in her place.

She turned to Lora and pointed to the white-uniformed chefs dishing out food along with advertising flyers. "If you're hungry, go ahead and see what they have to offer. I need to greet people before I eat."

"That's okay. I'll go with you. Our print shop could use more contacts."

Keri compressed her lips. She'd been after Lora to use her talents as a graphic designer to establish her own business, but Lora was afraid to spread her wings. Instead, she wanted the safety net of a stable job and a steady boyfriend. Rick had never encouraged her to soar. If anything, he'd clipped her wings and kept her grounded. Maybe with him out of the way, she'd look beyond the horizon for new opportunities.

Keri spotted a familiar face and waved. "Ossie is over there by himself. Let's go say hello while he's alone."

Ossie held a martini glass in hand. He peered at the crowd over his long nose with a sad expression on his face. Maybe he was thinking about Fiona.

"Hello, Ossie. This is my friend, Lora Wilson. Lora, meet Oswald Pittman, PHEADA's esteemed president." After the two exchanged handshakes, Keri touched his suit-covered arm. "It seems odd to be here without Fiona. I know everyone in your organization will miss her."

"We're all stunned by the news. Simply stunned." An attorney, Ossie spoke in a deep baritone voice that could carry across a courtroom. He had slicked-back dark hair and an arrogant tilt to his wide lips. "We were looking forward to celebrating her eightieth birthday. Isn't that right, luv?" He signaled to his wife, hovering nearby, to join them.

Hope Pittman's snug-fitting bronze gown left little room for movement. Its plunging neckline exposed her generous cleavage along with a glittering diamond necklace. Matching earrings dropped from under her bleached blond hair, styled in a fancy updo. She made the perfect eye candy on her husband's arm, an occupation that seemed to be her main goal in life. Keri had never had an intelligent conversation with her.

"What's that?" Hope asked in a slurred voice. She held a half-empty whiskey glass, making Keri wonder how many drinks she'd already consumed.

"We're talking about Fiona. Such a tragedy."

Hope pursed her crimson lips. "I can't say I'll miss her. She was always asking nosy questions and prying into everyone's life. If the old biddy wanted to make a difference, she should have joined the board of trustees."

Keri stared at her in shocked silence. *Talk about speaking ill of the dead.* She suppressed a retort while Lora stirred beside her. Her friend wasn't used to Hope's put-downs and might blurt out a nasty response.

"Fiona preferred to act behind the scenes," Keri said quietly, to quell the tension. She knew Fiona believed the trustees were puppets of the executive staff. Regardless, she'd let her views be known and had lobbied for her pet projects.

Then again, expressing an opinion differed from meddling in people's affairs. Purdy's words echoed in her ears. Hope certainly seemed resentful of Fiona's interference. Had there been a self-serving side to Fiona to which Keri had turned a blind eye?

Lora nudged her, and she realized she'd been remiss in an introduction.

"Hope, this is my friend, Lora Wilson. She's the graphic designer who did the invitations for this event."

Hope gave Lora a disdainful once-over. "Delighted to meet you, dear."

"Likewise," Lora murmured, handing over a business card. No doubt she'd relish talking about Hope when she and Keri compared notes later.

Ossie regarded Keri with a thoughtful frown. "I heard you were the one who found Fiona. You didn't mention that when we spoke earlier. It must have been a terrible shock."

Her throat tightened. "Yes, it was."

"What were you doing at her house?"

"I'd stopped by to deliver the groceries she'd ordered. The door was unlocked, so I let myself inside. She wasn't downstairs. I went looking for her, and that's when—"

"I heard it was a botched robbery," Ossie stated, narrowing his eyes.

"So it appeared. I can tell you that Fiona looked peaceful."

She hadn't noticed any signs of a struggle except for the disheveled covers and the pillow on the floor, but the discovery had rattled her too much for a closer inspection. That was the detective's job.

She'd rather remember happier times, like the Patron's Ball culminating last month's Fall Festival of the Arts. Fiona had looked regal in a black and gold sequined top with a long skirt. She'd had her silver hair freshly styled and applied her makeup with an expert eye. With her poise and grace, she'd reminded Keri of an aging movie star who retained a sense of dignity. She'd want to retain that dignity in death.

"Here are the testimonials I promised," she told Ossie, who'd been speaking to Lora while her thoughts wandered. She retrieved the folded papers from her evening bag and handed them over to him.

"Thanks." He stuffed them in his pocket. "I got your copy of Fiona's talk. It'll do very nicely and will honor her memory for me to read it."

His wife coughed. "Like you care. If you'll excuse me, I need another drink." She staggered away toward the bar.

"Sorry, she can be abrupt sometimes," Ossie said with a frown. Then he addressed Keri directly. "I meant to ask if you'll be involved with Fiona's funeral. Our staff would like to attend."

"I'm not sure yet, but I plan to offer my services to Garvan in that regard. He's Fiona's nephew," she told Lora.

"Are you talking about me?" a man's voice demanded from behind.

Keri spun around, recognizing Garvan Connor's petulant tone. She glanced at his portly form and round, flushed face. Strands of thinning, peppery hair brushed his shiny forehead.

"Oh hi, Garvan. I'm sorry about your aunt."

His dark eyes raked her with scorn. "Are you? I heard you found the body."

She bristled at his cold attitude. Conversations of partygoers faded into the background as she repeated her reasons for being at Fiona's house.

Garvan thrust out his double chin. "I hope you don't expect to get reimbursed from her estate for your efforts. I'll be calling her attorney on Monday. It's likely I'm her beneficiary."

She hadn't liked the man when they'd met before, and she liked him even less now. Squaring her shoulders, she gave him a level glance. "Is that right? If you're assuming her debts in addition to her money, you'll owe my agency the balance due on her account."

"I don't think so," he said, his florid complexion deepening. "Aren't you her party planner? Enid and I had been looking forward to celebrating her birthday next weekend. It's a shame the party will have to be cancelled."

"Actually, I thought you might want to apply her deposit to a lunch following the funeral. That way, she could still be with her friends in spirit, if not in person." And maybe it would bring Fiona a modicum of peace, wherever she was now.

"That's actually a good idea," Ossie told Garvan. He'd been standing by during their brief exchange. "You should hire Keri to help you. Our members would like to pay their respects to Fiona, whatever you decide to do." He regarded Garvan with a calculating gleam in his eyes.

No doubt Ossie hoped Garvan would make a generous donation to PHEADA in honor of his aunt's memory.

Garvan's mouth curved downward. "We'll see. Leave it to Aunt Fiona to be the talk of the town even after she's gone."

Of course, she'd be a topic of interest with her death fresh on everyone's minds.

"She was a true force in her own way," Ossie acknowledged. "Kindly notify our office when you've set a date for the memorial service. We'll send a memo out to our membership."

With a parting nod, he walked off and became engaged in a conversation with the mayor and his entourage. Keri had heard Ossie had political aspirations and believed those rumors to be true. He knew how to work a crowd.

"I'm not sure when we'll be able to schedule a service," Garvan said with a frown. "The police will have to release the body before we can make plans. I don't understand why they're holding things up."

"Who was it that notified you?"

"Detective Saunders. That call was a shocker. I never expected—"

"Sweetheart, I've been looking for you. Oh, hello Keri. And who's this?" Enid, Garvan's wife, spoke in a low, throaty voice as she joined them. She wore a sparkly blue cocktail dress and a heavy dose of perfume that reminded Keri of floral bouquets at funerals.

Keri introduced Lora. Enid gave her a brief nod and focused on Keri. "Weren't you planning Aunt Fiona's birthday party? I'm not sure what you did for her otherwise. She said you ran some kind of service."

"I own a personal concierge agency. I did a variety of jobs for Fiona."

"Did that include managing her finances?" Garvan asked, studying her with narrowed eyes.

"Those details are confidential."

"You'll have to tell me if I'm her heir. I'll want an accounting for every transaction. I understand you were selling things for her on eBay."

"Fiona has… had a houseful of collectibles and antiques that took up every space. She wanted to start decluttering."

"I hope she didn't sell too much of that junk because we could use the money."

Keri resisted the urge to grit her teeth. A nudge from Lora reminded her to be polite. "If you need help disposing of things, I have a buyer online who's been snapping up her goods as soon as I list them. I'll fetch you a decent price. That is, assuming you do inherit Fiona's personal possessions."

He gave her a considering glance. "I may take you up on your offer."

Fiona wouldn't like him referring to her treasures as junk.

Everything there had held sentimental value for her. As for Garvan, Fiona had said he had rarely visited unless he wanted something. Nor did Enid ever invite Fiona for the holidays. Fiona called her a cold fish and didn't care to spend time with either one of them.

Despite her distaste, Keri realized she shouldn't offend Garvan if she wanted to assist him with the funeral. He might skimp on the details otherwise, and Fiona deserved a proper sendoff.

She forced herself to be amiable. "Here's my card if you want my help with the memorial lunch," she said, handing one over. She got Garvan's contact info in return. "Is your son here? I'd been hoping to meet him." As far as she knew, he was Fiona's only other living relative.

"Hugh never comes to these charity events," Enid said with a sniff. Her note of disparagement made Keri wonder if he avoided society events in general. If so, was it because they didn't appeal to him or because this wasn't his crowd?

"How old is he?" Lora asked, posing aloud the question on Keri's mind.

"Hugh is twenty-four," Enid replied. "Don't look at him to be sorry about Aunt Fiona's death. She constantly criticized him. I hope she remembered him in her will at least."

"What, in addition to my share?" Garvan scoffed. "I wouldn't count on it. Oh, hey. There's Maurice. I should say hello to him. I'll be in touch, Keri." He scurried off to greet the organization's vice president.

Enid walked away without even the courtesy of a goodbye.

Keri glanced at Lora. "That conversation left me with a sour taste. Let's hit the bar. I need a drink to sooth my nerves."

"Me, too. Seems to me that the people we've met didn't like Fiona very much." Lora ticked them off on her fingers. "Hope Pittman didn't care for Fiona's nosy questions. Enid and Garvan want her money. Ossie seems to be the only one who appreciated her."

"Diane will be the most upset about her death. I haven't seen her. She must have been too broken up to attend."

"Who's Diane?" Lora asked, crinkling her nose.

"Fiona's surrogate daughter. Diane's mother and Fiona were best friends. When Diane's mom died, Fiona took Diane under her wing."

"Do you know her very well?"

"We've only met a few times. I'll give her a call during the week to offer my condolences."

They bought drinks, and then Lora headed toward the food tables.

Keri roamed the room to greet more guests and introduce herself as the party planner. She handed out business cards, feeling guilty for focusing on work when she should be mourning Fiona. But duty held sway tonight.

She realized she should thank the chefs for coming. Stopping by each table, she complimented them on their displays and expressed her gratitude for their participation.

A few of the food samples satisfied her hunger. Amazed at how quickly her wine glass emptied, she placed it on a tray and ambled toward the artists. Keri wished she could afford their spectacular paintings of Florida landscapes.

She did another round of thanks and ended up at Tatiana's display. Keri had invited the talented young artist to several of these events already. They shared an enterprising spirit, and Keri wanted to help her in any way she could. The willowy brunette wore an attractive maxi-dress and had pinned her long hair back from her face.

"How's it going?" Keri asked her with a friendly smile.

Tatiana grinned back, the warmth extending to her tawny eyes. "I've had a couple of sales, so it's been a successful night for me. Thanks so much for including me again."

"Thank you for giving your time to support our cause. I'm glad to hear you've sold some of your works, but I'm sorry Fiona isn't here to join us. She loved your scenes with native birds and would have bought something."

If they expanded next year to include other types of art,

perhaps Keri could afford to purchase a smaller item. The big donors could still buy the canvases, but then more people would have a chance to find something less expensive. She'd have to mention this idea to Ossie later.

That is, if his group meant to retain her services. She hoped Fiona's absence wouldn't negatively impact their connection.

Tatiana's eyes grew sorrowful. "It's hard to believe Fiona is gone. I miss her being here tonight. She always had a cheerful attitude and a good word for everyone."

"I know. She would have been pleased by the great turnout."

"Most of that was due to her influence. She convinced people to get involved. That was her superpower."

"You're right." Then again, were all these guests truly altruistic? Or had they shown up because Fiona had compelled them to attend? Purdy had planted seeds of doubt in her mind.

"Fiona was always kind to you, wasn't she?" Keri asked, hoping for confirmation of Fiona's magnanimous nature.

"Yes, of course. I greatly appreciated her support. People have been stopping by and asking about my work, thanks to her recommendations." Tatiana pointed to a silver-haired gent chatting with Maurice. Ossie must have greeted the veep and moved on. "Have you met John Beekman, the real estate developer? I was thrilled when he bought one of my paintings. I heard he's been gobbling up older condo buildings in town for redevelopment. Get this. I pitched him the idea of using some of my art on the walls. He said he'd pass my name on to their decorator."

"That's a wonderful idea. Here's hoping they go for it. Your scenes of native Florida would be much more appealing than the usual boring, generic pictures in building lobbies."

Keri glanced at Maurice and John Beekman. They appeared to be in a heated discussion. Maurice shook his head at something Beekman said, spat out a reply and stalked away.

Ouch. That clearly hadn't been a friendly talk.

"Tatiana," said a woman from behind just as Keri was about to take her leave.

Recognizing Winnie Marino's strident voice, she whirled around to see PHEADA's secretary bearing down on them.

"You need to come see me this week," Winnie said, wagging her finger at Tatiana. "You're late with your payment."

"I'm sorry," Tatiana replied, her voice strained. "I've tried to contact you, but you didn't return my calls. If I can have more time—"

"Impossible. We can't make exceptions, not when we have a waiting list."

What kind of payment did Tatiana owe her? Keri couldn't begin to guess, but it wasn't her place to interfere.

"Hi, Winnie. It's good to see you again," she said cheerily, hoping to defuse the situation. Not only was it her job to make sure things went smoothly tonight, but she also didn't like how Winnie was speaking to Tatiana.

"How are you, Keri?" Winnie's heavily made-up brown eyes did not disguise the circles beneath them. Her plum lipstick contrasted with her brassy hair and gave her a Goth vibe, especially with her pasty skin and shapeless black dress. Fashion earrings added a touch of gold to her austere outfit.

"I'm happy we got such a great turnout," she replied. She drew Winnie aside, aware of the grateful glance Tatiana cast her way.

"I had no doubts in that regard. Your firm always throws a good party."

"It's been a team effort. By the way, we need to review the details for next month's tea party honoring your donors. It's sad that Fiona won't be there to join us." She watched for a reaction, wondering if Winnie would be sorry that Fiona had passed.

Winnie's face fell. "I was shocked to hear the news about her. It's hard to believe she's no longer with us."

Keri nodded in commiseration. "I'll miss her terribly. She was a great help to me personally as well as being an influencer in the community."

"I know. Her absence will be deeply felt."

"By whom? Surely, not you," said Felicity Abbott, the association's treasurer. She sidled up to join them. Fine lines framed her intelligent green eyes, while tendrils of red hair escaped her French twist.

Winnie's mouth puckered, but she didn't respond.

"Fiona was very generous to your group's cause," Keri told Felicity, to fill in the gap of awkward silence. "Of the many other nonprofits she supported, yours was her favorite."

"If so, let's hope she remembered PHEADA in her will," Felicity remarked in her raspy voice. Keri had always wondered if she was a surreptitious smoker.

Winnie snorted. "That's one pie you wouldn't be able to dip your fingers into."

"Guard your words, darling. I could say the same about you."

Before Keri could consider what they meant, someone from behind tapped her shoulder.

Chapter Five

Keri spun around to regard Sarah Underwood, a neighbor of Fiona's. They'd met at previous events. Sarah wore an ivory ensemble that flattered her figure. With her ash-blond hair and pale complexion, she reminded Keri of a snow queen. Even her crystal earrings sparkled like ice in a sunbeam. The only jarring slash of color was her red lipstick.

"Keri, how lovely to see you. It's been a while," Sarah said, while Felicity and Winnie muttered their farewells and wandered off.

Sarah hadn't been present in the throng of neighbors the day Fiona had died, Keri realized. Perhaps she hadn't been home. Even so, she might have noticed if someone had been lingering by Fiona's house in recent days.

"Sarah, I'm glad you're here. I wasn't sure how many of Fiona's friends would still come tonight."

Sarah's eyes glistened. "She would have wanted the show to go on. This party is a tribute to her legacy."

"I know. Tell me, had you seen—"

"I want to introduce you to someone." Sarah signaled to a tall, sandy-haired man who hovered nearby. "Keri Armstrong, this is Jarek Marshall."

Jarek stepped closer to shake hands. His blue suit jacket enhanced the same hue in his eyes. With his square jaw and his slightly off-center nose, he looked like a dockworker and James Bond all rolled into one. Warmth seeped up her arm as he held on for a moment longer than custom dictated.

"Jarek is a chef who's opening a new restaurant in town," Sarah explained as he broke contact. "I told him about your agency, and he needs your help with publicity."

Aware she was staring, Keri's face heated. "What did you have in mind?" she asked him. She knew what kind of help she'd like to give this man, but was he single? She didn't want to be too obvious by glancing at his ring finger.

"Excuse me, I see someone I need to greet," Sarah said, leaving them alone together.

Jarek grinned, dimples creasing his cheeks. "I'd like to plan a launch party that ties in with local advertising venues. Sarah said your agency specializes in that kind of thing."

Keri nodded, stifling her excitement. This enterprise could give her business the income boost it needed to meet their rent increase. "We organize lots of parties and business events. What sort of restaurant is it?"

"Homestyle cuisine using regionally sourced ingredients. It's my first venture, so I hope your fees are reasonable."

"For special events, we usually ask for a percentage of the total cost. A grand opening celebration is very detailed-oriented and will be heavy on marketing."

He spread his hands. "Where do we start?"

"Do you want a daytime or evening event?"

"I'm thinking dinner hour."

"How soon will this take place?"

"Let's aim for February. We're still waiting on permits and licensing as well as equipment. Then there's the holiday rush. I'd rather take our time to get things right."

Keri's pulse raced at the possibilities. "We could tie the grand opening into Valentine's Day if that would work for you."

He gave her a thoughtful glance. "That sounds doable. We should set a meeting to get started on the details. How's your schedule for next week?"

Keri checked the calendar on her phone. "If you're free on Tuesday afternoon, I can fit you in then." She had a meeting with the catering director at the Parkhaven Hotel that day but could delegate it to Purdy instead.

"Okay, but in the meantime, how about joining me for dinner tomorrow night? We could start on the preliminaries."

"Oh. Um… I guess I'm free." Whoa, he'd knocked her off-kilter with that invite. Normally, she was the one who set parameters with her clients.

"Pencil me in for Tuesday as well," he said with a disarming grin. "I have a feeling we'll need to spend a lot of time together."

Struggling to keep her cool, she managed to agree on where and when to meet on Sunday night before they parted ways. The idea of seeing him again made her blood thrum.

Left alone, she scanned the room for Lora's blond head but didn't spot her anywhere. It was getting so crowded that she risked sloshing someone's drink if she turned too quickly. The noise level had risen, making her head throb.

Craving a moment of quiet, she headed outdoors to the rear garden. Its sculpted grounds were part of the museum's display. The encounter with Jarek had left her feeling so hot and flustered that she didn't even shiver in the chilly air. She couldn't decide if he was being flirty or sincere. Either way, she'd focus on his restaurant launch the next time they met.

A chorus of crickets calmed her nerves as she strolled along an illuminated path toward the gazebo. She paused when a figure over by a darkened patch of grass caught her eye. It looked like Sarah. Keri should thank her for the introduction to Jarek.

She'd veered that way when another person moved into the light. What was Ossie doing there? She stepped behind a tree, not wishing to intrude but curious as to why they were meeting removed from public view.

"How much longer will I have to wait?" Sarah's pleading words carried on the breeze. "You promised me—"

"I told you we have to lay low for now," Ossie snapped, "especially after Fiona's death. Don't cause trouble until things die down." He snickered at his pun. "You know what I mean."

Keri's eyes grew round. She supposed Sarah could have been referring to anything, but Ossie's warning concerned her. What did Fiona have to do with their private problems?

Before they could spot her, she turned away and hastened back toward the party. She'd tell Lora about their exchange and get her opinion. Inside, she searched for her friend, wondering how many of the guests' animated conversations masked troubling personal issues.

She turned to avoid a woman holding a filled martini glass and nearly collided with Calvin Foster. He backpedaled to avoid bumping into her.

"Jeez, Keri. Watch where you're going."

"Nice to see you, too. Is Diane here?"

He pursed his lips under a receding hairline and deep-set dark eyes. "No, she stayed home with the kids. After she heard about Fiona, she was devastated. She asked me to come tonight to support Fiona's cause."

"Who notified you?" Keri asked.

"Would you believe Garvan called to rub it in that he'd be inheriting everything? That guy is something else. He knows how much Diane cared about Fiona, but all that interests him is her money. I'd be surprised if he even informs us about a memorial service."

"Don't worry. I'll make sure you're included." While Garvan might realize Fiona favored Diane's family, she didn't think he would turn them away at her funeral. "Meanwhile, please give Diane my sincere condolences. I'll call her during the week."

The photographer she'd hired sauntered over and aimed his camera at them. He was chronicling the event for the group's website, social media, and newsletter. Various members of the press were present, too. They were taking pictures for the local society pages.

Cal threw up an arm and turned away. "Not me. I don't like my picture taken. Old family superstition."

Keri gave him a quizzical glance. She'd heard of people from other cultures who didn't like their photos taken, but Fiona had never mentioned this oddity regarding Cal. Then again, she hadn't noticed any pictures of him among the framed photos in Fiona's house. Most of their family pictures featured Diane and the kids.

Unfazed, she stepped apart and smiled for the house photographer. When he was done, she glanced around, but Cal had already left.

Just then, a microphone squealed and hurt her ears. Ossie's voice came on loud and clear.

"May I have everyone's attention, please? Fiona was supposed to make this speech, but the honor has now fallen to me." He segued into a glowing tribute to Fiona. Then he read her spiel, along with the testimonials from Keri. He concluded with a request for donations in her honor.

Drained of energy, Keri swiped at a tear about to run down her cheek. Seeking comfort, she searched for Lora in the crowd and spotted her in the corner, chatting with a bunch of women. Keri caught her attention with a wave and pointed toward the exit. She'd done her duty and wanted to retreat for the night before she was totally exhausted.

"I've heard some interesting things," Lora remarked as they headed outside toward the parking lot. "What about you? Did you learn anything new after we split up?"

Keri nodded, enjoying the scent of autumn leaves in the night air and the chorus of crickets. It was peaceful after the throng of people inside. The lilac fragrance she'd detected earlier had dissipated, or maybe it had been a figment of her imagination.

"I ran into Diane's husband, Cal," she replied. "He said Diane was too upset to come tonight, so he took her place. She's home with their kids. Garvan notified her about Fiona's death and gloated over his impending inheritance."

Lora's mouth turned down in the dim light from the streetlamps. "I knew Garvan was a prick when I met him."

Keri tended to agree on that score. "Even more interesting was the snippet of conversation I caught between Sarah and Ossie," she said, repeating the gist of it.

"That does sound odd, but they could be referring to a work-related issue. Is Sarah involved with the organization?"

"She volunteers at some events. But why would Ossie warn her to lay low and not cause trouble?"

"It's possible they're working on a project that will be affected by Fiona's absence."

"Perhaps," Keri agreed, mulling over this possibility. "Or maybe Fiona got wind of some scheme they've cooked up, and they got rid of her."

"By staging a robbery? Don't be ridiculous."

"It's not such a stretch. Sarah lives next door. She might have been familiar with Fiona's habits, like when she went to sleep."

"What then? She stole away from her husband and broke into Fiona's house?"

"Or she convinced Ossie to do it." Her brow throbbed, and she rubbed her forehead. She'd seen the dents in Fiona's rear door. Had the lock been jimmied, or had the intruder used a tool like a crowbar? It seemed unlikely a woman would do that.

Lora jabbed a finger in the air. "We're meeting Pam for brunch tomorrow. With her background, she'll come up with some good questions you can ask the detective the next time you see him."

Keri absorbed her words and fell silent. She'd dig as deep as necessary to discover what had happened to Fiona. She owed it to her friend to find justice and would do whatever it took to get the right answers.

****

Sunday morning dawned bright and sunny, and as usual, Keri and Lora met Pam for their power walk around Central Park. Planters filled with colorful crotons bordered the sidewalk, while moss-draped live oaks graced the grassy rectangle that made up the park. She heard the occasional toot of a horn from a train at the nearby Amtrak station.

"Lora and I attended the PHEADA party last night at the art museum," Keri began after they'd exchanged greetings. Pam hadn't been there to cover it for the *Gazette* because she'd had another assignment.

"How did that go?"

"It ran smoothly, considering Fiona's absence. Ossie—the group's president—read Fiona's fundraising speech. It was a nice tribute to her."

Pam tucked a loose strand of auburn hair under the wide-brimmed hat she wore to protect her freckled face. "Can you tell me what happened yesterday?"

Keri described her visit to Fiona's house and the ensuing disaster while Lora kept pace beside them. It pained her to relive the details, so she only related the highlights.

"I'm sorry. I know you were fond of her as a client and a friend."

"True. I miss her already, but at least her nephew has agreed to let me help with the memorial lunch. I'm glad I can look after her interests that way."

Pam gave her a keen glance from behind her sunglasses. "What do the cops say?"

"Detective Saunders wasn't very forthcoming."

"His hands are probably tied until he gets an official cause of death. It could have been a robbery gone wrong. Or not. That opens up other possibilities."

Keri frowned. "Purdy told me not everyone admired Fiona, and after talking to some of her so-called friends at the party, I'm wondering if he's right. She was always so kind and thoughtful to me, but maybe that was an act." Keri couldn't conceive of why Fiona might have deceived her, but she was beginning to doubt her perceptions.

"What exactly did people say about her?" Pam asked with a tilt of her head.

"I overheard an odd conversation between Ossie and Sarah." She filled Pam in on their brief exchange. "In our last phone call, Fiona said she couldn't trust anyone except me. Maybe she suspected those two of doing something unethical."

"You may be taking their conversation completely out of context. Then again, if it turns out Fiona was murdered, all her acquaintances become potential suspects. Is there anyone you know who might have had a grudge against her?"

"Ossie's wife, Hope, said Fiona had stuck her nose into everyone's business. Obviously, Hope didn't care for her, but she's only involved with PHEADA through her husband's role. I'd be more inclined to look at Winnie and Felicity. They're the group's secretary and treasurer, respectively. They made some strange remarks about dipping their fingers into the pie, whatever that means."

Pam skirted a woman pushing a stroller with a cute little Yorkshire terrier inside. "It could mean anything. You don't know them well enough to make assumptions. Did anyone speak kindly about Fiona?"

Keri nodded. "Ossie praised her generosity and contributions to our community. Tatiana, my artist friend, mentioned how she'll miss Fiona's patronage. And several others spoke well about her, too."

"I talked to Maurice, PHEADA's vice president," Lora said. Keri glanced at her in surprise. She hadn't mentioned this last evening. "He put on a sad face when I mentioned Fiona and said she would be missed, but I didn't get that vibe from him. If anything, he seemed gleeful that she was no longer around."

"Interesting," Keri said. "I saw him speaking to the land developer, John Beekman, and it didn't appear to be a friendly conversation. Maurice walked away in a huff. Who knows what that was about?"

Maybe they'd been discussing Fiona. Keri had detected undercurrents last night that she wouldn't have thought twice about before Fiona's death. But add in Purdy's insinuations, and they took on more significance.

"Maurice complimented your firm for organizing the event," Lora told her.

"Thanks, that's good to know. Fiona had acted as a liaison between us, and now I'll have to work directly with each board member."

Less than pleased by that prospect, Keri stopped beside a fragrant gardenia bush to tighten the shoelaces on her sneakers. "Maybe I can get more information from Detective Saunders. I have to stop by the police station to sign my statement and leave my fingerprints for comparison."

"Does he work on weekends?" Lora asked.

"Since this is a fresh case, I assume he'll be there. I'd like to know when Fiona's body will be released. I can't help Garvan plan her luncheon until we have a definite date."

"Even if he's there, he might not be willing to share the details about an active investigation," Pam said. "In that event, what will you do? I don't see you leaving things up to the cops when they might accept the most obvious explanation."

Keri thought about it as she resumed her pace. Didn't they usually interview neighbors when there was a crime? "I could pay Sarah a visit. She lives next door to Fiona and might have noticed someone lurking by her house. Or I could talk to the lady across the street. Saunders seemed to regard her as a conspiracy nut, but she still could have seen something important."

Lora poked Pam's elbow. "Hey, you're in the perfect position as a journalist to do some research. What if you suggest to your editor that you want to do a profile on Fiona? That would give you an excuse to dig into her life. She was a generous philanthropist whose loss will be felt throughout the community. I'd think that would be a good subject for an in-depth article."

"That's a great idea," Keri said, excited by this suggestion. "Fiona never spoke much about her past. What if you discover something in her background that led to her death? A scoop like that would allow you to show them your chops as an investigative reporter."

"I love it," Pam said with a grin. "Count me in, whether my editor approves or not. I sniff a story here. Let me know when the funeral is scheduled, and I'll go with you. That's the best place to start."

Lora's cell phone rang, and she pulled it from her bag. A glance at the caller ID made her wince. "Rats, that's the third call this morning. If Rick contacts you, you don't know where I am," she told Keri. "Okay?"

"Sure," Keri agreed, aware that if Lora's former boyfriend wanted to locate her, he had merely to follow her home from work. She hoped Lora wouldn't cave in to his excuses again.

Lora stashed her phone away. "By the way, I've been looking into rentals. It's a tight market, and I might need to stay at your place longer until I find something affordable."

"Don't worry. You can be my roomie as long as necessary." A moment's anxiety flashed through Keri's mind as she imagined Rick pounding on their door. With his temper, she was concerned he might become abusive, but despite the risk, she couldn't turn Lora away.

Lora's face brightened. "Thanks, it means a lot to me. I'll contribute to the utilities and will help with cleaning."

"Now that would be welcome," Keri said with a chuckle. She hated to clean. She'd debated hiring someone but didn't want to spend the money.

They quick-marched ahead. Their path curved around the rose garden, took them past the bulletin board listing community activities, and cut by the bandstand at the northern end of the park. A train whistle sounded as a line of railroad cars clacked its way past the Amtrak station.

When they reached their favorite café, they came to a halt. Customers were lined up by the door, waiting for a spot inside, and all the outside tables were filled.

"Oh crap," Lora said. "We should have gotten here sooner."

"It shouldn't be long. Look, people are coming out," Pam observed as six people exited.

When their turn came, Keri and her friends followed the hostess inside. A jolt of surprise hit her when she spied Ossie and Sarah sharing a table for two near the entrance. Judging from their intent expressions, they were involved in a deep conversation. Should she go say hello or pretend she hadn't seen them?

No way would she pass up this opportunity. Without further hesitation, she broke off from her friends and stepped in the pair's direction.

Chapter Six

"Hey, guys. Nice to see you again," Keri said, while Lora and Pam trailed after the hostess.

Sarah gave her a startled glance. "Keri. I, um, didn't expect to see you here."

"I came with my friends. It's our favorite breakfast place, despite the fact it's always crowded on weekends. How about you guys?"

Ossie cleared his throat, his face reddening. "We're discussing PHEADA business. With Fiona gone, we have a gap in our organization. I've asked Sarah to take charge of a particular project in her place."

"Oh? Which project is that?"

"We're still working out the details before we make an announcement."

"I see." From the way he avoided her direct gaze, Keri didn't quite believe him. "Good luck with it, then. Sorry to have interrupted. Enjoy your meals." She waved and moved on, not wishing to intrude any further.

As she turned, she noticed Ossie reaching across the table to grasp Sarah's hand, and somehow, she didn't think their meetup had anything to do with the nonprofit organization. But then, why else would they convene in such a public place?

She pushed aside her questions to admire the white latticework decorating the interior and the ceiling fans twirling overhead as she headed toward her friends' table. Smells of bacon and toast wafted in the air, making her mouth water. She was starving after their walk.

"What happened to you?" Lora asked when she'd rejoined them.

She sat and lifted her menu. "I stopped to say hello to Ossie and Sarah. They're sitting at a table by the entrance. Ossie said they were discussing PHEADA business, but he acted evasive when I asked for details. And when I left, I noticed he took hold of Sarah's hand."

"Isn't she married?" Lora asked, a crease between her brows.

"Yes, but her husband hasn't shown up, neither last night nor this morning."

"Do you still intend to drop by her house? If so, you could ask her for more info about this supposed new project."

"True. I'll have to find time to fit in a visit," Keri said, aware she had a tight schedule next week.

They paused their conversation when their server brought over steaming mugs of coffee and took their orders. She'd brought water glasses as well.

"Pam, do you have any suggestions as to what I should ask Detective Saunders when I see him?" Keri asked, sipping the hot brew after adding creamer.

Pam rummaged in her purse for a notebook and pen. "I should take notes while we talk. According to what you've said, Saunders likely believes Fiona to be the victim of a robbery gone wrong. But what if that's not the case? Does he have any alternatives?"

"Hmm. Garvan would top my list of suspects if he turns out to be her beneficiary. I suppose this means I'll have to give him the box of Fiona's goods I've stashed in my closet."

"What? You brought her stuff home?" Lora squealed, gazing at her in horror.

"What's the big deal? She gave me a bunch of things to sell, and I couldn't get to them all at once. Fiona said it would be okay if I took them home to catalogue." A defensive note crept into her voice. Why was Lora looking at her like she'd done something wrong?

"Did you tell the detective you've been selling off the victim's possessions?" Pam said, obviously on the same wavelength as Lora. "He might wonder where the money has been going, or if you've been fudging the sales figures."

Her shoulders tensed at the implication. "He knows I've been putting her things up for sale on eBay. I've offered him a copy of my inventory list. If he wants to verify my records, he can check the receipts. I have clear accounts of all sales and payouts."

Then again, would Saunders believe her if he learned about their office rent increase? That would give her a motive for needing money. "At any rate, we're getting ahead of ourselves. We should wait for the detective to officially announce the cause of death before we go off on tangents."

Lora took a noisy slurp of coffee. "Let's change the subject to a more pleasant topic. What do you have planned for the rest of the day, Pam? I'm going food shopping, since Keri has nothing decent to eat at home."

Pam grinned, her impish face surrounded by waves of red hair. "I'm getting my nails done for a party tonight. That reminds me, we need to plan a spa day together."

"That sounds wonderful," Keri said with a sigh. While she'd love to indulge herself, she'd have to postpone any spa dates until she made sure her budget would allow for it.

A sense of hollowness crept up on her. Fiona would have told her to take a day off and relax. She'd miss her wisdom and advice. Here she was, laughing and chatting with her friends while Fiona's cold body lay in the morgue. How could she forget her grief so quickly?

Lora gave them an oblique glance. "I'm afraid I'll run into Rick if I go out anywhere else. After I go grocery shopping, I'll stay in for the rest of the afternoon."

Keri bit her tongue to avoid making a snide remark. Lora needed to learn to stand up for herself. She kept making the same mistakes. Hopefully, she wouldn't let Rick sweet-talk her into coming back… again.

"Men aren't worth the trouble," Pam said with a dismissive wave. "Then again, I might take my chances on that guy walking through the door."

Keri's heart thudded in her chest as she recognized Chef Jarek. She surveyed his broad shoulders in a navy polo shirt, and her mouth went dry. Golden highlights streaked his head of fair hair.

"Hey, Keri. I didn't expect to see you here," he said, stopping at their table. His teeth gleamed white as he grinned at her.

Keri introduced everyone. "Jarek is a new chef in town. He's hired my firm to publicize his restaurant's grand opening," she added.

Pam offered him a brilliant smile. "Would you like to join us? We have an extra chair."

Lora raised her brows. "Yes, by all means. We would love the company."

"Thanks, but I'm meeting a friend." Jarek nodded at Keri. "I'll see you this evening. Nice to meet you, ladies." He loped off toward a lone man at a table in the rear.

"Holy hot potato," Pam muttered under her breath. "Have you been holding out on us? It sounded as though you two have a *date*."

Keri's skin heated. "Jarek suggested we meet for dinner to do a preliminary interview regarding his restaurant launch. It's strictly business."

"Oh, sure. Whatever you say. Hey, if you're not interested in him, tell him I'm available."

"You?" Lora scoffed. "Miss love-'em-and-leave-'em? You wouldn't stick around long enough for a relationship, especially with the erratic hours a chef keeps."

She and Keri both knew why Pam sought affection from romantic entanglements that never lasted. Her parents had regarded their only child as an accident not meant to happen. All she'd craved was their love, and when they ignored her for months on end, she looked for solace elsewhere. Likely that explained why Pam cut things off before the latest boyfriend could reject her.

"Excuse me?" Pam protested. "I stayed four months with

my last guy. Besides, I might even turn over a new leaf just for Chef Jarek."

"You're welcome to him. I don't date clients," Keri declared in a huff. *Yeah, right. He's a hunk. Maybe you should make an exception in his case.*

"Come on, Keri," Lora said in a coaxing tone. "Your fiancé might have been a jerk, but there are still some good men out there. You need to get back in the game."

"Oh, like you're the expert?" Pam quirked her eyebrows. "You cling to Rick even though he's a loser. You should let him stew in his own pot for a change."

"He's not all bad. He just needs to find the right path."

"Keep telling yourself that, hon. See how it works out for you the next time."

"Enough about men," Keri said, before their discussion escalated further. It wasn't a topic she liked to discuss when it applied to her. She'd dated Dave for two years in college. After graduating, they'd gotten engaged. She'd been excited to plan their wedding until she found her fiancé in bed with Angie Coppersmith, a sorority sister. His betrayal still stung like a splinter festering under her skin.

The waitress delivered their orders, and Keri poured maple syrup on her raspberry-and-brie stuffed French toast. She ate in silence for a few moments before restarting their conversation. To avoid controversial topics, she focused on upcoming social events and other plans.

Finally finished eating, she signaled the server for their bills. She couldn't linger with all the items on her to-do list for that afternoon.

"I'll meet you back at the condo," Lora told Keri as they rose from the table. "Is there anything you want me to get at the grocery store?"

Keri mentioned a few items. "Thanks, Lora. I appreciate it." She'd forgotten how nice it was to have company at home. "Pam, good luck in getting your article approved."

On her way out, she glanced at the table Ossie and Sarah had occupied, but a group of women sat there now, studying their menus. She still wondered what they'd been doing together aside from PHEADA business.

After exchanging farewells with her friends, she drove to the assisted living facility where her client resided and parked in their spacious lot. She'd brought along a pot of yellow mums to give to Mrs. Brody to brighten her room. The woman's daughter lived out of town and had hired Keri to visit twice a month. She was more thoughtful than most of the other residents' children.

Then again, not everyone could afford her services on top of the six grand per month plus extras that the ALF charged. Not all the residents had long-term care insurance to cover the costs.

She pushed open the front door with her hip and swung inside. The ground floor held a suite of administrative offices, a spacious dining room, and an auditorium for speaker presentations. It also held a library, salon, and small chapel.

A corridor branched off either end, with each wing holding private bedrooms. The second floor had a secure section for memory-care patients.

Despite its attempt at a cheery décor, with peach-colored walls and framed artwork, the place still had an institutional look and an ever-present smell of bleach. The latter was more pronounced down the residential hallways. An alcove held walkers and wheelchairs ready for use. Her mood dipped, as it always did at this place. It was sad how people had to give up their independence and privacy when they couldn't live alone anymore.

She nodded at the receptionist, who knew her by sight. As she passed the admissions office, she heard voices from beyond the slightly ajar door.

"I can't tell you how happy I am that you've accepted my mother," said a woman in a familiar raspy voice.

Startled, Keri halted. Was that Felicity, PHEADA's treasurer? And what was this about her mom? She'd never really spoken much about her personal life.

"I'm glad things worked out, Miss Abbott. You're lucky we had a vacancy," the administrator responded.

"Mom will be thrilled. This place is so much better than where she's living now."

"You won't regret your choice. We'll take good care of your mother. Let's get things started. Here are some papers for you to sign."

Keri hurried on before Felicity noticed her hovering outside. Hopefully, her mom had enough savings or an insurance policy to fund her housing needs. Otherwise, Felicity would have a hefty bill to cover.

A white-haired woman shuffled up to her. "Excuse me, miss. Can you show me the way to my room? I can't remember where it is."

"What's the number?"

"That's the problem. I don't know."

"Come with me. I'll find someone to help you." Keri passed the auditorium, where a staff member was arranging chairs for the afternoon event. A vocalist would be singing old Broadway tunes, and she knew it would make Mrs. Brody happy if Keri sat alongside her. She felt bad charging money for her time, but that's why she had Purdy handling those details.

She found a nurse's aide and handed the confused lady over to her. As she moved down the hall, Keri greeted Frank, a widower who spoke of his late wife as though she were still alive.

"Ann wants me to go to the concert," he told her, hunched over his walker. "Are you staying? It should be a nice performance."

"Yes, I'll be there. See you later, Frank."

Keri stopped by another resident named Judy, who was a retired teacher. She'd chosen to move into assisted living rather than burden her children. In her eighties, Judy liked the socialization aspect and participated in the activities offered by the social director.

"How's it going?" Keri asked her. "Did you win the Mah Jongg tournament the other day?"

Judy waved a gnarled hand. "Nah, I lost. But no worries. I'll win next time."

Keri moved on, saying hello to the former shoemaker who always commented on her footwear and then to another visitor whose aunt had suffered a stroke.

The warning signs came to mind unbidden—numbness or weakness on one side, blurred vision, slurred speech or trouble speaking, loss of balance, or a sudden, severe headache.

Her mother had suffered headaches. Several scans had come up negative for a brain tumor, but they had missed the slow leak that had ultimately caused her stroke. Another specialist might have found the aneurysm if Keri and her sister had insisted Mom get another opinion.

It was too late for that now, but she could still care for her clients. She entered Mrs. Brody's room with a cheerful air. The elderly woman sat in an armchair with a shawl wrapped around her frail shoulders. She wore a flowered top with black pants and a lonesome expression that brightened upon Keri's arrival.

"Keri, it's good to see you, dear."

"Mrs. Brody, how have you been? I've brought you a plant," she said, putting the pot down on the windowsill. As she gave the woman a gentle embrace, she noted that Mrs. Brody felt thinner than last time. She'd have to catch the nurse to make sure her client was eating enough.

"You're a sweetheart," Mrs. Brody said in a weak voice. "You don't have to bring me gifts each time you come."

"I like doing it. How are you feeling? You need to keep your strength up, or your daughter will be upset with me."

Mrs. Brody cackled. "Iris is always upset. She's annoyed that I won't move closer, but she has enough to do caring for her own family. I refuse to be a burden on her."

"It would be easier if you lived nearby. Don't you want to see your grandchildren?" Keri handed her the roll of stamps she'd bought on her behalf. Mrs. Brody wrote letters to her grandkids the old-fashioned way.

"Of course, I do. But my old bones can't stand the cold weather. I would hate the winters. All that dry air inside and frigid temperatures outside."

"We have hurricanes and humidity. It's a trade-off," Keri pointed out.

"True, but I prefer Florida." Mrs. Brody looked thoughtfully at the flowerpot Keri had brought. "Fiona used to like yellow mums. I heard the sad news about her."

"Fiona Sullivan? Did you two know each other?"

"We became friends when she moved to Florida. That gal enjoyed life to the fullest, but like almost everyone we know, she kept some things to herself."

"What do you mean? Fiona was a friend of mine, too. I was very fond of her."

"Did you ever meet Herman? He's in the room at the end of the hall," Mrs. Brody said.

"No. What about him?"

"He always made me laugh. He'd lost his son in the service, and after his wife died, he moved here. One day, they couldn't wake him up. Apparently, he'd saved his pills and took them all at once. We'd had no idea how lonely he must have felt," Mrs. Brody said, twisting her gnarled hands together.

"That's horrible. Poor guy."

"It proves that you never know what somebody is truly thinking. Like Fiona."

"Are you saying she was depressed?" Keri wouldn't forgive herself if she'd missed the signs. Could this be why Detective Saunders had asked her about Fiona's prescriptions?

"Not depressed. Regretful." Mrs. Brody leaned closer. "Did you know she meant to reopen her antique shop when she moved here? She'd even bought a property for that purpose but then decided to retire instead."

Keri gaped at her. "I knew Fiona had considered relocating her shop, but not that she'd gone so far as to purchase a place. She never mentioned it to me." A sting of doubt pierced her at this revelation. What else had Fiona neglected to tell her?

Mrs. Brody's eyes gleamed as though she were about to impart juicy gossip. "Fiona loved to brag about the foreign cities she'd visited and the things she'd bought. I envied her those experiences, but her face would grow sad when she spoke about the past. Something happened to take away her zest for life. She might have chatted about her parties and charitable works but mark my words. That woman was keeping secrets from us all."

Chapter Seven

"What kind of secrets?" Keri asked. Could this be about her lost love or something else entirely? True, Fiona had never talked much about her life up north, except for the antique store. Maybe there was a reason she'd been reluctant to discuss her personal history.

"She kept her past buried even from me, but it was plain as day that something troubled her," Mrs. Brody said. "I didn't want to dredge up bad memories, so I didn't press her for details." She struggled from her chair and reached for a water cup on the bedside table. Berating herself for being negligent, Keri rushed to assist her.

"Would you like some apple juice from the kitchen? Or some pudding for a snack?"

"No thanks, dear. They'll serve ice cream after the concert. You will stay, won't you?"

"Of course. This afternoon is yours." Keri poured her a cup of water and handed it over.

Soon it was time for the musical interlude. Shortly thereafter, Keri took her leave while promising to return in two weeks as scheduled. It was heartbreaking that Mrs. Brody wasn't near her family, but Keri could understand the disruption a major move would cause her.

Once in her car, she called the daughter and gave her a report on the day's visit. Next, she texted Detective Saunders that she'd be heading over to the police station.

I'm not in my office, but please stop by to leave your prints, he replied. I'll notify the front desk that you're on the way. As for signing your statement, may I visit your agency tomorrow morning at ten o'clock? I'll bring the papers for you to sign there.

Keri agreed and disconnected with a frown. Did he have a particular reason for wanting to visit her workplace? Maybe he had more questions to ask about her agency's function.

Hoping to get the first unpleasant task done, she swung by the police department and entered its intimidating walls to check in with the receptionist. A deputy took her inside and got her prints while chatting with her about the weather. She supposed it was his way of making her feel comfortable, but the whole time she felt like a criminal and quaked inside.

She had just exited the building when a client called.

"Keri, thank goodness I got you. This is Sandy. I'm at the restaurant for my daughter's Sweet Sixteen party, and nothing is set up. What happened to the decorator? Guests will start arriving in a half hour or so."

Her heart leapt into her throat. "What? Manuel didn't show up?" The party was scheduled for four o'clock, and it was already three. He should have had the place completely decorated by now. "Let me contact him to see what's going on, and I'll call you right back."

"I'm so sorry," Manuel responded after two rings. "My truck battery died, and I'm stuck on Fairbanks waiting for service. I'm kept my phone line open in case they try to reach me."

A rush of relief hit her that he hadn't been hurt in an accident. "You should have called me immediately. Do you realize how late it is? This could cost me a customer. I'm already in my car. I'll drive over and get the supplies from your truck."

She made a quick call to Sandy that she'd be there soon. Hopefully, they'd have enough time to put out the centerpieces and goody bags, but her skills did not include blowing up balloons. Her only option was to request Purdy's help.

"Hey, listen," she said when he picked up. "I'm sorry to bother you, but Manuel is stuck at Fairbanks with a dead battery, and Sandy's party starts in an hour. I can pick up the things from his truck, but can you meet me at the restaurant? I need help blowing up the balloons."

"Sure thing," he agreed jovially, as though happy she'd interrupted his day off. "I'll head right out. Don't worry about a thing. We'll get it done."

Bless his heart, and she meant it in a good way. He deserved a raise for always having her back, but then so did Staz. She wished she could afford it for them but that would have to wait.

She retrieved the supplies, met her client at the restaurant, and greeted Purdy when he arrived. While he blew up balloons, she set out the centerpieces and laid out the seating cards that doubled as take-home picture frames. On another table provided for that purpose, she laid out the goody bags and made sure space for gifts was available as well.

The aroma of garlic emanating from the kitchen made her mouth water. She'd had ice cream with Mrs. Brody but nothing else since brunch with her friends.

"Thanks so much for coming today," she told Purdy, after he'd directed the candy vendor where to put his station. "I really appreciate your help."

"No problem. I was just relaxing after last night."

"Oh, yes. How was the club?"

"Amazing. I met Svetlana there. She had me playing her tune in no time." He mimicked strumming a guitar.

Keri frowned at him. "I thought you'd mentioned a woman named Kitty. What happened to her?"

He shrugged. "She didn't show up. It's her loss."

She shook her head at his cavalier attitude. "I'm glad you had a good time. Look, I need to go home and change before my date tonight. Can you finish up here?"

Purdy pounced on her words like a car salesman. "You have a *date*? As in, with a man?" The astounded look on his face was almost comical.

A flush warmed her face. "I meant to say my appointment.

Chef Jarek is a new customer, and he's hired us to plan his restaurant's launch party. We're merely doing a preliminary interview. He's coming into the office on Tuesday to sign the contract."

"Where did you two meet? I don't recall this guy stopping by the office."

She pursed her lips at his persistence. "Sarah Underwood introduced us at the PHEADA party."

"Oh, yeah. How did that go? Did people miss Fiona?"

You could have asked about her sooner. "Yes and no. Some people seemed genuinely sad, and others made snide remarks." Glancing at her watch, she winced. She still had to shower, fix her hair, and change clothes before heading out again. "We can talk more about it tomorrow. If I don't leave now, I'll be late."

Keri arrived at the condo fifteen minutes later, tossed her handbag on the kitchen counter, and washed her hands. Lora was there, judging from the humming coming from the guest bedroom.

"Lora, I'm home," she called, noticing the clean countertops. They hadn't been this tidy when she'd left. It was handy having a roommate who liked to clean.

Lora wandered into the kitchen and straightened the blousy top she wore with a pair of distressed jeans. She'd secured her blond curls with a blue bandanna. "I hope you don't mind that I rearranged things a bit. You had no room in your pantry for my groceries, so I stashed your cookbooks in the linen closet. And why do you have so many canned goods? Hurricane season is over. You should consider donating the extras to a food bank."

Keri forced a smile on her face. It was nice of Lora to tidy the kitchen, but she wished she'd asked before moving things around. "I like to keep certain items in stock."

"Like baked beans, chicken noodle soup, and eight cans of tuna fish? You don't have a cat. Do you eat this stuff for dinner? Oh, I also took care of the trash and vacuumed. You should hire a maid service when I move out. All the dust made me cough."

"Thanks, I'll think about it. Now, I need to change before I meet Jarek so I'm not late." Keri dashed into her room to get ready and was lucky to be out of the house and on the road with time to spare.

By the time she reached the restaurant, it was six o'clock, and Jarek was already standing outside the entrance waiting for her.

"Nice to see you again," he said, grinning as she approached. His smile transformed his rugged features and heightened her senses in a way she hadn't felt in a while. She glanced at his blue sport coat that enhanced the intense hue of his eyes. Her skin heated as she noted the open top buttons of his dress shirt, giving her a glimpse of his hair-sprinkled chest.

"Shall we go inside?" she asked, trying hard to remain professional.

After the hostess seated them, she studied the menu, letting her hair shadow her face. It acted as a curtain, guarding her thoughts so Jarek couldn't observe how he affected her. They made small talk until the server took their orders.

Keri waited until their glasses of merlot arrived before pulling a notebook from her bag. "Let's get started. We've determined your grand opening will take place on Valentine's Day. Does this date still work for you?"

His eyes twinkled. "Yes, but only if you'll be there. There's no one else I'd rather celebrate the holiday with than a beautiful woman like you."

"Thanks, I think." How many times had he used that line before? "Tell me, what is it that makes your restaurant stand out?"

"Let's call it elevated comfort food featuring farm-to-fork Florida cuisine."

She creased her brows, uncertain what that meant. "Do you mean comfort food as in mac and cheese and meatloaf?"

"More like lobster mac and cheese with gruyere, cheddar, and freshly grated nutmeg. Or chopped sirloin with caramelized onions and roasted mushroom gravy. It's food people love and will recognize, but with a fresh twist."

"Sounds intriguing. What's the atmosphere? You know, will this be a family-friendly place, or an upscale setting better suited for date nights and special occasions?"

"Definitely the latter. The open kitchen will make guests feel as though they're part of the culinary experience. We'll have white tablecloths, votive candles, and fresh flowers on each table to invite intimacy. I hope it'll become a go-to destination for proposals."

"You sound like a romantic at heart." She took a sip of wine, savoring the flavor. "I think we have our theme. Food made with love. That fits in perfectly with Valentine's Day."

"I like it." He pulled a flash drive from his jacket pocket and offered it to her. "This has our basic info, including the menus, catering services, my bio and more."

"Thanks, that will be helpful." She tucked the drive into her bag. "Our firm will write the press releases, create flyers, design invitations, and do the mail-outs. You'll want to make a big splash about the launch on your website, too. Do you have a web designer, or would you like us to do this for you?"

"You can handle it. I'll send you the login info and our social media links. I need to focus on getting the restaurant ready and not all this marketing work."

"No worries. We'll take care of the advertising so you can do the things you love," she said in a confident tone. "Who will be managing the front end of the restaurant?"

"My business partner, Ronnie Pearson. He'll oversee dining reservations, staff scheduling, and other administrative duties."

"I'd like to stop by sometime to meet him and see your layout."

"Sure, that would be great."

She thought about what else they'd need. "How about music? Your opening gala should include a touch of elegance if that's the ambiance you want to project."

"What did you have in mind?"

"I know a guitarist who would blend in nicely with your theme. He'll give us a reasonable price." She didn't add that the musician was new in town and looking for gigs. It helped her business to connect clients whenever possible.

Like Fiona, she thought with a spark of insight. She'd connected people who had common interests and would have advised Keri on which people to invite to Jarek's event.

"What's the matter?" he asked. "You look serious. I hope it's not something I've said."

"No, it's not you." She fingered her wine glass. "I was thinking about Fiona. Remember, at the PHEADA event, Ossie spoke about her. She was known throughout town for her charitable activities. We were friends, and I miss her dearly."

"I'm sorry. I didn't realize—"

"No problem. Fiona would have suggested a charity tie-in for your launch party to attract media attention."

He nodded. "That's a great idea."

She was glad he approved. "I can email you a list of nonprofit groups that might be appropriate, unless you have a preference."

He buttered a slice of crusty Italian bread and took a bite. "I'd like to support sustainable farming, or if that's not possible, then feeding the hungry."

"Okay, this will narrow the choices." Keri considered how she'd delegate duties. Staz had her artsy side in addition to being the agency's IT person. She'd delight in using her creativity to spruce up the restaurant's website. Meanwhile, Lora could design the ads, invites and flyers. Keri would keep track of guests and handle the press. She'd let Purdy arrange for the flowers and hire the musician. It would require a substantial team effort.

If they did a good job, it would boost their visibility in town, not to mention the fees that would add to their bottom line. Purdy would be happy.

"Are you always this super-organized?" Jarek asked with a disarming grin.

She couldn't help smiling back at him. "It's my job to stay ahead of the game."

"You seem to enjoy what you do. How did you get started?"

Keri considered her response. She'd worked in corporate marketing where the high stress level hadn't concerned her until she began to get palpitations. Since her mom had died of a stroke and her dad of a heart attack, she worried that cardiovascular disease might run in her family. Getting laid off from her job proved to be a blessing in disguise.

"I'd worked in marketing and wasn't happy with the constant stress," she told Jarek, choosing a simpler explanation. "I noticed how everyone rushed around without taking time for themselves or their families. So, I left my job and set up the agency to help ease people's burdens. At least, that was my goal in starting out."

"It's an admirable objective, but it seems to me you're plenty busy. Have you shown the same care for yourself that you show for others?" Jarek asked with a perceptive gaze.

Thrown off-kilter by his remark, she fumbled for a reply. "I manage well enough, thanks."

Fortunately, the server chose that moment to arrive with their orders. She delved into her salad with fresh greens, sunflower seeds, golden raisins, and goat cheese.

They continued their discussion during the rest of the meal. Keri suggested giving a red rose to each lady who attended the launch party and Jarek approved the idea.

"I'm glad we were able to get started tonight," she told him. "We'll have a proposal ready for you to sign on Tuesday."

Jarek finished his steak while she polished off her grilled salmon. When he made a move for the check, she withdrew her credit card. "It's my treat. You're a client so this qualifies as a business expense." She hoped he'd continue to employ their services beyond his grand opening.

They took their leave in the parking lot. Keri was glad he hadn't tried to push their relationship in a romantic direction. As she'd told her friends, it was against her policy to get involved with a client, plus she still couldn't tell if this man was genuinely interested in her.

Lora was still awake when Keri got home. Her curly hair looked tousled as she meandered into the living room in her jammies.

"How'd it go?" Lora asked, settling onto the couch.

Keri hung up her keys on the set of hooks by the kitchen. "We got a lot accomplished. Now we have a definite direction to follow for Jarek's grand opening."

Lora's brows soared. "That's it? Did you find out if he's single?"

"We didn't discuss our personal lives." Keri couldn't deny Jarek's appeal, but she was determined to stick to business where he was concerned. "And now, I'm heading to bed. It's been a long day, and I'm tired. Plus, I have to get an early start tomorrow."

Lora's nose wrinkled. "Ugh, it's another day at the grind for me."

Keri had heard this refrain before. "If you're unhappy, find another place that will appreciate your talents. Or better still, start your own business."

"Not possible. I need the steady income and the benefits. It's too risky to leave."

Keri suppressed a retort. Sometimes you had to take a leap of faith to get ahead in life. That's what she had done in changing careers. But she understood Lora's need for security, especially when she'd just broken off with her boyfriend.

Suddenly, Fiona popped back into her mind, and she remembered her comment about a love interest. When Fiona had offered no further details, Keri assumed it was a painful topic. Now she wondered what had caused their split. Could it relate to the secrets Mrs. Brody had mentioned?

Chapter Eight

Monday morning found Keri at the office by nine o'clock. Both Purdy and Staz had errands to run, so she had the place to herself. She'd just finished typing up her notes from the interview with Jarek and printing out Fiona's inventory list when Detective Saunders arrived.

His presence made her nervous. While she had nothing to hide, she feared he might construe her closeness to Fiona as something shady. She'd known Fiona's routine, helped her with financial matters, and had knowledge of her valuables. If he was hunting for motives aside from a robbery, it wouldn't be a far stretch to look in her direction.

As he advanced, his keen gaze scanned the room while she examined him in turn. He wore a sport coat, crisp white shirt and tie, and had slicked his dark hair back from his forehead. He looked like a hawk searching for prey, making her hope she could avoid any missteps in their conversation that he might take the wrong way.

"I like your slogan out front," he said, dropping into the chair opposite her desk without waiting for an invite. "*If you can't do it all, give us a call. A Friend in Need Agency will take care of you.* Tell me, do you get walk-ins, or is it all referrals?"

She gave him an amiable smile, aware he was trying to disarm her. "We get most of our customers through networking, but there's a stack of brochures outside for passersby. People grab them out of curiosity. They'll call later when they need help."

"Good idea, since most people may not know what a

personal concierge is. How many employees do you have on staff?"

Keri gestured to the front row desks. "Only two. Purdy Jenkins is our office manager. He works with our vendors and does the bookkeeping. Staz—Anastasia Laurent—is our computer guru. She does the virtual assistant jobs, manages our website, and plans the larger functions. I like to work with clients on an individual basis to make their lives easier."

Staz was more than just an employee to her, as was Purdy. In a moment of friendship, Keri and Staz had bonded over drinks one night after work. Keri had told Staz about her mother's illness, while Staz had revealed her dream of becoming an event planner at a luxury resort in St. Barts. She'd fallen in love with the island after visiting there on a cruise. She'd taken the job at Keri's agency to gain experience, make connections, and add credentials to her resume.

"I can tell that you enjoy your role," Saunders said with a steady gaze.

"It's fulfilling to help clients who need us."

"Like Miss Sullivan." He studied her from under his bushy eyebrows. "Is there anything you want to add to your statement before you sign it? Any details you might have remembered?"

She shook her head. "I was too stunned to notice much of anything. Here's my inventory list from her house." She handed him the printed sheets of paper.

"Thanks, it'll be useful." He gave her the statement in exchange. She read it over, her stomach churning as she mentally revisited the scene. Pressing her lips together, she signed her name, dated it, and returned the document to him.

He opened his notebook and clicked on his pen. "I have a few more questions while I'm here. You said you'd picked up Miss Sullivan's prescription for sleeping pills last Tuesday. Can you explain why the bottle was nearly empty the night she died? She'd been given a thirty-day supply."

"That can't be right. Fiona only took one when she had

trouble falling asleep. The bottle should still be full." She stared at him. "Wait, do you think the intruder stole them?"

"It's possible," Saunders said with an impassive face.

She supposed the thief could have seen the container in the bathroom and taken the pills either to sell on the street or for personal use. But then, why not take the entire bottle?

"What about her meds for high blood pressure and cholesterol?"

"Those had the proper number of tablets."

A horrifying thought presented itself. The thief hadn't forced Fiona to take the sleeping pills, had he? "What is the official cause of death?" she asked in a squeaky voice.

Saunders regarded her with flinty eyes. "Miss Sullivan died from asphyxiation. It's considered a homicide case now."

Keri gripped her stomach. Even though she'd hoped for a different outcome, this confirmed Fiona must have been smothered. What a terrible way to go.

"I still believe an intruder is the most likely culprit," Saunders said. "Or, someone who knew her habits could have planned the whole thing. Garvan Connor suggested you were taking advantage of your relationship with his aunt."

Her jaw dropped. "What? How dare he say such a thing! My business depends on honesty and discretion. I'd lose my agency if I took advantage of clients. From my conversations with him, Garvan strikes me as someone who can't wait to get his hands on Fiona's estate."

Saunders didn't react to her assessment. "I'd like a copy of your transactions with Miss Sullivan, if it isn't too much trouble," he said, in a tone that indicated this wasn't a choice.

She bristled at his request. "I'll have Purdy compile the data into a file." A flash of anger speared through her. He should be focusing on other acquaintances of Fiona instead of her. Then again, she'd read about elder abuse. Unscrupulous caregivers forged checks, cashed in retirement benefits, or coerced patients to change names on their bank account, insurance policy, or property deed. Did Saunders really believe she would stoop so low?

Her blood ran cold at another thought. How would he react when he heard about the box of Fiona's goods she had stashed in her closet? Fiona had never issued any receipts for the things she'd given Keri to sell. Her budgetary concerns would only add fuel to the fire.

"I can't help wondering at Garvan's rationale for saying such a thing," she said, after struggling for a composed response. "He's hired me to help with the funeral luncheon. If he truly thinks I've behaved unethically, why would he want to work with me? He must be trying to throw suspicion off himself."

Saunders quirked an eyebrow. "Why is that?"

"He believes he is Fiona's beneficiary. At the PHEADA event, I met Diane Foster's husband, Cal. He told me Garvan had notified them of Fiona's death and gloated over his pending inheritance. This clearly gives him a motive, don't you think?"

"Perhaps, although it brings up the question, why wait until now to do the deed?"

"That's for you to find out." She paused. "Any idea when we can make plans for the memorial lunch?" Garvan might change his mind about using her firm if they waited too long.

"The body should be released later this week."

She nodded, considering the questions Pam might ask as an investigative reporter. Regardless of whether the crime was a straightforward robbery or a staged scene, someone had broken into Fiona's house. "Tell me, what's the difference between a robbery, a burglary, and a home invasion? I'm unclear on those points."

Saunders appeared to weigh his response. Was he wondering why she'd asked?

He leveled his gaze at her. "The simplest explanation is that burglary involves unlawfully entering a building with intent to commit a crime, such as theft. Robbery implies use of force or threat of force. The difference is that robbery is a crime against a person, while a thief merely steals something that belongs to someone else."

"And a home invasion?"

"In a home invasion, the offender enters a house with the intent to commit a crime, but either the owner is present, or the bad guy lies in wait for them. This offense also involves the use or threat of force."

Keri shuddered. No matter the definition, they were all evil. She could see a drug addict breaking in if he'd viewed Fiona as a vulnerable victim. Desperate for cash or jewelry to sell, they wouldn't care who they hurt to get what they needed. Finding meds with street value would be a bonus. That could explain the nearly empty prescription bottle, but not why the container had been left behind.

"Aside from a possible drug addict or neighborhood punk, do you have any other suspects?"

He smirked as though to say, *Aside from you?* "You've just mentioned the nephew," he said. "Who else would you include?"

She noticed how he'd deflected her question and countered it with his own. She considered Fiona's acquaintances. At least he seemed willing to listen.

"Felicity, the group's treasurer, may be supporting her mother in an assisted living facility. A room there costs over six thousand a month. I overheard Felicity talking to Winnie, the PHEADA secretary, at the party. They accused each other of dipping their fingers into the pie, whatever that meant. It did make me wonder if they were referring to the group's finances."

"Go on. Anyone else?" he asked, with a sardonic twist of his lips.

"I overheard Ossie, the group's president, talking to Fiona's neighbor, Sarah Underwood. Ossie warned Sarah to lay low after Fiona's death and not to cause trouble. I ran into them again the next morning at breakfast downtown. They claimed to be working on PHEADA business, but from their body language, the relationship seemed more personal."

He gave her a thoughtful glance. "You're very observant. Do you usually take such meticulous interest in people?"

"Yes, I do. It's important in my job to sense what my clients may need in addition to what they want. I imagine Fiona heard a lot of gossip through her social circles. Perhaps she overheard something not meant for her ears." When Saunders opened his mouth to reply, she forestalled his next inquiry with a wave. "And no, Fiona never shared anybody's secrets with me." *Or any of her own*, she thought.

"One more thing," she said, jabbing her finger in the air. "Are you researching Fiona's background? She never talked much about her earlier life. Maybe her past came back to bite her."

"Thank you for your suggestions." He snapped his notebook shut. "Let me remind you that this is an ongoing investigation, and you should keep our discussion private. Also, please don't go and play Nancy Drew to solve your friend's murder. That's my job."

"Understood." At least she'd given him some leads to follow. She rose, aware that Purdy and Staz would be arriving soon. She didn't want to subject them to an interrogation if Saunders was still here.

He stood, shook her hand, and took his leave.

Mulling over their interview, she formulated a takeaway of several points that she wrote down to share with Pam later.

Garvan didn't trust her motives, and she could say the same about him.

Fiona had died from asphyxiation, the most likely means being smothered by a pillow.

The bottle of sleeping pills was nearly empty when the prescription had just been refilled. Looking at it from the detective's viewpoint, she could have offered Fiona a glass of water with the tablets dissolved inside, murdered her, and staged the break-in. He'd assign her a motive, too, if he found out she needed money to keep her agency afloat.

Then there were the PHEADA people, and Fiona's neighbors to consider.

The phone rang, scattering her thoughts. She recognized a client's ID on the screen.

"Hey Keri, it's Clara Pearson. I have a meeting in South Florida next week, and I need to get my hair done on Tuesday. I'll be staying at the Sheraton Suites in Palm Haven. Can you recommend a salon nearby?"

Keri struggled to get her mind back to business. Palm Haven was a western suburb of Fort Lauderdale. "Sure. The Cut 'N Dye Salon is about five minutes from your hotel. Marla Vail is the owner. She's also an experienced stylist. Shall I give her a call and ask if she can fit you into her schedule?"

They had met when Marla came to town regarding a possible case of insurance fraud involving a friend. She had a penchant for solving crimes and often assisted her husband, a homicide detective. Keri had added her salon to their vendor list for that area.

"I'd appreciate it, thanks. Also, I'll want to take three colleagues out to dinner while I'm there. Can you make a reservation for us on Wednesday evening at a nice restaurant?"

"Of course. I'll text you when I have confirmations." After Keri hung up, she completed those tasks and then glanced at her watch. It was nearly eleven, and her stomach needed food. She went into the back room and grabbed a yogurt from the fridge. That would keep her going for a while.

Purdy arrived, they exchanged greetings, and he sat down at his desk. When she asked about his morning appointments before they got started on anything else, he opened his portfolio and withdrew a stack of papers. "The inflatable company has bounce houses, slides, and obstacles courses that'll be great for children's parties. Their company is licensed and insured and listed as a recommended vendor by the school board. I have their signed contract in hand."

"Good job." Keri was delighted to add another name to their

supplier list. "What about the housekeeping service? Were you able to ask the owner about the complaints we'd received?" Keri always preferred to work things out with vendors instead of dismissing them outright.

"I stopped by, and the proprietor promised to do additional training. She'll also assign the same crew to a house whenever possible. She seemed anxious to continue our relationship." Purdy cocked his head. "Hey, are you listening?"

Her thoughts had wandered, and she gave him a guilty glance. "Sorry. I was just wondering if anyone had notified Fiona's housekeeping service."

"O-kay. I don't think that's all of it. Do tell what else is on your mind."

She brought him up to date. "Saunders has ruled Fiona's death a homicide."

He adjusted his eyeglasses. "She must have woken up and startled the thief."

"It was only her bedroom that was trashed," Keri remembered. "I assume that's the first place a crook would look for jewelry."

"I hope the detective is considering other prospects besides a random intruder."

"You and me both. Garvan told Saunders I might have been taking advantage of Fiona. The detective requested a copy of our transactions with her, and I told him you'd prepare a file. But if he hears about our budgetary concerns, I'm screwed."

Purdy's mouth twisted. "Garvan is nasty piece of work. Hopefully, Saunders will see through his nest of lies. Don't worry about the budget. Jarek's business should give us the boost we need to cover our added expenses."

Staz breezed in and plunked down her purse. "Keri, you're here. How are you holding up?" She stepped over to give Keri a quick hug. She smelled citrusy, like her favorite verbena soap.

"I could be better, but I can't complain."

"I'm sorry again for your loss. You spent a lot of time with

Fiona. I'm sure you're going to miss her." Staz straightened the scarf that she wore with a camel sweater. "Have you learned anything new? Like, was it a home invasion like the newscaster said on TV? How terrifying."

"It seems that way, but I've asked my friend Pam—she's a journalist—to research Fiona's earlier life. She never spoke much about her past, and I think it's possible someone held a grudge against her. Hey, maybe you can do an Internet search to see what you can learn."

Two heads are better than one, right? Keri felt obligated to find out whatever she could about who had done this to her friend. And the two women wouldn't necessarily be working at cross-purposes. Pam would have resources that weren't available to Staz.

"I'd be happy to help." Staz's brown eyes glistened with sympathy. "The truth will come out in the end. I know you want to find out what happened to her."

Keri felt comforted by her words. "Here's the thumb drive with Jarek's restaurant information. Can you please add the launch party to his website?" Keri handed over the device, forwarded his login and password, then gave Staz and Purdy a brief rundown of her plans for his grand opening.

"I'll get on it. Lora can create a logo for him along with the printed materials."

"Sounds good." Graphic designs were right up Lora's alley. "Purdy, I'll need Jarek's contract ready by later today so I can look it over before his appointment tomorrow."

"Easy peasy." He turned back to his desk.

The office line rang, and Staz answered. "One moment, please." She pressed the Hold button. "It's for you, someone named Barf or Garf."

Staz knew his name well enough. Keri ignored her jibe, worried that Garvan had changed his mind about hiring her.

She grabbed her phone receiver. "Hello, Garvan. What can I do for you?"

"Have you heard when we'll be able to move forward with Aunt Fiona's memorial service?" he asked in his whiny tone. "The police detective hasn't gotten back to me."

Keri bit her tongue to keep from making a nasty retort. He hadn't even had the decency to greet her properly. "I checked in with Detective Saunders today. He'll be letting us know soon enough. Meanwhile, I'll call the restaurant to see if we can change our reservation."

"Don't forget to transfer the deposit."

Her hackles rose at his mercenary attitude, but she decided to be the better person. "Garvan, I run my business with high professional standards. Of course I will transfer the deposit. And I don't appreciate you insinuating I would do anything underhanded with respect to Fiona's account."

"You were selling her stuff. She wouldn't have noticed if you recorded a sale for less than the amount received."

"I have receipts to verify the transactions. And I don't steal from clients. If that's what you think, you might prefer to make the luncheon plans yourself."

"No, no, I still need your help." Now he was backpedaling at full speed. "My mind is clouded by grief. I'm just looking for some way to explain my aunt's death."

Keri didn't believe him for a second. She thought it more likely Garvan was trying to avoid giving Detective Saunders a reason to consider him as a possible suspect. "If you don't trust me, I can't work with you," she said a bit stiffly.

"I do trust you to do the job. I can't deal with the restaurant plans and the funeral home arrangements all by myself."

So ask your wife for help, she thought, but instead said, "I'll take care of it out of respect for Fiona's memory." It would be foolish to give up a paycheck due to pride. "Oh, and I'll need your credit card info for our retainer fee."

He cleared his throat. "You'll have to bill Diane for payment. Apparently, she's my aunt's executor and successor trustee."

Well, that was news but not a surprise. Fiona was closer to Diane than to Garvan. "How do you know this?" she asked.

"Diane called me this morning. It appears she has a valid copy of Aunt Fiona's estate documents."

"Is that so? Did she verify that you're the beneficiary?" She knew Detective Saunders would be interested in this development.

Garvan snorted. "You'll find out sooner or later, so I'll tell you now. My darling aunt cut my family out of her will and left everything to Diane."

Chapter Nine

"Your aunt didn't leave you anything?" Keri asked, flabbergasted. She'd known Fiona wasn't fond of her nephew but hadn't expected her to disinherit him entirely.

"Not a cent," Garvan replied with a growl. "Diane gets her personal property, her financial assets, and her house. I can't believe it. She's not even a blood relation. I've asked my attorney to challenge the will."

"I'm surprised you still want to plan the funeral, given those circumstances."

"I *am* my aunt's next of kin," he said bitterly.

Keri understood his resentment but also Fiona's decision. Fiona had spent holidays with Diane's family and regarded her children like her own grandkids, while Garvan and his wife had ignored her. Or so Fiona had said. Could Garvan's earlier remark be correct—that their estrangement had been her fault?

"What about your son?" Perhaps Hugh had a better relationship with his great-aunt.

"Diane didn't mention him, although she hadn't finished reviewing all the documents yet. Aunt Fiona should have thought of him, if not me."

"I hear you." It would have been a kind gesture on Fiona's part to give Hugh a small bequest. Then again, Keri didn't know how well they'd gotten along.

"Has Detective Saunders said anything more to you regarding his investigation?" Garvan asked. "The sooner things are resolved, the sooner we can get back to our normal lives."

Nancy J. Cohen

Fiona would never have a normal life again, but all you care about is her money. "He's considering it a homicide case at this point," she replied. "Can you think of anyone who might have wanted to harm your aunt?"

"Huh. It wasn't me, since I had nothing to gain."

Yes, but you didn't know that at the time. You could have murdered her to gain the inheritance you assumed was yours.

"There's still a chance it was a random robbery," she said. Hopefully, Saunders would investigate the different options and not just shuffle off Fiona's case as a botched break-in. In the meantime, she'd continue to keep her own ears open.

"Maybe Diane did it," Garvan suggested with a snicker. "She and her family followed Aunt Fiona to Florida. Why else would Diane coddle her, except for her fortune?"

"Diane regarded Fiona as a surrogate mother," Keri countered. "She might have been concerned that Fiona would be alone."

"Or she had an ulterior motive in moving closer. At any rate, I'll be in touch when I have more definitive news regarding a funeral date." Garvan signed off, and Keri placed the office phone down with a thoughtful frown.

"What was that all about?" Staz asked, spinning around in her chair.

"Yes, I'm curious, too." Purdy said, swiveling in his seat as well.

She took a moment to gather her thoughts. "Garvan said Diane is Fiona's beneficiary. He's pissed that his family was cut out of her will."

Purdy lifted an eyebrow. "That's new. Was Diane aware of Fiona's intentions?"

"I have no idea. When I spoke to her husband at the PHEADA party, Cal believed Garvan would inherit everything."

However, just because Cal was in the dark didn't mean Diane was clueless. Fiona may have mentioned her plans, in which case Garvan's accusations might hold merit.

"I'll give Diane a call now," she told her colleagues. First, she called the restaurant manager to alter their reservation. Fortunately, he agreed to apply Fiona's birthday party deposit to a funeral lunch instead. Keri promised to call him back when they had a definite date.

She rang Diane's number next. A soft-toned woman's voice answered. Keri conjured an image of Diane's strawberry-blonde hair, warm brown eyes, and friendly smile.

"Hi, it's Keri Armstrong. If you recall, Fiona employed me as her personal assistant. I'm sorry for your loss."

"Thanks. Cal mentioned that he ran into you at the cocktail party the other night. Fifi would have been happy at the turnout."

"Fifi?"

"My nickname for Fiona. I can't believe she's gone."

"I know. She always spoke of you with great affection."

"I loved her like my own family. Things won't be the same without her."

Her voice held genuine sorrow, and Keri's doubts about her motives fell away. "I'm helping Garvan plan the funeral lunch. He mentioned that you're Fiona's beneficiary and sounded surprised by the news."

Diane snorted. "Surprised isn't the word I would use. He had some choice words to say to me when I filled him in."

I can imagine. "Had Fiona informed you about her intentions?"

"Not at all. She'd asked if I would be okay being named as her executor, but I never expected her to leave anything to me. I had a thumb drive with her estate documents in a sealed envelope. She said I wasn't to open it until after her death."

That didn't sound as though Diane had anticipated an inheritance. "I presume the house belongs to you now. Has anyone notified Fiona's cleaning service, or would you like me to do it for you?"

"That would be great, thanks. I'll need them to keep coming for a while. I'm not sure who else to contact regarding the house's upkeep. It's all so overwhelming."

"Do you work outside the home?" Keri asked, remembering how time-consuming executing a will could be. She'd helped Zoey do it for their mother.

"I have a real estate license, but I haven't used it in years. The kids keep me busy when they're not in school, and I always have chores to do during the day. I didn't expect to have this responsibility so soon," Diane said, her voice ending on a choked sob.

Keri paused, hesitant to bring up the next matter. But it couldn't be avoided. "By the way, I have a box of Fiona's knickknacks to give you. She meant for me to sell them on eBay, but I hadn't gotten to it yet." The sooner she unloaded that burden, the better.

"All right. We should meet at Fifi's house as soon as the detective clears the scene. I'll need your help with things."

They hung up and she became aware that Purdy and Staz were regarding her expectantly. With a resigned sigh, she related the gist of her conversation.

"It would be great if you could get Diane to sign a contract," Purdy said, licking his lips over the prospect of a new client.

"Let's get past the funeral first, please."

"That event will give you another chance to hear what people thought of Fiona," Staz said. "Hopefully, it'll happen sometime this week. Otherwise, I looked up Fiona online. She didn't have much of a social media presence, except for press coverage of her charitable activities."

Keri nodded. "I'm not surprised. Fiona hated the time we spent on the computer together. She liked to do things the old-fashioned way. But keep digging. You might find something worthwhile buried among the news articles."

The rest of the day passed with errands and client visits. At home later that evening, Keri watched the news on TV. The police chief confirmed that Fiona Sullivan's death had been ruled a homicide. He released few details, except for the suggestion of a bungled robbery. The station did a brief profile on Fiona's life as a prominent citizen in the community.

Tuesday morning at the office, Keri reviewed the goals for Jarek's restaurant launch before his arrival. Her skin heated at the thought of his tall form walking through the door, and a flush of anticipation spiraled through her.

He showed up at the agreed-upon time, and she introduced him to her staff. As he sat in the chair facing her desk, she scanned his T-shirt from Hog's Breath Saloon in Key West that he wore with jeans. A faint whiff of his musk cologne drifted her way.

"Here's the proposal we've prepared for you," she began after they'd exchanged pleasantries. She handed him a printed copy. "Please look it over and let me know if you have any questions. Then, if everything is agreeable to you, I have a contract here for you to sign."

He perused the document while she studied him surreptitiously. He appeared to have an easy-going manner, but as a chef, she supposed he could be demanding in the kitchen. He couldn't be this laid-back when cooking under fire. However, his enthusiasm would belie any orders he barked at his staff. She couldn't deny his appeal. His customers would soon be avid fans if his food was as good as his menu descriptions.

After he signed the contract, they discussed ad placements, guests to invite to his launch party, charity tie-ins, and other details.

"Tell me about your agency," he began, once they'd been through all the plans. He crossed his legs and gave her a wolfish grin. "Do you really accept all jobs, large and small, like it says in your brochure?"

"Yes, we do, as long as it's nothing illegal or immoral."

"As the owner, is your job mostly managerial?"

"Purdy is our office manager. I prefer to work in the field with individuals."

His eyes warmed. "Then you're more like me. I work in the kitchen while my business manager handles the admin duties."

"I guess so. Staz takes care of our virtual tasks and group functions. She's a talented event planner. But we'll all pitch in where we're needed. Every day brings a new challenge, and that's what makes it exciting."

He winked. "I can see that I'll benefit in many ways from your services."

The innuendo didn't escape her. She hoped her colleagues didn't notice. Staz and Purdy remained glued to their monitors, but their hands weren't moving on their keyboards.

"Let's get past the grand opening for now, okay?" she said to Jarek. Despite his flirty manner, he was still a client. She had to maintain a professional attitude if they were to work together. "Reviews will be critical. If you have anyone else to add to our media and restaurant reviewer list, please send me the info. We still have lots of lead time, but the more we get done now, the better."

"I'm confident our opening will be a hit with you in charge," he said, rising. His tall presence seemed to dominate the room.

"I still need to stop by your place. I'll check my schedule to see when I can fit it in."

"That would be great. Don't wait too long, though."

With a sense of relief, she watched him swagger toward the exit. He had a disturbing ability to derail her.

"Whew, he's hot. Good move on landing him as a client," Staz crooned as soon as he'd left.

"I'll say." Purdy spun around and gave her a wicked smile. "How did your date with him go the other night?"

"It wasn't a date. We just had a business discussion to review the preliminaries."

"You went out to dinner with the guy. That's an unusual move for you with a new client."

Her toes tingled at the memory. "It seemed like an expedient way to get things started."

"Sure, Keryn. Just remember that business and pleasure don't always mix well together."

"Don't worry; I have my standards." Fortunately, her cell phone rang, saving her from the personal turn in their conversation.

"Hi Garvan," she said, recognizing him on caller ID. "What's up?"

"I've heard from the detective and called the funeral home. We've set Aunt Fiona's service for Friday at ten-thirty," he said, rattling off the location.

"Okay. Do you need help contacting people?"

"No, thanks. My wife will do that job."

"I'll call the restaurant to let them know." They discussed menu choices before disconnecting.

Keri phoned the place and set the luncheon time for noon on Friday. That would give mourners enough time to drive to the place from the cemetery.

She got busy with other tasks until Diane's name lit up on her phone.

"Garvan called me about the funeral," Diane stated without preamble.

"Yes, I meant to call but he beat me to it. I've made the restaurant reservation for twelve o'clock."

"That sounds about right. Would you be able to meet me at Fifi's house tomorrow afternoon at one? It's been cleared, and we're free to go inside."

Keri would have to hustle to get everything done on Wednesday, but it was doable. "Sure, I can be there."

"Good, I have some things to tell you. I'll see you then."

The prospect of meeting Diane reminded her of the forgotten photo in her purse. Perhaps Diane could identify the fellow with his arm around Fiona.

Her phone pinged with a reminder. Oh, right. She still needed to respond to her sister's Thanksgiving invite and quickly sent her a text to ask what she could bring to the family dinner.

She smiled when Zoey replied that she should make her popular sweet potato recipe. Several cute photos of her niece and nephew followed. She'd have to pick up some toys for the kids before the holiday and added this task to her to-do list.

Those pictures put her in a mellow mood so that when she

got home, she appreciated Lora's efforts to provide dinner. Her roomie had picked up a rotisserie chicken, a packaged rice mix, and a prepared salad. They shared the meal and chatted about their day.

"Things will be easier once Fiona is put to rest," Lora said, a thoughtful frown on her face. Keri had given her an earful of recent revelations.

"Let's hope so. I'm curious as to what Diane will say tomorrow. She may have her own theories about Fiona's death."

"Don't forget to chat up the neighbors about what they might have seen."

"Thanks. It's on my agenda." She may have a better chance of gleaning new info through the grapevine than Saunders would through official channels. The next few days could prove illuminating depending on who she persuaded to talk.

Chapter Ten

Keri pulled up to the curb at Fiona's house on Wednesday afternoon. She was running ahead of schedule. Judging from the empty driveway, Diane must not have arrived yet.

A glance at the front porch confirmed the crime scene tape was indeed gone. Thank goodness. She didn't wish to be reminded of that dreadful day.

Outside on the sidewalk, she straightened the rose sweater she wore over her black pants. The air had been chilly that morning, but it had quickly warmed up. As she adjusted the strap on her crossbody bag, she debated if she should retrieve the box of Fiona's goods from her trunk. It belonged to Diane now.

A movement from across the street caught her eye. She twisted to note Veronica Batten yanking weeds from a row of shrubs in front of her single-story house.

I should go talk to her since Diane isn't here yet. This is perfect timing.

And just at that moment, Veronica glanced up, noticed Keri crossing the street, and hooked her finger in a come-hither signal.

Keri hastened to close the distance between them.

"Hi. I'm Keri Armstrong, a friend of Fiona's," she said.

"I know. I've seen you visiting her house. I'm Veronica." The woman's aristocratic British accent made Keri wonder about her origins. Wisps of gray hair escaped the wide-brimmed hat she wore along with a buttoned blouse and navy trousers. She looked as though she'd be at home in a formal English garden.

Keri stepped into the shade under a leafy oak tree. "It's hard to believe Fiona is gone. I miss her terribly."

Veronica peered at her through a set of sunglasses. "You worked as her personal assistant, didn't you? Fiona spoke of you very fondly."

"Oh? I didn't realize you were friends." Keri hadn't known all of Fiona's acquaintances, just those she'd contacted on her client's behalf. As for the neighbors, Sarah was the only one Fiona had ever mentioned.

Veronica shrugged. "I'm a widow and Fiona was single, so we often got together to chat. Fiona knew how to serve a proper tea."

"This is true," Keri said with a sigh. "Things aren't the same without her." She fell silent, wondering if Veronica had just felt lonely and wanted to say hello. How could she steer the conversation toward the crime?

She tried another tack. "I'd feel nervous if there was a break-in across the street from where I lived. Had you noticed anybody unusual on the street recently?"

Veronica's eyes narrowed. "I've seen them. They think nobody notices, but I do."

Keri leaned forward, her pulse accelerating. "Who do you mean?"

"The bad eggs. They live among us. You should be worried, too." Veronica glanced up and down the street, then lowered her voice. "I dreamt about Fiona last night. She told me to warn you."

Keri's spine stiffened. "About what?"

"The weeds thrive in the warm weather. The ducks stay safe by the lake. The sour apples grow alongside the good ones."

"Huh?" Was Veronica being obtuse on purpose, or was she a few bulbs short in her garden—as Detective Saunders believed?

"You seem like a nice girl, so heed my words. They're watching. Fiona didn't listen and look what happened to her."

"Can you be more specific?" Keri asked, afraid they were veering down conspiracy lane.

"If I tell you, they might come after me next."

O-kay. Now we're really in woo-woo territory.

"I remember seeing you in front of your house after Fiona died," she said, hoping to discern truth from fantasy. "You held up a sign that said, *Go Home, Criminals. My Eyes Are On You.* Were you aiming those remarks at someone in particular?"

Veronica gave her a wily grin. "When you dig too deep in the ground, you run the risk of exposing snakes. You need to protect yourself, or they might bite you."

Her hat shadowing her face, she bent to pry loose a stubborn plant. After she yanked it out with unusual vigor, she found another stalk to pull. Her motions became jerky as she cleaned the shrubs of unwanted growth.

Keri sensed that Veronica was beating around the bush, literally as well as figuratively. If she did know something, she was acting elusive on purpose.

"Can you give me any names or descriptions?" she asked, as an earthy scent reached her nose.

"They know who they are. If I disappear, it's because the FBI kidnapped me as a witness."

Oh, boy. Are aliens the next baddies on your list?

"Was this the first break-in for your neighborhood?" she asked, hoping this would garner a lucid response.

"Huh. You should ask Sarah's husband that question."

Keri gaped at her. "You mean Bob Underwood? Why do you say that?"

"He's one of them. Their spies are everywhere. Look at the bad seed that got planted earlier. It took root but its growth is misshapen."

Keri gritted her teeth at yet more riddles. "How do you believe Fiona died?"

A curtain washed over Veronica's face. "The cops say a robber killed her."

"Do you agree with them?"

"The silver fox hides behind the trees. It goes undercover when the wolves circle close," Veronica said, pulling out another weed.

Keri barely heard her as a dog barked down the street and a cement truck rumbled past. Before she could think of what to ask next, a white SUV arrived at Fiona's house. That would be Diane.

"I have to go," she said, frustrated that she hadn't learned anything solid. "Thank you for your advice. Here's my contact info if you need to reach me." She handed over a business card.

Veronica took it then suddenly spun around and sucked on her finger. She must have pricked it on a plant. Across the street, Diane and her husband emerged from their car.

Diane spotted Keri and waved while Cal approached the house and let himself inside. Seeing Cal, Keri recalibrated her plans. Her agenda with Diane included the photo in her purse and the box of Fiona's goods in her trunk. She also meant to offer her professional services to Diane. But what was Cal doing here? Maybe Diane didn't need her assistance after all. Yet Diane was the one who'd asked to meet her there.

Veronica twirled back and tapped her arm. "Remember to keep your head down. Fiona can only keep the evil spirits away for a short time. They came through when the veil opened. Raise your shield and stay on guard."

Keri detached herself from this odd conversation and crossed the street. Now Veronica had added ghosts to the mix, but at least their conversation had served a purpose. Fiona's neighbor might have been enigmatic, but she didn't appear to believe Fiona had died from a robbery gone wrong. Otherwise, she might have been fearful of similar attacks in the community. Instead, she'd made cryptic remarks hinting at suspects that might or might not exist.

She strode up the walkway to Fiona's house and pictured her friend waving from the front porch, her silver hair in a swirl and her hazel eyes radiating affection. *I miss you,* she thought with a catch in her throat. *You were a rock in my universe. The world seems emptier without you.*

Taking a fortifying breath, she met up with Diane on the landing.

"Hi, Keri," Diane said with a warm smile. "It's good to see you, although not under these circumstances."

"I know." Keri gave her a quick hug, then stepped back.

"Let's go into the kitchen. I'll put on a pot of coffee unless you'd rather have tea."

"Coffee is fine. I only drank tea with Fiona because that was her preference." Keri paused. "I saw Cal is here with you."

"He's busy in the garage looking for insecticides. We have an ant problem at home, and we've run out of supplies. Then I've assigned him to clean out the fridge."

"Good idea. The perishables need to be tossed."

Diane led the way and halted at the stairway. "I don't care to go upstairs. I can't bring myself to look in the bedroom where… you know. The bedding will have to be removed."

"I know who to call, if you want me to handle it for you." That is, if Diane hired her. Purdy would get on her case if she didn't charge for her services.

Diane pressed a hand to her chest. "That would be great, thanks." She went into the kitchen and soon the aroma of brewing coffee filled the air.

Keri took a mug from a cabinet and filled it from the carafe. She wrinkled her nose upon sniffing the creamer from the fridge.

"This has gone bad," she announced, pouring the contents down the drain and throwing out the container. Fiona had kept a box of non-dairy creamer cups in the pantry, which she used instead. The hairs on her arms lifted as she pictured Fiona standing beside her. Maybe she was there in spirit, smiling at her and Diane being together.

After they'd sat down at the table facing each other, Diane broke the solemn mood and spoke first.

"I want to hire you to help me clean out the house, since you're familiar with the contents. I'll sell the place eventually." She regarded Keri with deep-set brown eyes above a longish nose. Strawberry-blond hair framed her face in soft waves, while hints of gray betrayed her at the roots. Keri put her age in the late forties range.

"I'll make sure Fiona's treasures find a good home," she said. "As you may know, I've been selling things for her on eBay. Here's a printout of our inventory list." She withdrew a sheaf of papers from her handbag and handed it over.

"I don't know where to start regarding her antiques," Diane said with a sweeping gesture. "Cal is more knowledgeable in that area than I am. I'm not a fan of older styles and have no idea how much these things are worth."

"Look at my spreadsheets," Keri said, pointing. "You'll find descriptions of each item, the initial cost, place of purchase, and current fair market value."

Diane glanced at the papers. "I'm impressed. You did all this research on your own?"

"Actually, Fiona kept detailed records of her purchases in a ledger. Were you familiar with the antique shop she'd owned in Manhattan?"

Diane's face grew wistful. "I have vague memories of the place. My mother was best friends with Fifi, so I'd often accompany her there. I remember our first visit to this house after we'd relocated. The place was so cluttered that we could barely move. I couldn't believe she'd kept all this furniture."

Not to mention the tchotchkes taking up every surface, Keri thought. Those collectibles had once been sought-after items, but her own generation had different tastes. At least her steady buyer on eBay appreciated them.

She took a sip of coffee. "Before I forget, I brought the box of goods Fiona had given me to sell. It's in my trunk."

"Do you know what's inside?"

Keri nodded. "It's an English tea set, with a teapot, bone china cups and saucers, dessert plates, and a cake platter."

Diane's eyes glistened. "Fifi was fond of her tea sets. I don't have any use for them, nor do we have room in our house for more stuff. Why don't you keep the box until I decide how to dispose of everything?"

"All right. I'm glad you're giving it careful thought. If

Garvan had inherited, he'd want as much money as he could get without respecting Fiona's treasures."

Diane grimaced. "You should have heard him after I told hm about the disposition of Fifi's will. He accused me of being after her money all along. That is totally untrue. I had no idea she'd included me in her estate plans other than naming me as executor."

Keri's gut clenched. "Garvan accused me, too. He hinted to the police detective that I might have been abusing my relationship with Fiona. I've kept accurate records of every transaction if you want to examine them."

"You don't have to defend yourself to me. Garvan is a worm. He intends to challenge the will." Diane scrubbed a hand over her face. "I've been in touch with Fifi's attorney. He said Garvan doesn't have a leg to stand on. According to the lawyer, she'd originally listed her nephew as beneficiary, but then she amended and restated her estate plans after Cal and I moved to Florida. Later she added a codicil with some additional bequests."

"Garvan wasn't wrong in believing he was the heir, then."

"Right. He just didn't know she'd made updates." Diane's dewy eyes regarded Keri with speculation. "I had another purpose in meeting you here today besides engaging your firm. Fifi mentioned you in the codicil."

Keri's mouth gaped. "She did? I wasn't expecting any-thing." Her throat thickened. Leave it to her dear friend to be generous in the end.

Diane grinned at her reaction. "Maybe you knew this already, but she'd bought a cottage, intending to reopen her antique shop near Hamilton Square when she moved to Florida. She changed her mind but still held onto the property. It's a small but cute little place, and now it's yours."

"No way. She left me a house?" Keri gawked at Diane, unable to fathom this turn of events. A place in that district, however tiny, would be worth a good amount due to the location.

"She wrote letters to several people along with her bequests.

Here's yours." Diane fetched an envelope from her bag on the counter.

"Thanks." Her mind reeling, Keri tore it open and quickly scanned the contents.

Dear Keri, she read. *I've appreciated all you have done for me. You've been like a granddaughter and have eased my burdens. I knew I could count on you for whatever help I needed. You have a kind nature and genuinely care about your clients. That's why I've left you this small cottage. It's zoned for mixed use if you want to move your place of business there. Then you won't have to worry about rent. With love, Fiona.*

Keri blinked, tears filling her eyes. In this heartfelt message, Fiona had validated her career choice and her purpose. How could she have died and left her to face things alone?

Speechless, she handed the letter to Diane, who'd reclaimed her seat. Diane's face softened as she read the message.

"This is sweet. I agree that your portion is well deserved."

"Wait until Garvan hears about this," she said, imagining his bitter reaction. "He'll have another reason to resent me." Plus, it would fuel his intent to challenge the will.

"Fifi appreciated everything you did for her. Don't mind him."

"She was lucky to have you nearby," Keri said with a smile. "She adored your children and being with you for the holidays. It meant the world to her."

"We were her only family here that mattered. And we live relatively close compared to Garvan."

Keri withdrew the photo from her purse. This gave her an opening to ask Diane about it. "Speaking of family, can you identify the people in this photo? The woman looks like a younger version of Fiona. It fell out from some papers she'd sent me."

Diane peered at it. "Yes, that's her. My mother had tons of pictures of the two of them together."

"Did you keep them? I'd love to see more photos of Fiona

in her younger days. We could use them to make a collage poster for her funeral."

Diane shook her head. "Unfortunately, we tossed out most of the old photos before we moved. I only kept a small collection."

"Who's the man in this picture?" Keri asked, hoping to solve this small mystery, at least.

"That would be Fifi's father, Crogher Sullivan." Diane's face darkened, and she handed back the picture. "My mother didn't like him. She said he was a bad influence on Fifi."

"How so? She spoke very little about her background when we were together."

"Mom wouldn't talk about it, and I didn't care to upset her by prying."

Keri waved the picture in the air. "I gathered Fiona sent this to me to display at her birthday party, but I never got the chance to ask her about it."

"You can keep it as a memento. I have enough pictures of her. It makes me sad to look at them now."

Keri tucked the photo back inside her purse. "This must be difficult for you. Has Cal been supportive?" She presumed he must be sympathetic since he'd come along to help her.

Diane's eyes glistened. "Cal has been wonderful. He's always been there for both of us. If Fifi needed any heavy jobs done, she'd call him to come over. He became like the son she'd never had. And since she died, he's made himself available to help me anyway he can."

"I'll bet he was surprised by your inheritance. When we spoke at the PHEADA party, Cal expected Garvan to be the beneficiary."

"Did I hear my name?" Cal appeared in the doorway. With his receding dark hairline, prominent nose, and sharp eyes, he reminded Keri of a crow. His black shirt and jeans enhanced the impression.

"Oh, hi Cal," she said. "Diane mentioned you were looking for ant killers."

He gave a low chuckle. "You wouldn't believe how many bug sprays and insecticide powders Fiona kept in the garage. She had enough to open a store."

Diane grimaced. "We'll have to clean out everything before selling the place. I'd like to donate the sheets and towels to an animal shelter. As for the furniture, shouldn't we leave some for staging purposes?"

"Probably, but let's not make any hasty decisions in that regard yet."

"It's going to take forever to sort through everything. Cal, did you pack the laundry detergent like I'd asked?"

His brows drew together. "Yep, that's done. I need to bring in more trash bags and boxes from the car before we get started on the food." He dipped his head at them and exited through the garage door entrance.

Diane turned toward Keri. "He took off work this morning, but I don't expect him to spend much time here. It's going to be painful for me to sort through Fifi's clothes and other personal belongings. After that, I'll think about the antiques. How do you suggest we handle them?"

Keri dove into this subject that was familiar to her. "We can either sell the individual items online like I've been doing or hold an estate sale. First decide what you'll be keeping. I know Garvan doesn't deserve it, but you might offer him some of the things you don't want."

"That's very thoughtful. No wonder FiFi liked you."

"Thanks. I do my best." Keri rose and took their empty mugs to the sink to wash. "Is there anything else you want help with today before I go?"

Diane's voice sobered. "There is another issue on my mind. I know it's not in your job description, but you're the only other person who cares. I want you to find out what happened to Fifi."

Keri turned toward her. "What do you mean?"

"I'm not so sure the robbery attempt was as random as the detective seems to believe. If that's true, why wouldn't the crook have waited until Fifi left the house? I don't agree that the killer was some dirtbag off the street."

"I've wondered the same thing," Keri said, as she put down the dishtowel in her hand and returned to her seat. "Did you notice Veronica across the street on the day Fiona died? She held up a placard that mentioned criminals. I just spoke to her, and although her responses were beyond weird, I think she knows something."

"You could be right. See what a good listener you are? That makes you the perfect person to investigate. Plus, the PHEADA people might be involved. I've heard them make snide remarks about Fifi behind her back. You have an insider advantage with them."

"I've overheard some negative comments from them as well. I'll keep my eyes and ears open," she promised, not willing to commit to anything further. "Meanwhile, I'll have my office manager draw up a contract for our services."

Outside, she paused on the front path and glanced at the open garage, intending to say goodbye to Cal. She noticed Fiona's car parked there, a sad testament to her loss. She didn't see Cal, though. He must have gone back inside the house.

She turned away, mulling over her conversation with Diane. She couldn't believe Fiona had left her a cottage. *How very generous of her to take care of me that way*. Usually, it was the other way around, with Keri caring for her clients.

She'd love to get a glimpse of the place, but Diane hadn't mentioned the address. Probably the property had to go through probate anyway before it was officially hers. She quelled her excitement to focus on more immediate matters.

Diane's suspicions about Fiona's death echoed her own. And not only had Diane hired her firm, as she'd hoped, but in addition wanted her to investigate the murder. Would she be up to the task? Nowhere in her job description did it say anything about solving crimes. And yet, she did know people around town and could dig into things on a subtle level.

Putting on her sunglasses, she considered what to do next.

Perhaps she should go talk to Sarah Underwood. If Sarah and Ossie had something unethical going on that Fiona discovered, they could have wanted her out of the way. Plus, Veronica had mentioned Sarah's husband.

It seemed a good place to start her inquiries, assuming Sarah was home. Without further hesitation, she veered toward Sarah's imposing two-story residence.

Chapter Eleven

Keri scooted up Sarah's front path, admiring the landscaping. Leafy green shrubs, blue plumbago and grassy liriope bordered the lawn. A flowering red hibiscus bush graced the side of the house, where a swathe of open grass separated the two residences.

The driveway was empty, but Sarah may have parked her car in the garage. She rang the doorbell and soon heard footsteps sounding from within. Then a shadow appeared at the glass insert.

"Keri, this is a surprise," Sarah said, swinging the door open. "What brings you by?"

"I was over at Fiona's house and thought I'd say hello. Do you have a few minutes to chat?"

"I've a meeting in a short while, but I can spare some time. Come on in."

Keri's glance took in her ivory sweater and pants, and sparkling crystal jewelry. She'd twisted her ash blond hair into a coil atop her head, making her look very cool and regal.

"I wanted to thank you again for introducing me to Jarek," Keri said, as Sarah closed the door behind them. It was a good excuse for her visit.

"You're welcome. I was happy to connect the two of you." They stood in a foyer that opened into a dining room with a polished wood table and eight chairs. A breakfront cabinet held an array of crystal glassware in various sizes. The living room was adjacent, with a glimpse of the kitchen beyond. "Come with me into the family room. Would you like a cold drink?"

Nancy J. Cohen

Sure, and I'd also love lunch. Keri realized she hadn't eaten since that morning and only now became aware that her stomach gnawed. Skipping meals was becoming a bad habit.

"I'll have a soda if you have any, thanks." At least the sugar content would help.

Sarah led the way to the rear, where French doors in a spacious room faced a covered patio and freestyle pool. Down a slope in the backyard, banana plants rooted near the lake's edge.

Keri sat on the sofa while Sarah disappeared into the kitchen. She returned with two glasses of cola and ice. Another trip brought a tray of cheese cubes and crackers, pitted green olives, and mixed nuts, which she placed on the cherrywood coffee table.

Keri's mouth watered. "This is quite a spread. You didn't have to go to so much trouble."

Sarah took a seat in an armchair. "No problem. How did it go with Jarek?"

"It went well. He's easy to please," Keri replied, before realizing how that sounded.

"Oo-la-la, tell me about it," Sarah said with a wink.

"No, I meant… I mean, he agreed to my suggestions for his launch party. How did you meet him?" she asked, to deflect her embarrassment.

"I belong to the town welcoming committee. When Jarek mentioned needing help with publicity, I thought of your agency."

Keri really should initiate a referral fee. She'd have to talk to Purdy about it. Meanwhile, she chatted about the upcoming launch while munching on snacks. Her hunger satisfied, she brushed off her hands and leaned back on the sofa cushion.

"That was great, thank you. I didn't realize I was so hungry. We've never had much of a chance to talk at PHEADA functions, but I know Fiona was always glad you attended." She needed to learn more about the board members, and Sarah could be a good source.

"Bob and I like to support the arts. You do a wonderful job of organizing their events. Fiona always spoke very highly of you."

"We worked well together. Did the group's officers appreciate her involvement? I got the impression she may have rubbed some people the wrong way."

Sarah's brow creased. "I shouldn't speak ill of the dead, but she wasn't always as kind as she appeared. That was an act she put on to gain people's confidence. Then she'd collect information about them and use it to her advantage."

"Are you speaking from personal experience?" Keri wouldn't allow her own opinion of Fiona to slip another notch, even though Sarah's words echoed Purdy's remarks.

"I'd rather not talk about it," Sarah said with a dismissive wave. "But since you're here, I'd like to get an estimate from you on the project I'm doing for PHEADA. I could use help putting the pieces together."

"Which project is that?" This must be the matter Sarah had been discussing with Ossie at the breakfast restaurant, Keri thought, aware that Sarah had deftly changed the subject. She'd wanted to ask *how* Fiona had manipulated people.

"It's the spring art festival at the botanical garden. Ossie wants to go bigger next year with musicians and food booths and children's activities. He'd also like to include other types of artists to broaden the appeal. Fiona had protested this idea, saying it would draw attention away from the true artistic talents."

"I agree with Ossie in that respect. I'll be happy to write up a proposal." If Sarah was right, Ossie had felt restricted by Fiona's influence. He would have more freedom to press his own agenda now that she'd left the scene.

On the surface, it appeared Sarah's meetings with Ossie were legit. Even their handholding at the restaurant might have been Ossie expressing his gratitude for her accepting the job. But then, why did he issue that warning on the night of the party? Did he mean that Sarah shouldn't make waves over their project until a suitable time after Fiona's death had passed?

Since she couldn't reveal that she'd been eavesdropping, she moved on to her other purpose in coming. "Since we're talking about Fiona, had you noticed anyone unusual observing her house lately? If it were me, I'd be nervous living next door to where a murder had taken place."

Sarah gave a visible shudder. "Thankfully, it's been relatively quiet around here."

"What about your husband? Could Bob have seen anybody?"

"I can ask him, but he wouldn't see an elephant if it were in front of his nose."

"O-kay. How about unusual noises outside? Did you hear any weird sounds or screams the night Fiona died that you might have overlooked?"

"Nope. I conked out that evening after watching TV. I didn't even hear all the commotion the next morning. Bob was concerned about why I was sleeping so late, but I guess my body needed the rest."

"Was he still awake when you went to bed?"

"He was working on some garage shelving. Bob is very handy around the house. He helped Fiona with things at her place, too."

"What does he do for a living?" Keri asked, taking a gulp of her soda.

"He owns a pool cleaning business. Most of his work is with commercial properties, but he does a few residential homes as a favor to friends. He took care of Fiona's pool. I guess he'll continue until he's notified otherwise by the new owner."

"I suppose this neighborhood gets a lot of workers who come and go, since it isn't a gated community. Have you heard about any other burglaries in the area?"

"Nuh-uh. We get some thefts from unlocked cars, but those are stupid people who park outside and don't lock their doors." Sarah's gaze sharpened. "Why do you care, Keri?"

"Fiona was a dear friend to me. I want to understand what happened to her."

"It was a shock to all of us, but we need to let the police do their jobs."

A car engine idled outside, and the garage door rumbled.

"Bob must be home," Sarah said, rising.

Keri gathered her handbag and stood, not wishing to overstay her welcome. She'd learned what she needed. Sarah had explained her reason for conferring with Ossie. She hadn't seen or heard anything noteworthy outside the evening of Fiona's death. And she had shed some light on Veronica's remark that Keri should talk to Bob. If he did handyman work for Fiona, that would give him a reasonable excuse for entering her house.

Bob joined them, having come in through the laundry room entrance. His acorn-colored eyes regarded her with curiosity. "Hey, Keri. I didn't realize you were here."

"I parked next door. Diane Foster hired me to help clean out Fiona's house. She's the executor on the estate." This would become public knowledge soon enough, so Keri wasn't betraying any confidences in telling them.

"I'm not surprised. We've seen Diane and her family visiting Fiona," Sarah said with a nod. "We know her and Cal from PHEADA functions."

"Is that why you're here? To tell us you're working for Diane?" Bob asked.

Sarah shot her husband a guarded glance. "Keri came over to thank me for introducing her to Jarek, a new chef in town. She's handling his restaurant's launch party."

His lips curled. "I see. It's good to know you're useful for something, darling."

Whoa, that wasn't nice. Did Bob suspect Sarah was dallying with PHEADA's president for purposes other than volunteer work? If there was any truth to that matter, maybe she was unhappy in her marriage. Keri could understand if Bob constantly demeaned her.

Or was Sarah's strained look because she feared he might say something that would throw suspicion their way regarding Fiona's death?

"I'll have my office manager send you a proposal for the

garden festival," she told Sarah with a bright smile. "Meanwhile, I hope to see you both at Fiona's funeral."

"We'll be there," Sarah said, prior to escorting Keri to the door.

A glance at her watch told Keri she'd better hustle or she'd be late for her next appointment. Luckily, her client didn't live too far away. Mrs. Veltri had hired Keri to help plan her family's Thanksgiving dinner with out-of-town guests. Keri had arranged for a personal chef to cater the meal and for a discounted hotel room block, but they still had other details to work out.

She pulled up to the curb at her client's residence in an affluent gated community. Her stay took longer than expected since Mrs. Veltri served coffee and cake in her kitchen while they discussed the holiday menu, table decorations, and place cards. Satisfied with the arrangements, Keri left with a wave and headed to her next job.

She was finally driving to the office when a call came through via her earpiece.

"Hi, it's Diane. I can't find some of the items on your inventory list, and they're not marked as sold."

Keri's neck muscles tightened. "Oh, really? Which items do you mean?"

"An antique German music box with a singing bird, a set of sterling silver cake forks, and a Chelsea ship's clock. I didn't go through the entire list, but what could have happened to them? Do you think the thief stole these things on his way to Fifi's bedroom?"

"I doubt it. That's an odd assortment to take, and the downstairs rooms weren't disturbed during the robbery. Only Fiona's bedroom was tossed."

She gripped the steering wheel tighter. Considering Garvan's accusation, she knew what alternative explanation Detective Saunders might offer. She could have sold those items on the sly and kept the money. But then, wouldn't she have deleted them from her list?

"Here's another possibility," Diane said. "Fifi may have gifted them to someone or donated them to a silent auction at one of her charities."

"That does sound like something she would do," Keri agreed. "I didn't think to include a column for gifted items. They may still turn up as we clean the house, though, so I wouldn't write them off as missing just yet."

"Okay. I'll put a mark beside each one, so we'll remember to look for them. Sorry to have bothered you."

"No problem. We can search together the next time I'm there."

Keri's brow wrinkled as she stopped at a red light. She didn't like having items unaccounted for on her list. Was it something she'd overlooked, or had Fiona neglected to tell her what she'd done with them? Hopefully, they'd find out soon enough.

Once at her office, she caught up on emails. She held perfunctory conversations with Purdy and Staz, not in the mood to discuss her latest findings. However, that evening after dinner, she shared her news with Lora as they relaxed in the living room with glasses of wine.

Lora sat curled up on the couch, her blond curls still damp from a shower. "It does seem unlikely that a thief would grab a few knickknacks rather than go straight for Fiona's jewelry. She might have stuffed those things in a drawer or forgotten to tell you she'd donated them. You could look for tax receipts."

Keri sat up straight in the chair opposite. "That's a great idea. I'll tell Diane to be on the lookout for them when she sorts through Fiona's papers."

Then again, maybe Fiona had given Keri the receipts to record in the latest package she'd sent to her office. She'd only glanced through the papers inside, meaning to get to them later. She should ascertain now if they included donation receipts.

"You could wait until morning," Lora suggested when she explained her plan to go check right there and then.

"I need to get this off my mind. I don't want Detective Saunders to think I stole anything."

Nancy J. Cohen

"I'll go with you," Lora offered, uncrossing her legs. "It's dark outside."

Keri surveyed her friend's pajamas. "No, thanks. This won't take long."

She changed into jeans and a sweater before rushing out. Wishing her shop had curbside parking, she found her favorite lot on a side street and claimed a space. She could have walked but didn't feel like making the effort.

Her low-heeled shoes clicked on the sidewalk as she rounded the corner onto Broad Street. The scent of decaying leaves pervaded the air and streetlights cast eerie shadows onto buildings. While most of the shops had closed, the restaurants were open, and boisterous diners occupied the outdoor seating.

She reached her office, unlocked the door and pushed inside. As she flicked on the lights, she took one glance and shrieked.

Desk drawers lay askew, their contents strewn across the floor. Overturned chairs sat on the ground. Even the filing cabinets against the wall had been opened.

Oh, God. She pressed a hand to her mouth, disbelief assaulting her. Who could have done this? She stared at the chaos, struggling for rational thought as her heart pounded in her chest.

The front window was intact. The lock had been secure. That left the rear door as the only means of entry.

Déjà vu, she thought with a chill, reimagining the scene in Fiona's house.

She turned and hastened outside to call Detective Saunders from a few doors down, where she sank onto a park bench by a sweets shop that was still open.

"It's Keri Armstrong. I'm sorry to call so late," she said when he answered. "There's been a break-in at my office."

He sucked in a breath. "Are you okay?"

"Yes. I'm sitting on a bench across from Kelly's Confectionary."

"Stay there. I'm coming over."

While waiting for his arrival, she pondered what the intruder might have wanted. Were they looking for something, or had the intent been to scare her? Either way, her world had been turned upside down. She shivered and crossed her arms over her chest, watching a couple emerge from the shop holding ice cream cones.

Saunders pulled up to the curb with a squeal fifteen minutes later and ignored the No Parking sign. Relief washed over her as he stepped from his sedan and hurried over. From his rumpled sport coat, it appeared he might still have been at work.

"Can you tell me what happened?" he asked as they walked together toward her office.

Her body trembled. She couldn't believe her business had been invaded. The intrusion made her feel sick and violated.

She mustered her strength. "The front door was locked when I arrived. I walked in, turned on the lights and saw the mess. Somebody had been inside and wrecked the place."

"Let me clear the scene and then you can join me." He disappeared inside the agency and returned a short while later, a frown on his face. "The rear door lock has been broken. I can dust for prints and take some photos, but for anything more, I'll need to bring in my team. The intruder has gone, so you can enter. Let me know if anything is missing."

While Saunders performed the tasks he'd mentioned, Keri did a cursory examination and determined all their equipment was present. "I won't know about our files until we sort through those papers," she said, gesturing at the floor after he'd rejoined her.

"What about your desktop computers? Do you use passcodes?"

"Yes, we do." She sat at each one of their stations and brought up the log-in screens. All appeared normal.

"What do you think the crook wanted?" Saunders asked.

Her lips quivered. "Maybe Fiona's killer was looking for something they didn't find at her house. Plenty of people knew I worked for her."

"Why were you at the office so late?"

I might as well tell him. "Diane said she couldn't locate some items on my inventory list. Fiona had sent me a packet of papers lately, and I wanted to see if they included tax receipts. She may have donated those things and forgotten to tell me."

She scanned the piles on the ground, looking for the telltale manila envelope. "Oh, there it is. Let me look inside." A quick inspection revealed signoffs from the vendors at their last function. "They're merchant records for me to file. No donation receipts." So much for that theory. It wasn't anything a thief would want, either.

"This incident may be unrelated to Miss Sullivan's case. Regarding other possible motives, can you think of a rival business owner, former employee, or dissatisfied customer who might hold a grudge against you?" Saunders asked, snagging her with his eagle eye.

Keri lifted her chin, resenting his suggestions. "Our clients fill out a satisfaction survey, and we haven't had a single complaint. I can send you copies if you want to see them for yourself. And check out our online reviews. They're all four and five-star ratings."

"Is that so?" He took out his pocket notebook and flipped through the pages. "Our department received an anonymous tip that you've charged for services that were not performed."

"What? That's a lie. Was it Garvan again? He's already accused me of cheating Fiona. He must have been really upset after hearing—" She stopped, realizing how Saunders would view her unexpected windfall.

"What?"

"He won't be happy that I'll be working with Diane," she finished lamely. "She hired me to help clean out Fiona's house." And find out who'd killed her, Keri thought but didn't say aloud.

She should tell Saunders about the cottage, but her tongue stayed glued to her mouth. She'd inform him later, after the funeral. Surely, Diane would have notified anyone else mentioned in the will by then.

Saunders's scrutiny made her squirm. "Who else have you spoken to lately?"

"I talked to Veronica across the street from Fiona's house. She warned me to be careful, but I couldn't get her to be more specific. I think she knows something important."

"Yeah, so she says every time she calls us on the tip line. Is that it?"

"I stopped by Sarah Underwood's house to thank her for a client referral. We had a nice chat until her husband, Bob, came home. He worked as Fiona's pool cleaner and handyman."

Could Bob have taken offense by her presence and done this? Or maybe Sarah had told Ossie about Keri's visit. If they had some kind of affair going on, Ossie might have trashed her place as a warning not to expose their secret. While those possibilities seemed unlikely, she shouldn't discard them.

"What about personal issues? Can you think of anyone who has a reason to resent you?" Saunders asked, his pen poised over his notebook.

Her heart leapt into her throat as Rick came to mind. No! This hadn't been his doing, had it? He might be furious at her for sheltering Lora. He could even be the one trying to smear her reputation.

"I should mention that my friend, Lora Wilson, is staying with me for a while. She just broke up with her boyfriend. He could resent my interference."

"What's his name?"

"Rick Lager. He works as a mechanic at Hanson's Garage."

"I'll have a chat with him. Meanwhile, I'll write up a police report on this incident. It's up to you if you want me to bring in my team for a more thorough sweep. I did get a good print from the back door. Do you have a cleaning crew that comes in at night?"

"You're looking at her, Detective." Keri's shoulders lifted in a sheepish shrug. "As for the rest of the place, our prints will be on every surface." She didn't care to have black dust to clean up, since nothing had been stolen.

"I'll need your staff to give us their fingerprints for comparison. Meanwhile, I'd advise replacing the rear door lock and adding a security system."

"Good advice. I'll get on it." She'd call the alarm company in the morning. She hadn't felt one was necessary before, but now it had become a priority.

"Let me walk you to your car."

"Thanks, I'd appreciate it. I'm sorry I disturbed your evening, but I didn't want to call nine-one-one with all the hullabaloo that would have caused."

"No problem. You still look shaken up. You should go home and get some rest."

Once he'd left and she was safely in her car, Keri texted Purdy and Staz to fill them in.

Purdy called her back. "I'll take care of the locksmith. We need to secure the place before anything else. I'm glad you're okay."

"Thanks. I'll handle the alarm system. Oh, and guess what? Detective Saunders received an anonymous tip that we've charged for services that weren't performed."

"Are you kidding? That's absurd. Who would spread such lies?"

"I'm thinking it was Garvan or maybe Rick, my friend Lora's ex-boyfriend." She explained her reasoning. It didn't matter whether the complaint was real or not. If word got around town, her business would suffer.

"You should ask Detective Saunders to check their alibis for tonight."

"It's his job to follow through on any leads. I don't want to bother him any further."

Weary to the bone, she said goodbye and turned on the engine. As she drove home, she glanced at her rearview mirror. She'd have to be extra cautious until Fiona's killer was caught. While the break-in at her office more logically pointed to Garvan or Rick, it could be related to the murder case. In that event, she didn't want to put herself in the crosshairs next.

Chapter Twelve

Keri told Lora about the intruder as soon as she got home. Her friend had waited for her, popping up from the couch when she entered. Lora looked sleepy with her curly hair askew and her eyes heavy-lidded.

"That's awful. It's a good thing you weren't there when the guy broke in."

"I know. Do you think Rick could have done it? He must be upset that I invited you to stay here," Keri said, sitting in the opposite chair.

Lora's nose wrinkled. "He gets angry, but it's all verbal. He's never hit me or thrown things. Although, there is that one time he let the air out of my tires."

Keri heard the uncertainty in her voice and kept Rick on the suspect list. It brought to mind a news story she'd read once about a man who'd strangled a lady lawyer from the backseat of her car. She'd been friends with his wife and had encouraged her to divorce him. The killer had blamed the attorney for their split-up. That story had haunted her as it brought home the danger of women leaving an abusive partner.

"More likely, it's Garvan's fault," Lora suggested with a jab of her finger. "He's been cut from his aunt's will and is looking to cast blame."

"True, but we *are* working together on the funeral lunch. Why would he risk offending me?"

"You said Detective Saunders received an anonymous tip against your firm. That sounds like something Garvan would do.

You'll see him at the funeral. Maybe you can slip these things into the conversation and get him to confess."

Keri yawned as fatigue set in. "Let's revisit this another time. I'm too tired to think straight anymore."

"You need to rest. Tomorrow will be better. You'll see." Lora ushered Keri into her bedroom and then retired for the night herself.

True to Lora's words, by the time Keri reached her office in the morning, Purdy had righted the chairs, straightened the drawers, and cleared the floor. Her heart rate, which had increased upon her arrival, settled into a slower rhythm under his calming influence.

"The locksmith is due to arrive any minute," he said without preamble. He'd slicked his hair back from his brow and wore a navy blazer. She felt disheveled in comparison, having tied her hair into a hasty ponytail and thrown on the first decent pair of pants and top that caught her eye.

"You're a gem, Purdy. Did you notice if anything was missing?"

"We'll know more after we put away these papers." He gestured to the stacked piles on each of their desks.

Staz walked in and winced at the scene. "Ouch. What a disaster."

"You should have seen it last night," Keri said. "Purdy has already cleaned up most of the mess."

"Who would do this to us?"

"I'm sure it was aimed at me. It could have been Lora's boyfriend, Rick, getting revenge for my taking her in, or Garvan, who did it out of spite. Either way, be careful and watch your backs."

"Have you been talking to people about Fiona?" Staz asked, plopping her purse down on her desk. "Maybe you should let the detective handle things going forward. If not Garvan or Rick, the intruder could be someone related to the murder."

I had that same thought. "If so, it makes me even more determined to learn the truth. Meanwhile, I'll get a security system installed. Hopefully that will serve as a deterrent in the future." Or was it too little too late? Better now than never, she figured.

Purdy scowled at her. "You do realize an alarm bill will increase our monthly budget?"

"It's a necessary expense." She settled at her desk and turned on her monitor. The pile of papers Purdy had dumped there could wait until later.

"Listen to this," Staz said, her eyes brightening. "I found out the name of Fiona's antique shop in Manhattan. It was called Fiona's Treasure Trove and was located on Tenth Street before she moved it to Greenwich Village."

"Good work." Keri knew so little about Fiona's background. She'd preferred to speak about current events or to focus on Keri's news.

"There's more." Staz brought up the file on her phone and read from it. "'Fiona's Treasure Trove dealt in Georgian and Regency period furniture and other decorative arts. Customers described the place as a veritable Aladdin's Cave, with exotic objects hiding in a warren of rooms. The owner, Fiona Sullivan, traveled the world to add eclectic works of art to her inventory. Her shop had an international clientele and shipped worldwide.'"

"That's impressive," Keri said. "I'll bet it was a fun place to visit."

"Right? It sounds like Trader Mae's. You never know what you're going to find each time you go. I'm not into vintage pieces, but they have fun home décor items."

Keri pressed her lips together. Should she tell them about the cottage? She'd meant to wait until after Fiona's funeral, but she couldn't hold off any longer.

"This is confidential, but Fiona had bought a cottage near Hamilton Square. She'd intended to reopen her antique shop there but decided to retire instead. According to Diane, she left the property to me."

Purdy's jaw dropped. "That was very generous of her. Is this place vacant or rented out?"

"I have no idea. In fact, I don't even know the address."

"It will take some time for the estate to settle, at any rate." He squinted at her. "Is Detective Saunders aware of this bequest? He could construe it as a motive."

Keri grimaced. "I'm not sure. He'd have to obtain a copy of the will unless Diane told him."

"I think it's exciting," Staz said, clapping her hands.

"Wait until you get the bills for property taxes and insurance. And who knows what condition it's in? Heavy renovations might be required," Purdy said, always the pragmatist.

He was right. What sounded like a windfall could turn into a costly burden. Keri would assess the situation once she saw the place.

She made her call to the alarm company while Staz went to work, and Purdy conferred with the locksmith. Then other tasks occupied her for several hours.

She took a break when Diane's face lit up on her phone's screen.

"Hey, Keri. I cleared out Fifi's safety deposit box. Not much was in there except for a bunch of documents, including the title for her Volvo. It's still sitting in the garage."

"Oh, right. I assume you can get the title changed once you have the death certificate. Will you sell it?" Fiona had offered Keri the use of her vehicle for their errands together, but Keri had preferred to drive her own car.

"Here's the thing. In her latest codicil, Fifi left the car to Hugh with the stipulation that he can have it only if he's kept himself out of trouble."

"Garvan will be pleased that she thought of his son." But what did Fiona mean by her caveat? Was Hugh a troublemaker? She recalled Enid saying Fiona had constantly criticized him. Did she have a reason to do so?

"I need to notify him," Diane said. "There's a sealed letter for Garvan as well."

"You have a lot to do. Remember that I'm here to help with whatever you need."

A person's death led to many sorry tasks. She and Zoey had shared the burden when their mother died. They'd had thank you notes to write, service people to notify, accounts to close. That didn't even include clearing out her house. It had taken months to get everything done and the legalities concluded.

"Listen, I have news." Keri filled Diane in regarding the break-in at her office.

Diane sucked in a breath. "It's fortunate no one was hurt."

"If Garvan is getting back at me, he might come after you next. He's the spiteful sort."

"True, but you don't know it was him for certain. I'm just glad we're a team. Cal is helpful, but he goes to work every day. Anyway, I have to get the kids from school. I'll see you soon."

Keri hung up and then called Pam to relate her latest news.

"That's terrible, Keri. Do you have any idea who might have done it?"

She mentioned her theories. "I'm hoping it wasn't Rick. That could mean he's turning violent."

"It's more likely you've riled someone with your questions about Fiona."

"Have you learned anything new in that regard?" Keri asked. "Staz discovered her shop in Greenwich Village was called Fiona's Treasure Trove."

"Sorry; I haven't had the chance."

"On another note, Detective Saunders received an anonymous tip that our agency bills for services that aren't rendered. Have you heard any gossip to that effect?"

"No, but don't worry. I'll add some glowing reviews about your agency in my profile on Fiona. What time should we meet at the cemetery tomorrow?"

"The graveside service starts at ten. Let's arrive by nine-thirty. It should be interesting to see who shows up."

****

Friday started as an auspicious day with a clear blue sky, moderate autumn temperatures, and low humidity. A tent had been erected and chairs set up at Fiona's plot. Guests stood about in clusters, murmuring in low voices. The immediate family and the coffin had yet to arrive.

Keri felt a swell of sadness. Tears made her blink rapidly as she remembered Fiona and the friendly visits they'd shared. The loss left her with a hollow feeling.

Pam arrived shortly afterward, looking professional in black pants with a matching blazer. Keri had chosen a modest dress appropriate for a funeral. They exchanged hugs, then Keri led Pam over to Diane and Cal to introduce them while they waited for the service to start.

"Nice to meet you," Diane said, clutching a tissue in her hand. She looked pale and clearly distressed.

Cal greeted them with a somber nod. His skin had a grayish tinge in the sunlight.

"How are you doing?" Keri asked Diane, tapping her on the arm.

"I'm managing. I knew this day would come at some point but not so soon." She swung her attention to Pam. "How did you know Fiona?"

"Actually, I didn't." Pam tucked a strand of auburn hair behind her ear. "I work for the *Sunny Grove Gazette* and I'm doing a profile on her role in the community. Would you care to give me a quote?"

"Maybe later, if you don't mind. Keri, when can you meet me at Fifi's house again? I'm going over there tomorrow to get more work done. Cal said he'd take the kids to a movie."

Uncertain about her weekend plans, Keri dodged a definitive reply. "I'll check my schedule and let you know."

She and Pam stepped aside as a black car and a hearse pulled up to the road. Garvan got out with his family and followed the pallbearers carrying the casket. As they took their seats in the front row, Keri felt her pulse accelerate at the thought that Garvan might truly be acting behind her back to discredit her.

She presumed the young man next to him was his son, Hugh. Enid's eyes were partly shrouded by a veil attached to her chic black hat. They all sat stone-faced, looking toward the minister.

Diane and Cal claimed seats behind Garvan's family, while other guests drew closer. Keri noted the board members from PHEADA were present, along with several leaders of the community. Sarah and Bob joined the crowd, the only neighbors of Fiona's that she recognized. A cool breeze stirred, as though Fiona approved of the assemblage.

As the workers positioned the coffin in place on straps over the grave, a lump clogged her throat. Fiona was about to descend to her final rest.

While the clergyman led a series of prayers, she scanned the throng, looking for anyone who might appear smug or suspicious. From the corner of her eye, she noticed Detective Saunders threading his way over among the graves. At his side was his partner that she'd seen on Fiona's stoop the day she'd died. She wondered if they planned to attend the luncheon afterward.

Her attention returned to the official, who spoke about the many good deeds Fiona had done for the town, and about her favorite pursuits and interests. Then he called upon members of the congregation to share some thoughts about the deceased.

Diane got up as everyone else remained silent, including Garvan. "Fiona was my mother's best friend," she said in a trembling voice. "Growing up, I knew her as a special person who always had a kind word for me and who respected me even as a child. When my mom died, she grieved with me and helped me fill the void in my heart. I could talk to her about anything, and she would listen and offer an encouraging word." Her voice broke, and she visibly fought to regain her composure. "I'll miss our conversations and her wise advice."

She spoke briefly about Fiona's sense of civic duty and how she'd led by example. Then she dabbed at her eyes and resumed her seat.

Nancy J. Cohen

Ossie rose and moved up front. He gave an inspiring speech about Fiona's contributions to the community. "PHEADA was Fiona's favorite charity, and if you want to support her cause, there would be no better way than to make a gift in her memory," he concluded.

Really? Couldn't you at least have waited for the luncheon to ask for donations? Keri looked around at other people's reactions. Some guests appeared affronted by his pitch while others gave approving nods. How many of them had truly cared more about Fiona than her money? Ossie's colleagues didn't appear too sorrowful. They huddled together in a group off to the side.

"Does anyone else wish to speak?" the minister asked, looking pointedly at Garvan.

Fiona's nephew shook his head and sat rigidly in his seat. It figured he wouldn't have anything good to say about his aunt.

After the service concluded, Keri brought Pam over to Garvan and introduced them. Enid had wandered off, and he stood alone with his son, whom she'd yet to meet.

"I'm sorry for your loss. This is my friend, Pam Teague. She's a reporter for the *Sunny Grove Gazette* and is doing a profile on Fiona."

Garvan gave Pam a scornful glance. "Don't believe all the good things you hear about her. She cut us out of her will, including my son, Hugh. She might have thought of him, if not us."

Keri bit her tongue to avoid mentioning Fiona's bequest to Hugh. It was Diane's news to share. Besides, she had other things on her mind.

"My agency was broken into earlier this week," she told him, gauging his response.

His eyes bulged. "Really? That's unfortunate. I hope no one was hurt. Was anything stolen?"

"Not to my knowledge." She looked at him pointedly but said nothing further.

He didn't miss the silent accusation. "You don't think I did it? You probably made some client angry at you."

"Is that what you want people to think?"

He looked at her as though she'd left her brains at home. "Why would you say that?"

"Somebody is spreading malicious rumors about my business practices."

"Don't look at me, although I might agree with them. Hugh, find your mother and meet me at the car. We need to get over to the restaurant."

He hustled off before Keri could say more, and Pam walked away to greet some people she knew. Hugh didn't leave right away, though. The opposite of his portly father, he was tall and lean, with a thick head of wheat-brown hair and a scruffy jaw. Right now, he stood glowering at her. Her shoes sank into the soft earth as she shifted her feet.

"You'd better not make trouble for my dad," Hugh said. "I'll bet what he says about you is true. Aunt Fiona wouldn't have known if you'd overcharged her."

Keri bristled. "Fiona was my friend. I wouldn't have done anything to abuse our relationship. How about you? Did you ever visit her or call to ask how she was doing?"

"I'd stop by when I was in town. Otherwise, she rarely invited us over."

While Keri considered the possible truth of his statement, Pam returned to her side.

"Whew, the sun is getting hot. I should have worn a hat." Pam shaded her face with her hand and cast a glance at Hugh. "You're from St. Augustine, right? What do you do there?"

He glanced at the cars pulling away from the curb. "I help people. If you have aches and pains, I make them go away."

"You're a physical therapist?"

He laughed out loud. "Not quite."

"I'm afraid I don't understand."

"Then let me give you a word of advice. You don't want to know more about me."

Keri gazed thoughtfully after him as he turned and hastened

to retrieve his mother as requested. Was he always that rude, or had they struck a nerve?

"Did he just tell us he's a drug dealer?" she whispered to Pam.

"I wouldn't be surprised. He gives me a creepy vibe."

"Maybe he's the one behind everything instead of his father." That was an angle to pursue, especially in light of Fiona's remark about him staying out of trouble. "Oh look, here comes Detective Saunders and his partner. I can introduce you."

"Hi, this is my friend, Pam Teague. She's a reporter for the *Sunny Grove Gazette.*"

"This is my partner, Detective Alex Petroff," Saunders said with a nod of acknowledgment.

The younger man had light brown hair, keen eyes, and a square jaw reminiscent of Clark Kent. Keri's quick glance noted the absence of a wedding ring. Pam must have noticed also, because she stepped closer to him.

"I've always wondered how someone becomes a detective," Pam said with a coy smile. "Is it something you learn on the job, or do you have to take classes?" She drew him aside, either to have a private word with him or so Keri could have a moment alone with his senior partner.

"I figured we'd see you here today," Saunders drawled in the awkward pause between them.

"Likewise. Is there anything new about Fiona's case that you can share?"

"We're running the prints from your office through our system. I'll need your colleagues to stop by the station so we can get theirs for comparison."

"Oh, right. I'll let them know. Is that all?"

Saunders's voice lowered. "We got the tox report back on Miss Sullivan. She had a trace of sedative in her blood but not an unusual amount."

"What does that mean?"

"She didn't take an overdose of sleeping pills. Either the

intruder stole them or dumped them down the toilet to confuse the issue."

"Have you spoken to Garvan's son, Hugh? Pam just asked him what he did in St. Augustine, and he said he helped treat people for their aches and pains. Maybe he's a drug dealer and Fiona found out. He murdered her and then took the sleeping pills to sell on the street."

"That's a broad assumption to make. As you know from personal experience, it's best not to make unfounded accusations."

His words hit like a bucketful of cold water. She was searching for a proper retort when Pam returned and nudged her.

"Didn't you want to check the setup at the restaurant before everyone gets there?"

"Yes, we'd better hustle." They gave their farewells to the detectives and turned away.

"Detective Petroff is cute," Keri said to Pam as they headed toward their cars.

"I agree, and he's single. He moved here from Pittsburgh because he couldn't stand the cold winters anymore, and his brother lives in Florida. But right now, he's focused on this case. What did Saunders have to say?"

"So far, the tox reports have been negative. This means the killer may have dumped her sleeping meds to fool the cops or stolen them to sell. I mentioned Hugh's remarks and that Saunders might want to check him out, but he cautioned me against making unfounded accusations. I just want him to investigate all the possibilities."

"Is he attending the luncheon?"

"Yes, he'll be there." Maybe she'd find someone else at the event who knew more about him. At least then she could inform Detective Saunders that she wasn't making things up. He needed to start taking her seriously and not write her off as another looney friend of Fiona's.

Chapter Thirteen

Keri found a parking spot at the restaurant, which was starting to get crowded. Pam pulled in right after her, so they walked inside together. After showing Pam the private room where the event was being held, Keri excused herself to use the restroom.

She scrubbed her hands under the cool water, washing away the symbolic residue from the gravesite. A sense of relief that the funeral service was over lifted a weight from her shoulders.

The water in the faucet stopped, gurgled, and spat out again. That was odd.

It happened again, only to her faucet and not the one next to hers when another guest turned it on. Could this be Fiona sending her a message? Using water to send a sign would be appropriate for her, considering how many times she'd filled a teapot during Keri's visits. Fiona must be there in spirit, letting Keri know she was okay.

With a smile on her face, she entered the private dining room to check on the setup. Her expert eye surveyed the Italian buffet and dessert tables. Satisfied with the display, she turned her attention to the guests. Garvan and Enid greeted people by the door as they arrived. More of Fiona's friends filtered in and grabbed seats at one of the black-clothed round tables.

Diane and Cal claimed a corner to themselves, while the PHEADA crew drifted towards the bar. Sarah and Bob showed up and meandered over to join them.

A sudden swell of tears caused Keri to blink. This should have been Fiona's birthday party. Her friends would have been congratulating her on reaching eighty, and she'd be laughing and opening presents. Instead, they'd opened her grave.

I'll find out what happened to you, she promised silently. Diane was the only one who seemed to care. Everyone else would just as soon pay their dutiful respects and move on.

Seeing that Enid was inspecting the food, she headed over to forestall any criticism about the preparations. "I hope you and Garvan are pleased with the setup."

Enid's heavy perfume scented the air. "It's good enough. By the way, Hugh said you asked him some nosy questions. I'd advise you to leave him alone."

Keri kept silent rather than making a sarcastic reply. Hugh shouldn't have baited her and Pam. It only strengthened her resolve to learn more about him.

"Have you spoken to Diane?" Enid asked, gesturing toward the buffet. "She'll be reimbursing us for this meal from Fiona's estate. That's the least she can do, considering how she tricked Fiona into making her the beneficiary. Or was that your influence?"

Keri stiffened, resenting her remarks. "I don't believe there was any trickery involved. According to what Fiona told me, Diane was more of a family to her than you and Garvan." She knew that statement would ignite a response.

"Nonsense. We just didn't live as near as that little gold digger. Have you seen Cal's face? He's grinning like a sports fan whose favorite team just won the Super Bowl."

Keri glanced over at him, realizing Enid hadn't risen to her bait. Instead, she'd cast aspersions on someone else. Sure enough, Cal wore a smirk that quickly wiped off his face when he noticed her looking his way.

"Maybe he's thinking about how pleased Fiona would be that so many people showed up to honor her," Keri suggested. "Cal told me he didn't expect Diane to inherit anything. Her inheritance came as a surprise to them both."

"It was more than a surprise to us. Before Diane moved to Florida, Aunt Fiona told Garvan that if he expected to inherit her money, we should be nicer to her. We assumed that meant she favored him as her heir. Then recently, she mentioned an announcement she planned to make at her birthday party and dropped hints about an endowment to PHEADA."

"Oh? She didn't say anything about it to me."

"Garvan was afraid she would change her will and leave everything to the nonprofit group." She gave Keri a sly glance as though she could confirm this notion.

"I wouldn't know. We only discussed her social activities and other obligations." Either way, if Garvan believed he was the sole heir, this would have given him a strong motive to secure his inheritance early.

Someone tapped Enid's elbow, and Keri took it as an excuse to wander toward Cal, who stood alone. His complexion seemed overly pale, almost ashen. "How are you holding up?" she asked, concerned for him.

"I'm okay, but I feel bad for Diane. It's like she's lost her mother all over again." He pointed to where she was talking to some society ladies over by the buffet table.

"I can relate. Fiona meant a lot to me as well, although I didn't know her as long as you and Diane. Did you ever visit her antique shop in Greenwich Village?" she asked, hoping to learn more about Fiona's background.

His brow wrinkled. "I went there a few times before she moved to Florida. The place was cluttered like an attic, but customers loved to browse the aisles. Fiona shipped most of the contents to her new house after closing the store."

"I understand she meant to relocate the business but then decided to retire."

"That's right. Now Diane has to get rid of her stuff. It's good she hired you to help her organize everything. I'd be happy to offer my expertise if you need a hand. With my experience in silver restoration, I'm familiar with heirloom pieces. Here's my card if you want to contact me at my jewelry store. I specialize in silver, if you're ever interested."

"Thanks, I appreciate it." Keri had some clients who might benefit from his services. "Actually, there is one thing you can do for me right away. Can you polish Fiona's coffee set that's on her cocktail table? It looks tarnished and will be easier to sell if the pitchers are nice and shiny. That is, unless Diane wants to keep it."

"I'll ask her." His gaze lit with curiosity. "Why did Fiona suddenly decide to sell things on eBay? Did she give you a reason?"

"She told me it was time for her to declutter the place. Would Diane want to hang onto any of the furniture?" she asked, thinking it might be difficult to sell the heavier pieces.

He squinted in the overhead lighting that brought out the streaks of silver in his hair. "I doubt it. Diane has modern tastes, and we don't have any more space available in our house."

"She shouldn't rush sorting through things," Keri advised. It had been a difficult task for her and Zoey to decide what to keep and what to discard. Each item that had belonged to their mother held sentimental value. She'd only let go upon realizing material things weren't as important as the difference you made in people's lives and how they might remember you. She'd taken photos of objects that had meaning for her, accepting that those would have to suffice along with her memories.

"Do you have a plan for selling Fiona's goods?" Cal asked, his gaze narrowing. Was he wondering if she'd drag things out to pad her bill?

"I've mentioned the possibility of doing an estate sale to Diane," she replied, to set him straight. "That would be the simplest route. I wish we could find Fiona's ledger, though. It would save us time in researching each piece."

He nodded. "Diane mentioned a record book, but she hasn't found it so far. Maybe Fiona stashed it somewhere and forgot where she put it."

"She had been getting more forgetful lately. It made her happy to have you and Diane nearby. She talked about your kids as though they were her own grandchildren. Whose idea was it to relocate?"

He scratched his neck. "It was mine. Diane was heartbroken when Fiona announced she'd be leaving the area. My work is something I can do from anywhere. I figured Florida would be a great place for a restart with all the senior citizens. They value their heirlooms, unlike today's generation."

"I imagine it was difficult for Fiona to make new friends once she settled here," she said, envisioning the stress of moving to a new state and starting over.

Cal waved a hand. "Nah. She got involved in her charitable activities and met people that way. Her social life filled up very quickly. It's just too bad she and Tony didn't reconnect since he'd moved to Florida as well."

"Who's Tony?"

"Tony Salvatore is Diane's uncle on her maternal side. Didn't my wife mention him to you? Fiona had been in love with him back in the day."

Keri's eyes widened. "Fiona said she'd once loved a man, but it hadn't worked out. I didn't realize Diane's mom had a brother."

"Fiona's father forbade the match," Cal explained. "She obeyed his wishes, afraid to risk his wrath for Tony's sake. You didn't go against Crogher Sullivan if you wanted to live."

Whoa, that sounds ominous. "What do you mean?"

"It's not my tale to tell. You'd best ask Diane."

"Is Tony still around?" Keri asked.

"He lives in Sarasota. Diane called Tony to let him know about Fiona's death. He's unable to travel, or he might have attended the funeral."

Keri chewed on these words. "Was this why Fiona stayed single? Because she still carried a torch for Tony after all these years?"

Cal glanced beyond her toward the bar. "Tony didn't waste any time after their break-up. He got married and had kids with another woman. The sting of his betrayal might have turned Fiona off toward other relationships. Anyway, it's history at this point. Can I get you something to drink?"

"No, thanks. I need to eat lunch. I'm starving."

True to her words, she made a beeline for the buffet while Cal aimed for the bar. She filled a plate with steaming baked ziti, chicken Parmesan, garlic bread, and Caesar salad.

She looked for Pam, but her friend was busy chatting with the PHEADA group and Keri didn't want to interrupt them. While she was glancing around for an empty seat, Diane sidled up to her. Fatigue lines etched her face.

Diane lifted the coffee cup in her hand. "I see you're finally getting lunch. The food is delicious. You did a great job in planning this event."

"Thanks. I like this restaurant for special occasions. They always meet our expectations." Keri spotted an empty table and inclined her head for Diane to follow.

"I noticed you and Cal having a conversation," Diane said, once they were seated.

"Is he okay? He looks rather pale."

Diane waved a hand. "He's exposed to high levels of silver in his job. It causes a blue-gray discoloration of the skin called *argyria*. It's not harmful but it can become permanent."

"Interesting." Keri spoke between bites. "Cal told me your Uncle Tony and Fiona had once been in love."

A rueful look entered Diane's eyes. "Uncle Tony came to her shop whenever he had the chance. They were crazy for each other, but her father wouldn't permit him to court her."

"Why was that?"

"My mother said the gulf between them was too wide, whatever that meant."

"O-kay. Why didn't Fiona and Tony reconnect after she moved to Florida? Cal said Tony lives in Sarasota."

"Fifi refused to see him, even after his wife died. Poor guy was distraught when I told him Fifi had passed away." Her expression brightened. "I have an idea. You should visit him, Keri. I'll pay your travel expenses."

"For what purpose?" Keri didn't understand what they'd gain.

"He can tell you about her earlier life. It's possible her history relates to current events."

Hmm, a visit to Tony could be useful. He might offer insights into Fiona's character. She'd like to discern which version of Fiona was the true one, the altruist or the manipulator.

"Why don't you go see him for yourself? He's your uncle."

"No, thanks," Diane said in an emphatic tone.

That had touched a nerve. "Are you two not on good terms?"

Old pain entered Diane's eyes. "It hurt Fifi terribly when he married someone else. In my opinion, he should have fought harder to win her hand instead of abandoning her. Here's his address. He's eighty-two and still lives at home."

Keri copied the info into her cell phone. "We'll see if he agrees to talk to me. It could be difficult for him to dredge up the past."

"It might also bring him closure. Fifi was his first love." Diane gathered her purse and stood. "Let me know what happens when you call him."

Keri considered these revelations as she finished her meal. While a past romance might not be relevant to the murder case, she should learn more about Fiona's earlier years. Who knew what other nuggets might arise?

She disposed of her tableware, then glanced around. Winnie and Felicity were hanging out together. Great; she could catch them alone.

"You did a terrific job in setting this up," Winnie said with a warm smile. She wore a black pantsuit, brightening her appearance with a slash of coral lipstick and a strand of chunky beads.

"Thanks, although I wish we were celebrating Fiona's birthday instead."

"It's sad, but she would have been pleased by this luncheon in her honor."

Keri nodded. "True. Her absence will leave a gap in town. I know she played a big role in your organization. She was generous with her donations and her volunteer time."

Felicity had been ogling a handsome stranger who'd entered the room. Now she swung her gaze Keri's way. "Volunteering gave her the means to meddle in people's affairs."

"Oh? How so?" Keri asked in wide-eyed innocence.

"She stuck her nose where it didn't belong, same as you. Sarah told us you'd stopped by to see her. I suggest you let Fiona rest in peace and stop annoying her friends."

Do you consider yourself one of them? If you genuinely cared, you'd want to learn the truth.

"I wanted to thank Sarah for a client referral. But I'll take your advice under consideration," Keri said, realizing she needed to be agreeable to work with these ladies on upcoming events.

She excused herself before she blurted out something she'd regret. Time passed as she greeted people and made sure the dishes at the buffet were refilled. Finally, guests started to trickle out as the luncheon wound down.

Her cell phone rang. Lora's face showed on the screen.

"Keri, I don't know what to do. Rick is here. He says you sicced the cops on him. Detective Saunders showed up at his garage and asked him questions. He's banging on the door. Should I let him inside to calm him down?"

"What? No way! Keep the door locked and do not open it. How did he get into the building? You didn't buzz him in, did you?"

"I expect he followed someone into the lobby."

Keri's heart thumped. She didn't want Lora to do something stupid. Was Rick there to harm her or to convince her to come back to him?

"Listen, I'm on my way home. Let me try to defuse the situation. If Rick gets more violent, call the police." She hung up and hurried over to Pam, who'd been talking to a local councilman.

"I need to go home. Rick is pounding on our door, and Lora is thinking about giving in to him. He could be dangerous if she lets him inside."

Pam's eyes rounded. "Do you want me to come with you?"

"Thanks, but it's best for you not to get involved."

"Okay, but be careful, you hear? Call me when you're safe."

Pam's warning stayed on her mind as she left the restaurant and speed-walked to her car.

When she arrived home, Rick was pacing back and forth in the hallway with a scowl on his face. Clutching her keys, Keri glanced down the corridor. Not a single neighbor was in sight. Her heart beat a staccato rhythm while her fingers went cold. She didn't care for confrontations, especially with someone bigger and in a mean frame of mind.

"Go away, Rick. Lora doesn't want to see you," Keri said with false bravado.

"I just need to clear the air with her. Let me in." He plowed his fingers through his spiked hair.

Keri waved her arm. "What's there to make clear? She's over you. You never keep your promises. You lied about taking college classes. You've been stuck in the same job for years. If you really love Lora, you'd want to take care of her. Instead, you always put your needs first."

He stepped toward her, making her aware of his height and muscle. "I am thinking of her needs. She wants me. Now open the door."

Shaking inside, Keri held up her cell phone. "Not until you leave, or I'll call the cops."

"Didn't you do that already? A police detective showed up at my workplace. You're trying to get me in trouble, aren't you?" he snarled, balling his fists at his side.

"Somebody broke into my office the other night. Was it you?"

"You'll think I did it no matter what I say." He took another step closer.

Keri's heart lurched. "Be aware these hallways have video cameras. Your actions are being recorded." Like that would be a deterrent if he meant her harm.

"All right, have it your way." He spread his hands and backed off. "I'll catch Lora at work instead. She'll come to her senses. You'll see." With those parting words, he pivoted and stalked down the hall.

Keri pressed a hand to her chest. Her heart raced so wildly that she feared it might jump out of her ribcage. If Lora had any sense, she would wash her hands of this guy permanently and stop making excuses for him.

"Lora, it's safe. Rick has gone," she said, knocking on the door. She heard the latch turning and entered the foyer.

Lora hovered by the kitchen with a panicked expression on her face. "Thank God. What should I do to get rid of him the next time?"

"A restraining order might be a good idea." Keri dumped her purse on the kitchen counter and joined Lora in the living room. The coffee table had a polished sheen and smelled of lemon oil. Lora tended to clean when stressed.

She claimed an armchair while Lora collapsed onto the couch. It had been a tiring day, even though it was only early afternoon.

"So far, Rick has been all bark and no bite, but there's always a first time." Lora hugged a throw pillow and cast her eyes downward.

"I hope you're done with him for good. He's a loser, Lora. You can do better."

"I know, but I feel bad for not listening to what he had to say."

"You've given him enough chances, and he's never changed. You need to cut him loose."

"We'll see. Enough about my problems. I'm sorry I dragged you away from the funeral."

Keri shrugged. "The luncheon was nearly over anyway. Oh, I promised to let Pam know when you were safe." She sent a text, then related to Lora what she'd gleaned from the day.

"So, Diane's Uncle Tony was in love with Fiona?" Lora said when she'd concluded.

"That's right. He lives in Sarasota." A brilliant idea came to her. It would get Lora out of harm's way for a few hours. "Diane asked me to pay him a visit. If he's home and agreeable, I could make it there by dinnertime. Would you like to join me? I'd rather not make the long drive by myself."

Lora clapped her hands. "Oh goody, a road trip. We could visit Michelle while we're there."

"Great idea. Let me call Tony first."

When he answered directly, Keri identified herself. "Hi, my name is Keri Armstrong. I'm… I was a friend of Fiona's. Diane said I should give you a call."

"What's this about?" he said, his voice wary.

"Diane and I have some concerns about the way Fiona died. I live in the Orlando area, but I could drive down to see you this afternoon if you'll be home."

A lengthy pause ensued. "Sure, I'll be here."

"I'm bringing a friend, if you don't mind." She got his address and then rang off. Next, she texted Michelle to see if she was available. Keri, Lora, Pam and Michelle had rented a house together during their college years. Michelle had moved away after getting a job at the Sarasota museum as an art historian.

"Good news," Keri told Lora after reading their friend's response. "Tony will see us, and Michelle can meet us for dinner. She's invited us to stay over her place until Sunday."

"This will be fun. Do you think Pam would want to come?"

"Let me ask." Keri relayed their plan and read the reply. "Pam says she can't go but we should call her when we're all together."

"I'll go pack a bag." Lora bounded up from the couch and loped to her room with a springy step while Keri rushed to get ready.

She was glad to kill two birds with one stone. She'd get Lora away from Rick while he cooled off, and she'd talk to Tony about Fiona's history.

Chapter Fourteen

Tony's address was a couple of blocks from St. Armand's Circle in Sarasota. By the time Keri and Lora arrived, the sun had started its nightly descent in a blaze of crimson glory.

She pulled up to the curb by a single-story house with a shingle roof and a clean coat of eggshell paint. A gaunt, silver-haired man wearing a pair of khakis and a Cuban shirt answered the door. His weathered face broke into a smile as he swung the door wide.

"I'm Tony. You must be Keri and…?"

"It's nice to meet you. This is Lora. Thanks so much for seeing us."

"Come on in. We can sit out back." Tony leaned on a cane and led them through his living room. Traditional furnishings, paintings of Florida landscapes, and shelves full of books gave the impression of homey comfort. "I don't get young ladies like you visiting me too often, unless they're from physical therapy. I'm recovering from hip surgery."

"You seem to be doing well," Keri said politely.

Tony indicated they should sit at a glass-topped patio table with a wicker base. "Can I get you gals something to drink?"

"No, thanks. We'll be going out to dinner from here." Keri admired the view that overlooked a yard lush with banana plants, red hibiscus bushes, and areca palms. The sweet fragrance in the air must have been coming from that flowering Hong Kong orchid tree.

"You have a lovely home," she said. "Do you have family in the area?"

"Yes, my daughter Cassie lives nearby. She's married with two kids. I moved to Florida to be near her after my wife died."

"Of course, you'd want to be close to your grandkids. Is Cassie your only child?"

He shook his head. "I have a son who lives in upstate New York, but it's too cold for me there. I'd managed fine on my own until my hip got worse. The doctor said I was ready for a replacement, otherwise I'd end up in a wheelchair. I suppose this is better, eh? But I'm not allowed to drive yet, and I have therapy three times a week. It's damned inconvenient."

"Maybe so, but you need to heal properly. It's tough when you're on your own. Fiona hired me to drive her to appointments and assist her in other ways. We became close friends, and I valued our time together. I still can't believe she's gone."

Tony's eyes saddened. "It's a loss for us all. How did she die? Diane didn't give me any details."

"An intruder broke into her house while she was sleeping."

"That's horrible. Did she have a heart attack out of fright?"

"She was murdered. The police think it might have been a drug addict off the street. I'm guessing Fiona woke up while he was in her room."

"Good God." Tony fell silent, his expression ranging from horror to grief. Finally, he addressed her, his eyes moist. "You said on the phone that you and Diane had concerns about her death. In what way? And how do you think I can help?"

"Her house was the only one broken into on the street," Keri explained, glancing at Lora. She appeared content to listen quietly.

"Are you saying this wasn't a random robbery? That Fiona may have been targeted?"

"Exactly." She gave him a level glance. "The whole robbery scenario might have been staged, although I'm not discounting the drug addict theory. Otherwise, could somebody from her past still hold a grudge?"

"Like me, you mean?" A haunted look entered his eyes.

"Diane believes I caused the rift between us, but she doesn't know the entire story."

Keri leaned forward, eager to hear his side of the tale. "I know Fiona was best friends with your sister. Is that how you met each other?"

He gave a vigorous nod. "We hit it off at first sight even though we came from opposite sides of the track, as it were."

"Meaning?"

Tony's gaze darkened. "Crogher Sullivan—Fiona's father—was purebred Irish. I'm from Italian stock. That might not seem like much of a difference to you, but it mattered back then. Crogher didn't care to taint his bloodline."

I don't like the sound of this guy at all. "Did he realize how you felt about Fiona? Were you dating?"

"He forbade us to see each other. Crogher made it clear I'd be sorry if I defied him."

"What made him so fearsome?" she asked.

"I'll get to that in a minute. I'd accompany my sister, Teresa, whenever she visited Fiona at her antique store, which was the only way we could be together."

"So, Teresa acted as your go-between?" Lora asked. Her rapt expression indicated she'd been absorbing every word, even while she appeared to be soaking in the view.

"That's right." Tony's glance followed a lizard scooting across the old-style Chattahoochee floor. The sealant-coated pebbles glistened in the sinking sunlight.

"Teresa knew what was going on but pretended she didn't," Tony continued. "She was afraid for me. Crogher was a crime boss for the Westies, an Irish-American gang that ruled over Hell's Kitchen in New York City. They called him The Crocodile because his enemies ended up in the Hudson River. Their gang had a rivalry with the Italian Mafia."

"No wonder you didn't want to cross his path," Keri said. Gang wars were a good reason to steer clear of conflict. She didn't blame Tony for not pushing the romance under those circumstances, although she wished his story with Fiona had a happier ending. "Was your family involved on the Italian side?"

"No, we were just poor shopkeepers. I worked as a butcher, same as my father before me."

"Did you ask Fiona to marry you?"

"I did, and she turned me down. She was terrified her father would kill me, but that wasn't the only reason."

"Then Fiona was the one who broke things off?" Keri asked, needing clarity on this point.

Tony bobbed his head. "She said she wouldn't risk my life. The Irish gangs were growing too powerful, and she was fearful of her father's reaction if I continued to see her. But I understood her true reasons for rejecting me. She didn't want to lose Crogher's support. He financed her trips around the world to stock her shop."

"You could have eloped," Lora said, her eyes dreamy. She was lapping up his story like a puppy with a bowl of water.

His lips twisted. "Then Fiona would have had to give up her lavish lifestyle. She loved going to parties and being the center of attention. If she married me, we'd be shunned. She would have had to leave all that behind to face an uncertain future."

Keri's brow wrinkled as she considered Fiona's motives. "If I'm getting this right, you're saying Fiona was unwilling to give up her cash cow, meaning her father's funding."

"Yes, that's my belief, at any rate."

"What happened after she broke things off?" Lora asked, folding her hands in her lap.

"I realized we had different priorities and stopped coming around. Fiona had chosen her path, and I wasn't part of it. I moved on." A smidgen of guilt entered his eyes, and he glanced away.

"How sad for both of you," Keri said. It appeared Fiona wasn't willing to sacrifice her easy lifestyle, and Tony didn't try hard enough to convince her otherwise. Diane was right in that regard, not that it would have made a difference. Fiona's fears for

Tony were only the excuse she used to disguise her true reasons for backing off.

"You said you had two kids," Lora remarked. "You were fortunate to find someone else to marry."

He leveled his gaze at them. "That's right. I met Rose, a wonderful woman who brightened my days. She cooked the best lasagna in the world. What man could resist?"

"I don't understand why you haven't explained all this to Diane," Keri said. "She seems to blame you for leaving Fiona."

He harumphed. "Diane idolized Fiona, and I don't want to spoil her image. When Rose passed away, Diane urged me to call her. I did ask her out, but she said it was too late. Diane always felt I should have been more persistent."

She needs to hear your side of the story, Keri thought before changing the topic. "Tell me, does this Irish mob still exist? I'm wondering if Fiona learned some of their secrets, and they sent someone to eliminate her."

"At this late date?" Tony scoffed. "Most of those gangsters are dead. Plus, she'd risk exposing her own role if she ratted them out. She was one of them. For example, Teresa and I dropped by her shop one day, and she seemed nervous about us being there. She shoved something under the counter that she didn't want us to see. I figured Crogher must have given her a bauble to sell on the sly."

"Didn't she choose the goods for her store?"

"Not always. She and Crogher seemed to have an unspoken agreement. Fiona sold certain things he gave her to private collectors, and in return, he gave her money to spend abroad."

This didn't sound like the Fiona she'd known. She'd reconcile it all later when she had time to think. Meanwhile, Keri retrieved the photo from her purse and showed it to him. "Do you recognize this picture? Diane said it's Fiona and Crogher."

He peered at it and gave a curt nod. "That's them, all right. Looks like they're at a party."

"Do you recognize the brooch she's wearing? Diane hasn't found it among her jewelry."

He gave the picture a closer examination. "Nope, I'd remember that star design with the pearl in the center. But this photo was taken years ago. She could have long since sold it." Just then, a buzzer sounded from somewhere inside, and Tony leveraged to his feet. "There goes my timer. I need to get my dinner out of the oven."

Keri rose and signaled to Lora to do the same. "We need to leave to meet our friend. I really appreciate you sharing a bit of Fiona's history. I know it wasn't easy for you."

Tony paused to regard her. "It helped to unburden myself, so I have you to thank for coming to see me. I hope you're able to find out what really happened to Fiona."

"I'll tell Diane we had a nice chat. Do your families ever get together for the holidays?"

He shook his head. "I'm afraid we've drifted apart. Aside from Diane's resentment toward me, her husband has never been the friendly sort. I think she made a mistake in marrying him."

Keri gave him a startled glance. "Oh? Why is that?"

"There's something shifty about the guy. I can't put my finger on it, because Cal treats her well and adores their kids. But their marriage was a whirlwind affair. Diane should have waited until she knew him better."

Really? How long had they been together before he proposed? Keri would have to ask Diane. For now, she wished Diane and Tony would mend fences. It would benefit them both.

"Sarasota isn't so far from Orlando," she said. "I'd bet Diane would be thrilled if you suggested a get-together with her cousins."

His brows lifted. "We're doing Thanksgiving this year at Cassie's house. Maybe I'll suggest that she invite Diane's family to join us."

"That would be great. Thank you again, Tony. Here's a business card with my phone number if you remember anything to tell me. I'm still trying to get a sense of who might have wanted to harm Fiona, aside from a random thief."

"I wouldn't worry about the past so much if I were you," he said, his eyes narrowing. "You're better off looking closer to home."

Before she could ask him to elaborate, he hustled them out the door.

She walked in silence alongside Lora until they reached the car. Lora's curls had frizzed in the humidity, while Keri's hair hung straight and flat.

She turned on the engine and relished the blast of air-conditioning. "Tony had a lot to say. It's sad that he and Fiona had a chance for happiness twice, and she let it slip through her fingers. She should have given him a second chance."

Lora fastened her seatbelt. "At least Tony moved on. It sounded as though his marriage was a happy one." She looked thoughtful, and Keri hoped Lora wasn't thinking about giving Rick a second chance. Although in his case, it would be the fourth or fifth time around.

They were overdue to meet Michelle. She drove downtown, the streets brightly lit with streetlamps and storefront lighting. They were lucky to find a parking space in front of a bookstore.

Outside, a balmy breeze ruffled the hairs on her arms. A lone owl hooted. The sky had darkened, but the street buzzed with activity.

At the restaurant, they found Michelle, who'd claimed a booth with a window view. Lively chatter competed with the clatter of dishes and the clink of glassware. After hugs all around, they sat and ordered drinks, along with appetizers.

"You look good! I love your outfit," Keri commented, surveying her friend's Lilly Pulitzer maxi-dress and turquoise jewelry.

"Thanks. What's been happening with you two?"

Keri filled her in on Fiona's death and what she'd learned so far. Lora mentioned her break-up with Rick.

"You did the right thing," Michelle told Lora. "Don't give in to his demands this time. You can do better."

They paused while the waitress delivered their starters. Then Keri swung the conversation back to Fiona.

"Our talk with Tony was enlightening. According to what he said, Fiona's father funded her trips abroad. In return, she sold goods he gave her to private buyers. In other words, she acted as a money launderer and a fence for her gangster father. I can't believe she's the same person I knew."

Michelle dipped a chip into the cheesy spinach and artichoke bowl. "Do you think she understood what she was doing? If so, maybe her philanthropy when she moved here was an attempt at redemption."

"That's a good theory, but her initial plan had been to reopen her shop in Florida. Maybe she meant to go legit but decided to quit the business altogether."

Keri sipped her chardonnay, exhaustion stealing her energy. This had been a long day. First the funeral and the luncheon, and then the long drive to interview Tony. His revelations had been the final stomp on her mental powers.

Or else she was merely hungry. Her appetite surged as their meals arrived. She dug into her Jamaican-style mahi-mahi. The spicy sauce left a kick on her tongue.

"Didn't you say you've been selling Fiona's stuff on eBay?" Michelle asked, concentrating on her steaming chicken fajita.

"Yes. Why?"

"Maybe Fiona still had some items from her father that she wanted to unload. Or else she needed the cash. Her financial resources might have shrunk with inflation."

Keri stuck a corn chip in her mouth and crunched down on it. "I doubt she'd have me advertise things online that had dubious origins. Although, it is peculiar that the same man has been snapping up everything of hers that I've put on sale."

"Have you tried to track him down?" Michelle asked, taking a sip of water.

"His name doesn't bring up anything on an online search. The mailing address is in Clermont. I'll have to look that one up."

Clermont was west of the greater Orlando area. Actually, it wasn't far from Winter Garden, where Diane and Cal lived.

She fell silent while finishing her meal, unable to shake the feeling that they were missing something. Her talk with Tony had sparked an idea but she couldn't quite grasp it.

"We should call Pam," she said. "She wanted us to contact her when we were all together."

Keri initiated the video call, and after Pam chatted with Lora and Michelle, she listened to Keri's update.

"Get this," Pam said. "I came across an interesting article in our newspaper archives. Did Fiona ever mention that when she moved here, she sold goods on consignment through an antique dealer on Morse Avenue?"

"No, she didn't. Do you mean things from her former shop, or new merchandise?"

"You can ask the owner. She's still around, although she closed her store a few years ago. I could set up an interview if you want. Maybe she'll give me a quote for my profile on Fiona."

"That would be great. I'll get back to you after we're home."

They disconnected, and Keri let her shoulders sag. She should relax and enjoy the break from her routine. Just thinking about her agenda for next week gave her a headache. She decided to focus on her friends and put aside her worries for the next few days.

Their weekend ended with hugs and promises to get together again soon. Keri and Lora headed out in light Sunday traffic toward Orlando.

"I wish I didn't have to go to work tomorrow," Lora said with a groan from the passenger seat. She slumped against the cushion, looking defeated by the prospect.

"Are you afraid Rick will show up? He'd better stay away."

"It's not only that. I feel like this job is a dead end."

"Then why don't you quit? You're a talented graphic artist. You could find a better position elsewhere." They'd had this discussion before, and it always ended in frustration for Keri.

"I need to find a rental apartment, and I'll have to list my job on the application. The timing isn't right."

"You can stay with me until you find another position. Your creativity is being stifled at the print shop. You'd be happier if you could spread your wings."

"I don't want them to think I'm a quitter."

"They won't see things that way if you have a better offer. But it won't happen unless you're more proactive."

Lora didn't respond. With a sigh, she turned and stared out the window as the scenery sped past. Keri didn't want to irritate her further and remained silent.

Several hours later, they arrived home. Just to appease her curiosity, she looked up the eBay buyer's street address in Clermont. It brought up a UPS store.

She could always offer another item of Fiona's for sale and see who picked it up, but that was impractical. She couldn't hang out for days watching the place.

Tony's advice had been to look closer to home. Maybe he was right, and the culprit was someone known to both her and Fiona. In that case, they were one step ahead of her. She needed to up her game and learn the truth before the killer set his sights on her next.

Chapter Fifteen

Monday morning, Keri checked into the office, reminded her colleagues to visit the police station to leave their prints and, after meeting with the security guy who came to install their alarm system, went out to do a few errands for clients.

Pam called when she was getting into her car after her last field appointment.

"I scheduled a meeting with Mrs. Hawkins, the antique shop owner," Pam said. "If you're free, she'll see us both at one-thirty."

"That's great. Do you want to do lunch before we head over?" She'd gotten ahead of her schedule and had some unexpected free time.

"Okay. We should catch up on things anyway before we see her."

They set a time and hung up. As Keri drove back to her office, she felt energized by the prospect of meeting the woman who'd sold things on consignment for Fiona. These interviews offered a glimpse into Fiona's past. Maybe Mrs. Hawkins would reveal a darker side to her life, the same as Tony.

At the allotted hour, she met Pam at a French café a few blocks away and ordered her favorite chicken and mushroom croissant sandwich.

"We can walk to Mrs. Hawkins's place from here," Pam said between bites of her strawberry and arugula salad.

Keri took a sip of iced tea. "I can't wait to hear what she says. I guess I'm finally ready to admit there was a part of Fiona that I never knew. It's disappointing, to say the least."

Pam's hazel eyes softened. "From people's comments at the funeral lunch, I gathered she was genuinely dedicated to the arts. She joined PHEADA shortly after she moved to Florida. But when I tried to dig deeper into her role in the group, their officers gave me evasive replies. There's something fishy about that bunch."

"I agree. I need to stop by their headquarters. Fiona had acted as liaison between us, but now that I'll be working with them directly, it may be helpful to determine how much she pushed the board members to do things her way. Like, how badly did they want her out of the picture?"

"Maybe she discovered something about them that led to her death," Pam suggested. "That's another possibility."

"You could be right." Keri got busy eating, resolving to make time to visit PHEADA's offices.

She picked up the tab in gratitude for Pam arranging the upcoming interview. Outside, a Sun Rail train rumbled past the nearby Amtrak station and Keri glanced across the street at Central Park. The rose bushes at the far end looked short and bare, pruned like Fiona's life. She set a brisk pace, anxious to meet another one of her mentor's acquaintances.

"How did you get Mrs. Hawkins to agree to our meeting?" she asked Pam as they dodged a woman pushing a small dog in a stroller.

Pam grinned under her sun hat. "I told her I was doing an article honoring retired merchants in the area. She seemed flattered that I would include her."

"That's an interesting topic. Maybe you should write about it from a different historical perspective."

Pam shrugged. "I can propose a piece to my editor when I have more information."

"What did you tell Mrs. Hawkins about my coming along?"

"I just said you were a friend of mine. She didn't object. Turn right at the corner. Her condo building should be two blocks ahead."

Mrs. Hawkins lived on the third floor of a multi-unit structure. Keri saw a shadow at the door's peephole before it swung open, and a plump woman with a beehive hairdo and pleasant smile greeted them.

"Mrs. Hawkins?" Pam said. "I'm Pam Teague from the *Gazette*, and this is Keri Armstrong."

She and Pam handed over their business cards. "I own a personal concierge agency in town," Keri explained. "I'm here to help if you ever need an extra hand."

"That's good to know. Please, call me Sally. Come in, girls."

Sally led them into a living room with traditional wood furnishings. Fiona would have felt comfortable there with the Lenox pieces on display, the Christmas village on a sideboard cabinet, and the oil paintings on the walls. Sally must have also liked fake flowers, because various bouquets adorned the room, including a red poinsettia plant. Apparently, Christmas décor came early in the fall season for Sally Hawkins.

After they took seats, Pam retrieved her notebook and began her interview with questions regarding Sally's arrival in town, her antique shop, and her social life.

"Were you acquainted with Fiona Sullivan?" Pam finally asked.

Sally's gaze hardened, a telling clue that her impression had not been favorable. "Indeed, I was. Fiona had some lovely things—wood carvings from Africa, German music boxes, New Guinea art, plus a collection of vintage lamps and assorted clocks. I sold them on consignment in my store, but I rejected her offer to become a partner."

"Why was that?" Pam asked, leaning forward with an intent expression.

Sally tucked a strand of gray hair behind her ear. "Fiona was so sweet and charming that I totally bought her story of how she'd acquired her goods. It was clear that she'd traveled the world. But then she brought in some estate jewelry."

"Go on." Pam's scrape of the pen on her notebook came to

a halt while Keri's ears perked up. Sally's tone had changed, and her mouth curved down.

"I wondered why she didn't go to a jeweler where she'd get a better price, so I did some research. The diamond and ruby neck-lace had been reported as stolen from a collection years earlier."

Keri's stomach clenched. "Stolen? From where?"

"Some foreign country. I don't remember the details, except it had been part of a set. That's all I needed to know. Although Fiona denied knowledge of its origins, I told her I'd restrict my inventory thereafter to my own acquisitions."

A pit opened in Keri's gut at the tarnished image of her friend. She desperately wanted to hold onto the kind person she'd known, but it was becoming increasingly difficult. She'd be naïve to believe otherwise.

Her cell phone rang, and she groaned inwardly as Detective Saunders's name popped up. What did he want?

"Sorry, I have to take this," she said, rising. She walked toward the foyer for privacy. "Hello, Detective. What's up?"

"I'm afraid I have bad news." His solemn tone made her nape prickle with dread.

"Oh? What's happened now?"

"I regret to inform you that Miss Sullivan's neighbor, Veronica Batten, is dead."

Keri's throat closed. "Oh, my God. That can't be true. How did she die?"

"It appears the lantern on her front porch broke off and fell on her head as she stepped underneath. A neighbor saw her lying there this morning and called it in."

Keri couldn't imagine such a freak accident. It would depend on Veronica walking under the lamp at just the right time. Or… was it truly an accident? It had been only days since Keri had talked to her. This couldn't be a coincidence, could it?

"Are you sure someone didn't bash her on the head and make it look like an accident?" she asked, suspicion tinging her voice.

"The M.E. will determine the cause of death. Would you mind stopping by the station? I've some more questions to ask you about Ms. Batten."

What kind of questions? She'd already told him all she knew. "I can come by around three, if that would work?"

"I'll be here." He hung up, and Keri's thoughts spun.

How could Veronica be dead? Suddenly, the woman's befuddled warnings rang true. Somebody must have been watching her, after all.

She returned in a daze to the living room and sank onto the sofa.

Pam cast her a concerned glance then filled her in on what she'd missed. "Sally said Fiona should have done her due diligence regarding the necklace's provenance, but Fiona claimed her father had given it to her."

Sally plucked a speck of fuzz off her trousers. "Apparently, she'd often sold art works or jewelry for her dad, but the whole thing sounded strange to me. She never questioned where he'd obtained them."

Keri figured Crogher had acquired the goods through illegal means and used Fiona to fence them to private collectors. After he died and she moved south, she must have wanted to get rid of the remaining stock. Using another shop as an intermediary had been a brilliant idea, but it hadn't worked out well for her.

Maybe she'd hidden her ledger on purpose, if it revealed the illicit origins of certain items. She wouldn't want Keri to learn the truth about her sullied past.

Sally glanced at a clock on the mantel and stood. "Is there anything else? It's nearly time for my canasta game."

Pam stuffed her notebook into her bag. "I think we're done. Thank you for seeing us. I'll send you a copy of the article when it's printed."

Drained by recent events, Keri murmured a farewell to their host on her way to the door. Outside on the sidewalk, she donned her sunglasses.

"Did Sally say anything more after I left the room?" she asked, avoiding the most recent news she had to relate to Pam.

Pam started along at a brisk pace toward Broad Street. "She said Fiona weaseled her way into people's confidences. She had a gift for charming people into telling her things while revealing very little about herself."

"That's true." Keri took a deep breath and plunged into the next topic. "I have bad news. The call I took inside was from Detective Saunders. He informed me that Veronica Batten is dead. She had a fatal accident this morning."

Pam halted in her tracks. "Wasn't she Fiona's neighbor who lived across the street?"

"That's right. A porch lantern fell on her head. It's very weird that this happened so soon after Fiona died. I'm thinking someone hit her on the skull and made it look like an accident."

Pam resumed her pace. "If so, it'll show up in the autopsy report."

"Saunders wants me to stop by his station for more questions."

"Good. Then you can ask him for the details. Let me know what happens. And be careful. If there's a killer on the loose, they might come after you next."

"Or you. You've been nosing around same as me."

They parted ways, and Keri stifled her sense of unease to complete her next task, which entailed heading to the Sheraton to view the banquet room for a client's proposed Christmas party. Normally, she'd have assigned Staz to this job, but her colleague already had a full schedule for the day.

Lora called right after she'd left the hotel.

"Hi, what's going on?" Keri figured she must be at the print shop.

"I sent you an email with Jarek's proofs. Look at your office inbox."

"Okay, thanks. Are you calling me from work?" Lora could have sent her a text. What else did she want?

"I'm reorganizing your pantry since it's a disaster again. I don't know how you can find anything in here. You can't just stick things randomly on the shelves."

"You're at the condo?"

"Rick was waiting outside the print shop. I turned around and came home."

Oh my God. Keri's hands curled at her sides. "You really need to get a restraining order against him. He's stalking you, Lora. This can't go on. He needs a clear message that your relationship is over." She didn't mean to be harsh, but Lora needed a wakeup call.

"I'll get to it. Do you realize that some of your soups have expired? Why do you buy them and then let them go to waste?"

Keri gritted her teeth. "The best-used-by dates don't always mean they're no longer good."

"Yes, but this grated parmesan cheese is two years old. And it's yellow, not white."

"Okay, you can toss that one." A sheepish flush crept over her face. Maybe she hadn't been as diligent with her groceries as she should be.

"I don't mean to be critical," Lora said. "I'm grateful you're letting me stay here, but I've noticed how you make time for clients and not for yourself. I can at least help you organize your clutter."

Maybe it's clutter to you, but I know where to find everything. Or at least I did before you arrived. Still, she supposed it was nice to have a friend who cared.

"All right, but don't neglect your work," she advised. "You can still clock in from home."

She ended the call, exasperated at Lora's lack of focus. She should be looking for a better job and detaching herself from Rick instead of messing with Keri's things.

Feeling frustrated on all fronts, Keri headed over to the Sunny Grove Police Department for her appointment with Detective Saunders, who came downstairs to escort her to his glass-enclosed office on the second floor. She surveyed the papers strewn on his desktop, the dusty bookshelf, the battered file cabinet, and the overflowing garbage can. No doubt he had more important things to do than tidying up his space.

"I still can't believe the news about Veronica," she said, taking the seat offered. "I just talked to her a few days ago."

He sat in a leather desk chair and gave her an assessing glance. "A neighbor spotted her when he went out to get his newspaper. Tell me again what she said to you when you spoke with her the other day."

Keri repeated the riddles that she remembered offhand. She should have written them down. "The weeds thrive in the warm weather. The ducks stay safe by the lake. The sour apples grow alongside the good ones." She shook her head. "None of them make any sense."

"But Ms. Batten gave you a warning?"

"That's right. She said *they're watching* but didn't give any names or descriptions."

He flipped through his notes. "You'd said she mentioned Bob Underwood."

"She must have seen him entering Fiona's house, but as her handyman, he had a logical reason for being there. Her other comments could have referred to anyone. While she had some wild theories, she was observant. Do you really believe her death was merely an accident?"

His lips compressed. "It's a fresh case. I can't discuss the details. Who else have you spoken to since Miss Sullivan's funeral?"

Pleased he had asked, Keri told him about her interviews with Tony Salvatore and Sally Hawkins.

He wove his hands together on the desk. "Let me get this straight. You believe Miss Sullivan was fencing stolen goods?"

"Not recently, but in the past. It would help if I could find her ledger. She wrote down each item and where she got them."

"Let me know if it turns up. Is there anything more you can tell me?"

"I don't think so. How about you? Did you have a chance to look into Hugh Connor's background?" She still felt Garvan's son was a viable lead.

His shoulders hunched, as though she'd hit upon a point of interest. "We're still checking him out. Meanwhile, I appreciate you coming in today and sharing your information."

Realizing she'd learn little else by remaining, she made her departure. Outside, she considered her next move. She'd promised to call Diane to make another appointment. If they could meet at Fiona's house tomorrow, the maids would be there, and Keri could question them about their former employer.

She also had to fill Diane in on what Tony had told her. Then there was Veronica's death. Dread pitted her stomach at the thought of relating this news.

She placed the call and was relieved when Diane answered promptly.

"Hi. Would you be able to meet me at Fiona's house tomorrow?" Keri asked. "I've seen Tony and have things to tell you. It's best said in person."

"Sure, that works for me," Diane replied wearily. "I need to bring more packing boxes over anyway."

After they arranged a time and Keri rang off, she called the PHEADA office and made a date with Winnie for Wednesday to review their upcoming social events. That would give her an excuse to swing by and chat up the board members who were present.

"I'll see you then," Winnie said before ending the call.

At least they still wanted to work with her, Keri thought. She needed to delve deeper into their relationship with Fiona. Her insider role there gave her an advantage over the cops in that regard.

The rest of her day passed quickly with paperwork and other chores. Back home in time for dinner, she brought Lora up to speed while they ate baked salmon and roasted vegetables.

"I can't believe Fiona's wacky neighbor is dead," Lora said, swallowing a bite.

"I know. It makes me wonder what we're overlooking. Meanwhile, as Veronica said, somebody out there is watching."

Chapter Sixteen

Tuesday whirled around faster than Keri could blink. That afternoon, she parked in front of Fiona's house. Diane's car took up space in the driveway along with another vehicle belonging to the maid service.

Her glance inadvertently swung toward Veronica's house. It looked quiet, without any yellow crime scene tape stretched across the front porch. Any remnants of a broken lantern were long gone, but Veronica's suspicious manner of death rang a loud alarm bell in her mind. If she'd been murdered, the woman's conspiracy theories might be valid.

Wondering how much Diane knew, she rang the doorbell. Diane answered the door promptly, looking comfy in a rose-colored sweater and jeans.

"Hey, Keri. Come on in." She gave Keri a quick hug. The scent of vanilla accompanied her.

Banging noises sounded from above, and Keri glanced at the interior.

"Maggie and Inez are working upstairs," Diane explained. "Come with me so I can introduce you."

Keri climbed after her, thinking they'd need to find a quiet spot in the house for their private discussion. She didn't care to have the maids overhear them.

Maggie Rodriquez was a pleasant, heavyset woman with black hair tied in a bun. Her partner, Inez, was a perky blonde with a petite frame. Inez waved a greeting and went back to work dusting the baseboards.

"You are the lady who found Miss Fiona?" Maggie asked with a slight accent.

"That's right." Keri glanced toward the bedroom, her gut roiling. Had they disposed of the bedding? It smelled decent in the hallway, like pine trees and lemon polish.

Maggie noticed her face. "Do not worry. I cleaned the room, and it is freshly aired out."

Good, that's another thing out of the way. Keri had arranged for the mattress to get picked up last weekend.

She exchanged pleasantries, then segued into her lineup of questions. "Tell me, how was Fiona's mood when you were here last? Did she seem fearful at all?" Keri remembered Fiona saying she might have made a mistake. Since she'd also indicated Keri was the only person she could trust, did that mean she'd made a mistake in trusting someone else?

Maggie grimaced. "The only time she got upset was when that no-good young man came around. He called her Auntie Fiona."

"You must mean Hugh. He's Fiona's great-nephew."

"Yes, that is the one. He has bad karma."

"Did he come here very often?"

"No, but when he did, he made Miss Fiona angry. They would sit on the patio where they thought we could not hear them, but their loud voices carried into the house."

Keri exchanged a glance with Diane. "Could you make out what they said?"

Maggie shook her head. "I could tell he was not a nice person. I saw him once outside in his car, racing down the street as though the devil rode his tail. A duck was crossing the road. He ran it down and kept on driving."

Keri squeezed her eyes shut. How could he have cared about Fiona when he lacked compassion for innocent animals?

Wait a minute. What was it Veronica had said?

The ducks stay safe by the lake. The bad apples grow alongside the good ones.

Had she meant Hugh?

Before she could follow that train of thought, a knock sounded on the front door.

"Shall I get it?" she asked Diane, who stood on the upper landing looking thoughtful.

Diane visibly shook herself. "Would you, please? I want to check the drawers up here. Those missing items still haven't turned up. Maybe Fifi stuck them into one of the bureaus."

"Okay." Keri left Diane and headed for the foyer. When she opened the door, she took a step back. A muscular man stood there. He wore a dirt-stained T-shirt, faded jeans, and a frown on his face.

"Ma'am? My name is Lyle Lanier. I'm the lawn guy. Sorry for your loss."

"Thank you, but I'm not—"

"I thought I'd do my regular cut for today. If you like, I can keep you on my schedule, but I'll need to know where to send the bill."

"Come in, please. You'll want to talk to Diane Foster. She's in charge here. I'm Keri Armstrong, a family friend."

She eyed him thoughtfully as he entered, an earthy smell accompanying him. He might have been coming here every week. Could he shed any light on Fiona's recent activities?

"Did you have much personal contact with Fiona?" she asked, pausing in the foyer.

"Not much, ma'am. She'd send me a check in the mail every month. She only came outside if she wanted something done, like those bushes cut back further or a new plant put in."

"Had you noticed any unusual visitors in the past few weeks?"

His brow furrowed. "Once or twice when I pulled my truck up, I noticed a gray Dodge Hornet parked in the driveway. When I drove around back on my mower, I'd see Miss Fiona sitting on the patio with a young fella. Light brown hair, mean-looking face."

That must be Hugh. "Did you hear any of their conversation?"

"Not with the noise from my machine. But I saw the guy again when he left by the front door. Miss Fiona looked angry when she said goodbye to him. He stomped off to his car."

When Diane came downstairs and joined them, Keri introduced her to Lyle, still ruminating over his comments about Hugh. It confirmed what Maggie had told her about Fiona's relationship with Hugh. It appeared none of their encounters had been pleasant ones.

"I'd like you to continue the lawn maintenance, but can you switch to another day when the maids aren't here?" Diane asked Lyle.

"Sure thing. I'm back in this area again on Thursdays, if that would work."

"That's good, thanks. What do you do about billing?"

"Excuse me," Keri cut in. "While you work out the details, I'll see what else needs packing in the kitchen." She scuttled away, aware that Diane had many people to contact. If she missed one or two, they'd all show up on the radar sooner or later.

A quick glance inside the pantry told her that Diane had almost finished emptying the contents. She took over the task, her vision misting as she stuck a juicer into an empty box. Fiona wouldn't be needing the popcorn maker, griddle, or immersion blender anymore, either.

Finally, the front door shut, and light footsteps approached.

"You've made good progress," Diane said, halting in the doorway.

Keri made a sweeping gesture. "There isn't much left, except for the things in the cabinets and Fiona's cookbook collection. Are you donating these appliances?"

"I don't need any of them. How about you? Feel free to take whatever you can use."

"Thanks, but I'll pass." She kept Fiona in her heart, and that was enough for now.

"Let's sit. I can't wait to hear what Tony told you." Diane gestured to the kitchen table.

"I thought we'd talk about Veronica first." Keri took a seat and inhaled a deep breath to fortify herself. "If you recall, she was the neighbor across the street who had been friends with Fiona."

Diane's gaze sharpened. "What about her?"

"She's dead."

"No. You're joking."

"She died from a freak accident, or so it appears. The porch lantern fell on her head when she stepped outside."

"That's horrible. How could that happen?"

"Perhaps a wire got loose, and when the lantern fell, one of the corners hit her in the wrong spot." She winced at the image but quickly banished it as being unlikely. "The alternative is that someone bashed her on the head and staged the whole thing."

Diane gasped. "The same way somebody made Fifi's death look like a thief killed her?"

"Exactly. I don't believe in coincidence. Veronica was observant about her neighbors. Maybe she saw something important and was silenced because of it."

"Such as?"

"I wish I knew. Speaking of secrets people wanted to keep, Fiona had a few of her own. Tony gave me quite an earful when I visited him."

"Oh, do tell." Diane jostled in her seat, an avid expression on her face.

From upstairs, Keri heard sounds of vacuuming. The maids wouldn't be coming down anytime soon.

"Fiona's dad, Crogher Sullivan, was a kingpin in the Irish mob. Fiona fenced things for him through her shop. In return, he funded her buying trips abroad."

She related the gist of their conversation but didn't mention the relationship issues between Tony and Fiona. That was his story to tell.

Diane's eyes registered disbelief. "My mother spoke about

Fifi's travels to purchase things, but I just assumed their family was wealthy. I had no idea Crogher was connected to The Mob."

Keri cleared her throat. "There's more. When Fiona moved here and decided to retire, she sold things on consignment at a local antique store. The owner is still around, so my friend Pam and I interviewed her." She related the shopkeeper's concerns about selling stolen goods.

"That doesn't mean Fifi knew where that necklace had come from. Her father gave her jewelry to sell. She may never have questioned their provenance."

Or, she could have been fully complicit. We may never learn the truth.

She'd prefer to believe Fiona was following her father's orders rather than being an active participant in his schemes, but the more she learned, the more she doubted Fiona's innocence.

She sought a way to reassure Diane that Fiona still had a good side. "Regardless of Fiona's complicity with her dad, she cared for you and your family."

"True. It's too bad she didn't feel the same way about Tony. He gave up on her too easily. She probably never forgave him for marrying someone else."

"You should talk to him and hear his side of the story. Family is important, Diane. Don't miss your chance to make amends, or you'll be just like her."

The front door opened and closed, and Cal's voice boomed from the foyer.

"Hi Diane. I left work early so I could come help you. Where are you?"

"I'm with Keri in the kitchen." As he stepped into view, Diane regarded him questioningly. "I thought you had customers to see this afternoon."

Cal shrugged. "One came sooner than expected and the other cancelled. I figured you could use another hand here today." He gave Keri a wave.

"I've plenty of help. The maids are here, too. I've asked

them to pack Fifi's clothes. They can take what they want, and I'll donate the rest."

A thump sounded from above, followed by a string of irate Spanish. In the distance, a hedge trimmer whined.

"It's a regular circus around here," Cal said with a chuckle. "Did you see the cars across the street? What's happening over there?"

Keri shot up from her chair and hurried into the living room to peer out the window. A couple of cars were parked in front of Veronica's house. Possibly her family had come to secure the house.

"I gather you haven't heard the news," she said to Cal in a morose tone. He and Diane had trailed after her. "The homeowner across the street, Veronica Batten, was found dead yesterday."

Cal gaped at her. "What? That's terrible. Had she been ill?"

"No, it was an accident. The front porch light fell on her head."

"Good God. What a weird thing to happen. Poor woman."

"The sooner we sell this house, the better," Diane said with an anxious frown. "When word gets out, people will think this neighborhood is jinxed."

Cal grabbed a porcelain figurine off a shelf. "It's going to take a while to clear things out. These knickknacks may be a hard sell. Nobody wants them anymore."

"Some of them may fetch a fair price," Keri commented. "I have a buyer online who's been snatching up Fiona's goods as soon as I offer them for sale. I figure he's either a collector or a reseller. An estate sale would save us the time and effort, though." *And money, she thought, since my fee is based on an hourly rate.*

Cal lifted his eyebrows. "I can help determine their current market value. People bring in silver serving trays and other pieces to my shop for restoration, but they also want opinions on what their other items are worth."

"You should have gotten your license as a certified appraiser, like I suggested," Diane said, wagging her finger at him. "Then you'd get paid for your advice. Customers take advantage of you."

"It's good for business to be helpful. Word of mouth is how I get new clients." Cal put down the statue. "How about if I continue to clean out the garage? We could use the rakes and pruning shears I saw in there, and the shovel is bigger than the one we have at home."

"Be my guest. And thanks for stopping by to help us," Diane said quietly. After he disappeared, she picked up a crystal cat from a shelf and stared into its emerald eyes.

Her protracted silence prompted Keri to inquire if all was well between them.

"Cal says he wants to help me," Diane replied, "but his behavior lately has been erratic. I think he feels guilty and is trying to make it up to me."

"Guilty about what?"

"He stays at work late and has become more distant. I'm worried he might be seeing someone else."

Keri's heart sank. She'd hate for someone as nice as Diane to be hurt. "Have you asked him about it?"

"He says he's working on a special project. Cal is a wonderful father and he's always been so thoughtful. I want to trust him, but I have this gut feeling that something is off."

Keri hoped Diane's suspicions were groundless. "Why not give him the benefit of the doubt until you have evidence otherwise?"

"I'll try." She opened a cabinet in the shelving unit and took out a pile of folded tablecloths. "I don't want to keep any of these. You can donate or sell them, if you think they're worth anything."

Keri unfolded a few of them. The ones with lace or embroidery could possibly sell. She divided them into two groups, while Diane opened another cabinet to discover a collection of candlesticks. They sorted through those as well.

Time passed quickly until Cal returned with a bucket containing small gardening implements.

"Hey, Diane, look at these. Andrew's school can use them for their vegetable garden."

"Good idea. His class is learning about sustainable farming," she told Keri with a proud smile. "Andrew loves it. We take him to farmer's markets on weekends."

"That's great," Keri said, realizing she'd never met Diane's children. She'd seen pictures of them around Fiona's house, though. "Refresh my mind, please. How old are your kids?"

"Landon is fourteen and Andrew is ten."

"I'll bet it's challenging having a teenager."

"You're right," Cal replied with a grin. "That boy needs to be reined in sometimes. Anyway, I'm going to head out. It's my turn to pick up the kids today," he reminded Diane.

He seemed to be a considerate partner and Keri hoped Diane had nothing to worry about. Perhaps he was just working on a special project like he'd said.

Shortly after he left, the maids descended. They'd finished their work and promised to return in two weeks as per their regular schedule.

Keri helped Diane box up the table linens and candlesticks they'd chosen for donation. Then Diane signaled Keri to follow her into the kitchen. "Let's do Fifi's cookbooks next. There's some I want to keep, but I'll take the rest to the library for their book sale room."

"I can do that for you. I know you have a busy schedule."

"Thanks, that would be great."

A half hour later, Keri's cell phone rang and she recognized Lora's number. Now what? She excused herself and hurried into the hallway, hoping Rick hadn't shown up at the condo again.

"Hi, Lora. What's going on?"

"I made it to the print shop, and Purdy called. He said Tanner Tree Service would like your firm to send out their Christmas cards this year, and he wants us to do the design and mailout."

A sense of relief washed over her. This was about work, then. So why hadn't Lora replied directly to Purdy? "Okay. Did Purdy send over their logo?"

"Yes. I can probably get him a proof by tomorrow."

"That's fine. Is this the only reason you called?"

"I can cook dinner tonight if you don't have any plans," Lora offered cheerily.

Oh, so that's why you wanted to touch base. You're trying to be helpful.

"I'd love it, thanks, but let's talk later. I've got to go." She hung up, glanced at her watch, and realized she'd better hustle to finish her agenda for the day.

"I have to leave," she told Diane. "Let me know when you want me to come over again. I'll just load the donation boxes into my car."

Diane assisted her and promised to check her schedule for another free date.

Once alone outside, Keri noticed the cars across the street had left. Too bad. She'd have walked over to express her condolences to Veronica's family, if they'd been there. How sad that the neighborhood had suffered another tragic loss so soon after Fiona's death.

A glimmer from next door drew her attention toward Sarah's house. How did she feel about somebody dying again so close to home?

Maybe I should knock on her door and ask her.

As she crossed the yard, another flash of light came from a side window. Keri hesitated as she noticed Sarah coming into clear view and beckoning to someone. Her eyes popped as she recognized Ossie Pittman's profile. Were they working together on the PHEADA project?

She stepped behind a palm tree, hoping they hadn't spotted her. While she watched, feeling like a voyeur, Sarah tugged Ossie close and kissed him on the mouth. It wasn't only a friendly peck, either. They clung together like a pair of love bugs.

Huh! This little scene confirmed what she'd suspected all along.

She turned on her heels and slunk back towards her car. After starting the engine, she drove slowly down the block and spotted Ossie's shiny Lexus parked at the curb farther along.

Her mind conjured Sarah and Ossie outside the night of the cocktail party. Ossie had warned Sarah not to make trouble, saying they'd have to lay low after Fiona's death. Could Fiona have discovered their affair, and Ossie killed her to cover it up? He wouldn't want to risk his reputation being smeared with his political aspirations.

Then what about Veronica? Working outside in her garden, she could have spotted the furtive couple together. Or maybe Fiona had mentioned it to her when they'd had tea one day. Veronica might have suspected they'd killed her friend and threatened to tell the cops.

Keri couldn't pass up this opportunity to get more answers. She waited in her car with the motor idling until Ossie left. Then she pulled into Sarah's driveway.

"What is it, darling?" Sarah said, yanking open the door when Keri rang the bell. Her face reddened when she spied Keri on her front stoop. "Oh, it's you."

Keri noted her loose hair, flushed skin, and half-open blouse. Usually, Sarah was so put together, but not this time.

"I was next door helping Diane clean out Fiona's things and figured I'd stop by to say hello," she said. "Was that Ossie I saw leaving just now?"

Sarah began buttoning her shirt with fumbling fingers. "Yes, we were working on the PHEADA project."

"That's not what it looked like to me."

A heavy silence ensued, while Keri shifted her feet on the porch with its stately white columns. An owl hooted in the distance, and the aroma of decayed leaves scented the air.

Finished making herself decent, Sarah glared at Keri. "You and Fiona were two of a kind, weren't you? No wonder you got along so well. You stick your nose where it doesn't belong same as her."

"I only want to learn the truth about why she died." Keri peered beyond Sarah's shoulder. "Is Bob around? I have something to ask him."

"He's on one of his business trips and won't be back until tomorrow. He thinks I don't know why he goes away so often." She gave a bitter laugh. "If he's having fun, why shouldn't I?"

Keri gasped at Sarah's bluntness. "You think he's being unfaithful?"

"Why else would he be so secretive? Listen carefully, darling. If you breathe one word of my private concerns to anyone, you'll soon find yourself blackballed in this town."

Chapter Seventeen

Before Keri could think of a suitable reply, her cell phone pinged with a text from Purdy.

Heather Warrington cancelled her contract. She said you hadn't gotten back to her within the promised timeframe.

Oh, no. She'd forgotten to return Heather's call. Her client had wanted Keri to book a room at the Gaylord Palms for her brother's family and to get them tickets for the ice attraction. That was bad. She'd lose more business if she forgot about her regular clients. Then being blacklisted in town would be her own fault.

"Excuse me, I have to answer this message," she told Sarah, relieved to have an excuse to cut their conversation short. "We'll talk another time."

"Don't count on it," Sarah said, slamming the door in her face.

Keri replied to Purdy that she'd get in touch with Heather. Then she called her client to apologize but got sent to voicemail. After leaving a message, she headed to her car and was about to start the engine when her cell phone rang.

Surprise gave her pause as she recognized Ivy Morrison's name on her screen. She'd thought it might be Heather phoning her back right away.

"Hi, Ivy. What's up?" She knew Ivy was holding a fundraiser at her home that evening, which Keri's agency had planned. Hopefully, all was on track.

"The caterer is here setting up, and the decorations arrived, but no one is able to pick up our guest of honor from the airport," Ivy said in a frantic voice.

"I thought your daughter was doing that job."

"She had to take her Beemer into the garage for repair. Her husband loaned her his car, but she'll have to pick him up from work. Would you be able to get LuAnn and bring her here? I'll pay you double your hourly rate."

Keri's temples throbbed as she glanced at her watch. She still had several more jobs to complete before the end of day. "I could send a ride service, if that would work."

"Nuh-uh. I promised LuAnn we'd personally meet her at the airport. She doesn't trust the ride apps or the taxi service."

"All right, I'll be happy to do it," Keri said, not wanting to risk failing another client. "What time does the flight arrive?"

"The plane lands at four-thirty via Southwest. I'll text you the flight info. Since you're bringing LuAnn here, why don't you stay for the party?"

"Thanks. I can hang out for a little bit." She'd at least check in with the caterers while there to make sure all was well. However, her change in plans would affect Lora's dinner preparations.

Feeling guilty about cancelling, she messaged Lora that she wouldn't be home until later due to a last-minute work commitment. Then she rushed around town to perform the rest of her scheduled activities before heading to the airport.

By the time she'd picked up LuAnn, whose flight had been delayed, and they arrived at Ivy's house, it was nearly seven o'clock. Inside, she introduced the guest of honor to her hostess. LuAnn would be staying overnight, and then Ivy would drive her to the airport in the morning.

On her own again, Keri wandered into the kitchen to greet the catering staff. A few canapés made their way into her mouth. Next, she checked the décor and the table settings.

Ivy's six-bedroom residence was located on a lake in Windermere, an affluent suburb just southwest of Orlando. Her house had an outdoor kitchen on a screened patio facing the water. A rectangular pool sparkled in the glow from overhead spotlights.

An open set of French doors invited guests to claim a seat

outside at one of the rented round tables. Vases of fresh flowers and white tablecloths added a touch of elegance. At the far end, a bartender handed out drinks along with cocktail napkins.

Self-conscious in her day clothes, Keri avoided the clusters of women in fancy dresses with jewelry dripping off their arms like ripe fruit and instead introduced herself to the bartender and servers before meandering back inside. Local artists displayed their works in the spacious living room. As prearranged, ten percent of their sales would go to Ivy's favorite children's charity.

"Tatiana, it's great to see you again," she told the willowy artist, who sat beside her easels. Since Staz had handled the details for this event, Keri hadn't seen the list of participants.

"Mrs. Morrison likes my work, so I was happy to get the invite. I didn't expect to see you here tonight."

"I brought the speaker from the airport and decided to stay. How's it going for you?"

Tatiana raised her wispy eyebrows. "I've had a couple of sales. At least it's only a ten percent donation this time. I didn't mind giving twenty the other night at the PHEADA event, but when I'm trying to make money, that's tough on top of Winnie's application fee."

"What application fee?" Keri asked with a frown.

A string quartet began playing, making her lean closer to hear what Tatiana said.

Tatiana regarded her askance. "Don't you know? PHEADA charges artists a hundred dollars to participate in their fundraisers. The form we fill out says it's used for administrative purposes, including publicity."

Keri stared at her. "This is the first time I've heard about any fee. Who collects it?"

"That would be Winnie, their secretary."

"They aren't supposed to charge anything extra." Keri's muscles tensed. How did Winnie slip in an added fee without her knowledge? It added an extra burden to the artists, who were already donating a percentage of sales, not to mention their time.

"Maybe you can ask about it," Tatiana suggested in a timid voice.

"I certainly will. This should have been disclosed to our agency." It made them look bad not to be informed, plus the artists might hesitate to sign up for future events.

With another worry on her head, Keri offered a platitude and then walked away. Good thing she'd already made an appointment to see Winnie in the morning. They'd have a lot to discuss.

This unhappy prospect, along with the swelling music and loud chatter, made her temples throb. Perhaps she should leave. She'd done her duty and had no further reason to remain.

Somebody tapped her arm. "Excuse me, are you the woman who organized this party?" said a tall blonde with a toothy smile. Her plum dress ballooned out like a flyaway sail.

"Yes, I'm Keri Armstrong, owner of *A Friend in Need* Agency." Wishing she could change into a gown like Cinderella, she withdrew a business card from her purse and handed it over.

"My name is Jesse Hamilton, and I could use your help." The woman's scratchy voice sounded like a smoker's rasp. "I'm in over my head this year for the holidays. We're having out-of-town guests, and I promised them tickets to the Nutcracker Ballet. That's in addition to hosting our annual open house. Can I call you this week?"

"Sure. I'd be happy to discuss your plans." She wasn't thrilled about organizing last-minute holiday events, but it wouldn't be wise to refuse a new client with Heather Warrington off their list. She'd been a steady customer for the past two years, and it hurt that she might not accept Keri's apology.

When Jesse's friends began swooping in for introductions, Keri handed out her cards and made a mental note to put more in her purse. She tried to steer the conversation toward the charity being favored that evening, intending to ask their opinions about Fiona, but all they wanted to talk about was where to get the best facial.

Finally extricating herself, Keri dashed to the bathroom before the drive home.

As she emerged into the hallway, she heard a familiar voice from around the bend. She paused, not wishing to be seen on her way to the front door.

"I hate playing the waiting game," said Maurice Chauvel, PHEADA's vice president.

"Me, too, but at least we don't have to worry about Fiona's interference anymore."

Keri stifled a gasp. Who was this and what did he mean?

"You're right, John, but it still won't be an easy sell."

Recognition dawned as Keri remembered Tatiana pointing out John Beekman, the building developer, at the cocktail party. What business did Maurice and Beekman share that Fiona had known about?

"Don't worry," Beekman said. "The zoning committee meets in two weeks, and we have their votes in our pockets."

"You hope. Have you seen that journalist who's been sniffing around? She's a friend of Keri Armstrong, our event planner."

"I've noticed. My people are watching them, but they won't be a problem. Come on, let's go to the bar. I need a drink refill."

Keri's knees buckled and she steadied herself against the wall. *Oh my God. I'd better warn Pam. Something's going on here and I haven't a clue what it means.*

She held her breath until their footsteps faded away, then scurried toward the exit. The path to the front door proved to be an obstacle course of guests, but she made it without being stopped.

As she hustled outside into the night, her skin prickled and she glanced around to see if anyone took undue notice of her. A couple of men stood in the driveway, smoking cigarettes, but they didn't appear the least bit interested in her movements.

Nonetheless, she zipped to her car at a quick pace.

A sixth sense made her spin around again. She caught a glimpse of plum fabric disappearing into the brightly lit house. Was that Jesse, her alleged new client? Remembering her scratchy voice, Keri figured Jesse might have come outside for a smoke.

Or did Beekman send her to spy on me?

Now she'd be paranoid about anyone she met. Once safely inside her car, she texted Pam to fill her in.

I'm investigating a story concerning a land deal that may provide a link between those two, Pam wrote back. Meanwhile, hang tight. We'll figure it out.

I have an appointment tomorrow with Winnie at the PHEADA office. Maybe she knows what's going on with Maurice.

Sounds good. Let me know what you learn.

They broke contact and Keri headed home. By the time she reached her condo, Lora's bedroom door was closed. Disappointed that they couldn't talk things out, Keri got ready for the night. Sleep didn't come easily with her dreams reflecting her tangled thoughts.

She greeted Lora in the kitchen the next morning, where her friend was pouring herself a glass of orange juice.

"Sorry I missed your dinner last night," Keri said. "Ivy Morrison needed my help at her soiree. You won't believe what I overheard." She summarized the conversations.

"The real estate guy must regard you and Pam as a threat, but why? Is he afraid of what Fiona might have told you?" Lora asked.

"It's possible. I texted Pam to be careful. She's investigating a story that might be related. Meanwhile, I'm concerned about an extra charge Tatiana mentioned." Keri explained about the hundred-dollar admin fee.

"It is odd that Winnie never mentioned it to you."

Keri put a coffee pod into her single-brew machine and pressed the button. "I have a lot of questions to ask when I see her today."

Lora sat at the kitchen table. "Is there anything I can do to help?"

"Not right now, thanks. Your flyer for Jarek's grand opening was perfect. I've been meaning to stop by his place to review the details and to see the layout in person."

"Oh yeah?" Lora shot her a teasing glance. "Is that the only reason?"

Keri's face heated. "It's strictly business." Yet she couldn't help experiencing a thrill of anticipation at the thought of seeing him again.

To change the subject, she reviewed the points she wanted to make with Winnie later that day. Lora acted as her sounding board as they ate breakfast. It was helpful having a roommate to listen to her concerns.

Finished in the kitchen, Keri got dressed and headed to work. She checked in with her colleagues, caught up on email, and got busy with other tasks until it was time to meet Winnie.

A short drive later, she approached the squat building that housed PHEADA headquarters and halted just inside the lobby. Winnie usually manned the reception desk to greet her, but this person was a stranger. The woman who gave her a warm smile had a firm chin, clear complexion, and soft, honey-colored hair that couldn't belong to Winnie.

"Hello, Keri. You're punctual as usual."

Her eyes widened as she recognized Winnie's voice. "Whoa, it is you. What have you done to yourself? You look fabulous." She meant it, too. Winnie looked years younger.

"I had one of those lifestyle lifts." Winnie pointed to either side of her face under her ears. "You know, the quick kind you see advertised on television."

"No way? It really works." Keri couldn't believe the transformation.

"Also, I did a full makeover at the salon. I love this hairstyle, don't you?" She fluffed her short bob, the fresh tint bringing out the gold flecks in her brown eyes. She'd even given up her dowdy clothes in favor of an updated style.

"I'm impressed," Keri said. "What made you do it?"

"I've wanted to get work done ever since my eyelids started sagging and my face began to wrinkle. When I glanced in the mirror, I looked like my mother, and who wants that? I'd hoped to do it sooner but couldn't afford the doctor I wanted. He requires an upfront fee, so I had to wait until I had the money."

"You seem happy with the results."

"I've had more men look at me in the past week than in the last year," Winnie admitted.

"Oh? Are you in the market?"

"I wasn't ready before, but now I'm open to meeting someone. I'd like a lasting relationship, unlike Felicity, who seems to prefer a different flavor every month. Anyway, let's get down to business, shall we? We can talk in my private office." Winnie pressed her hands on the reception desk and rose.

Keri followed her into the spacious room with a window and took a seat opposite Winnie's desk. A potted plant in one corner added a touch of greenery. Framed cat photos and a collection of coffee mugs sat on a tall bookshelf.

They reviewed the details for upcoming events, then Keri addressed the topic foremost on her mind. "By the way, I ran into Tatiana last night at Ivy Morrison's fundraiser. She mentioned an application fee that PHEADA charges artists."

Winnie shrugged. "It's a standard administrative fee. Nobody objects to it."

"Nonetheless, I wasn't aware PHEADA charged the artists to display their works at our fundraiser events. This wasn't disclosed to my agency."

"What's that?" Felicity ambled into the room carrying a folder. She wore a teal blouse and a short skirt that showed off her long legs.

Winnie threw her a nervous glance. "Tatiana, the artist, told Keri about our participation fee. They met at another event."

Felicity's green eyes chilled. "Processing the artists involves added paperwork. They're happy to share in the publicity for events."

"That may be, but you shouldn't be charging them extra and not telling me about it. I need to disclose this fee when I book the talent. Our artists already donate a percentage of their sales to the heart disease fund. It's not fair to charge them twice."

"Well, now you know," Felicity snapped. "It's merely the cost of doing business with us."

That doesn't mean it's right, Keri thought. She'd have to come up with some way to get them to drop this fee or they'd risk losing the artists. Their mission was to support the talent, not take advantage of them.

Felicity forestalled any further questions by dropping her folder on Winnie's desk and departing without another word.

A glimmer of suspicion about this added fee entered Keri's mind. Winnie's makeover must have cost a bundle, and Felicity might need money for her mother's care in the assisted living facility. They could have instituted this fee to make some extra cash on the side, if they didn't report it to Ossie or Maurice. But fifty dollars each wouldn't get them too far.

Or did it go deeper? Could Winnie and Felicity be skimming funds from the group's accounts while covering for each other? If this were true and Fiona had found out, that would have given them a motive for murder.

Chapter Eighteen

"There's something I've been meaning to ask," Winnie said in an amiable tone. "If you have any vendor booths available during the holiday season, I'd be interested."

Keri shook herself out of her morose thoughts. Perhaps paranoia was getting to her again. She couldn't prove any of her theories. "For what purpose?" she asked, figuring Winnie might want to hand out brochures for PHEADA.

"It's a personal matter." Winnie withdrew a brightly colored ad from a desk drawer and handed it over. The flyer promoted a holistic health tonic called Vivonin. "I'm a sales rep for this product, and I swear by its effectiveness. Not only has it improved my skin, but it's made me feel much more energetic. I've never felt better."

Her skin did have a glow to it, but couldn't a good foundation do the same thing? Keri scanned the ad, her disbelief growing with each of the claims.

As America's Number One All-Purpose Health Supplement, Vivonin contains forty-eight percent natural resveratrol, an antioxidant that repairs cellular damage. It improves genetic regulators, promotes mitochondrial biogenesis, and extends longevity. Vivonin can lower your blood pressure, reduce the risk of cancer and diabetes, and slow age-related cognitive decline.

"This sounds like a miracle drug," she said, unable to keep the skepticism from her voice. "Are there any scientific reports to back up these statements?"

"Look on the website for a certificate of authenticity and for testimonials." Winnie rummaged inside a bottom drawer. She straightened and held out a small vial. "Here's a four-ounce-sized container if you want to try it."

"That's rather small. How much is one dose?"

"You take one teaspoon per day. This size costs sixty-seven dollars, or you can get an eight-ounce bottle for a hundred and thirty bucks. I'll give you a discount on a bulk order."

"No, thanks. That seems like a lot of money for a small amount." *Especially if it doesn't work*, she thought.

"Good things come in small packages, and resveratrol is expensive to refine."

"Who makes it? A pharmaceutical company?" Keri hadn't noted any recognizable sources on the flyer.

"Nutrious Industries. They're based in St. Augustine. Vivonin contains water from the same aquifer that supplies the fabled Fountain of Youth."

"How did you learn about it?"

Winnie gave her the look a teacher would give a recalcitrant child. "Garvan Connor introduced me to the product. We know each other through PHEADA events, and he mentioned Vivonin when we were discussing the dangers of sun damage to the skin. They needed reps in this area."

"So you took on the job?" Keri found it interesting that Garvan was involved. He did live in St. Augustine, so maybe he'd heard about it there.

Winnie nodded. "I get a commission on each sale, along with a nice discount on my own purchases. It's been a profitable little side business."

How many do you have? Keri wanted to ask. *Isn't extorting money from the artists and possibly stealing from PHEADA enough?*

"Thanks for the offer. I'll think about it. Meanwhile, I'll let you know if any vendor spots open up at local festivals." That was unlikely, considering how late in the season it was already.

She should put another bug into Detective Saunders's ear to

examine the group's finances. If Fiona had discovered some misconduct going on, she might have threatened Winnie or Felicity. One of them might have taken steps to remove her. Somehow, she couldn't see Winnie doing the deed, but Felicity had a callous side to her that could prevail under desperate circumstances.

"Is Maurice in the building?" she asked. "I'd like to have a word with him before I leave." She meant to see what she could find out about his relationship with the building magnate.

Winnie drummed her fingers on the desktop pad. "Maurice is out of the office. Can I help you instead?"

If you don't ask, you won't get an answer. "I saw Maurice hobnobbing with John Beekman at Ivy Morrison's soiree. Any idea what's going on between those two?"

Winnie snorted. "Mr. Beekman consults Maurice whenever he needs to get a ruling passed, like zoning changes or permit approvals. Maurice knows a lot of city council members. It's a matter of influence."

"I'm not sure I understand."

"They help each other through their connections with the movers and shakers in town," Winnie explained with a patient sigh. "Mr. Beekman's company caters to wealthy businessmen. He's introduced Maurice to some of our best donors."

Maybe so, but what did Maurice gain personally from these introductions? Or perhaps Beekman provided other benefits under the table, such as paid vacations or sports tickets. And how did Maurice sway the councilmen's votes anyway, assuming that was his role?

"What does Maurice do for a living? His duties here aren't full-time like yours."

Winnie arched her eyebrows. "I'm surprised you don't know with all your contacts. His family owns a French perfume empire. He emigrated here to start a line of discount perfume stores at the outlet malls."

"That's cool. Those places are always popular with tourists."

That dashed her theory that he craved luxuries he couldn't afford on his own.

"Yes, and his enterprise is doing very well. Would you believe his new shtick is expanding into pet care products? They have an awesome shampoo that washes away the doggie smell."

"Animal lovers will like it." A thought struck her. Maybe she was looking at things the wrong way. Maurice was a bachelor. Could he and Beekman have a more personal relationship? "Is Maurice married?" she asked, since Winnie seemed willing to gossip. "I don't recall him ever bringing a plus one to our functions."

"No, he's had a slew of girlfriends, but nobody special."

"What about Mr. Beekman?"

"He has a wife and four kids."

So much for that theory. "If not Maurice, is Ossie here?" Keri craned her neck to peer at the hallway, but the corridor appeared quiet.

"He had a deposition this morning."

"Oh, right. I keep forgetting he's a lawyer."

"He has a golf game later. That's where he schmoozes with people and acquires new donors. Take a lesson from him, Keri. If you want to meet people who can afford your concierge services, hang out where they tend to gather."

That wasn't a bad idea, although she didn't only cater to affluent clients. She also strove to ease the burdens of working parents and the elderly, even if just for a few hours a week.

"I'll keep it in mind. Does Ossie's wife ever stop by when he's working here?" Keri wouldn't bring Sarah into the conversation but maybe Winnie knew something.

"Hope keeps busy with her own activities. She rarely comes into the office." Winnie's face brightened. "I should tell her about Vivonin the next time I see her. It would help erase those lines on her forehead."

Keri stood and collected her purse, figuring she'd wrung Winnie dry of anything useful about her colleagues. "I think we're on track for our upcoming events, but if you can think of anything else, please give me a call."

Winnie lifted the vial of Vivonin. "Don't forget to check our rave reviews online. I hope you can find a vendor booth for me at a local festival. I need to make more sales by the end of the year to earn a bonus."

Keri let herself out, disappointed that she hadn't been able to meet with Ossie or Maurice. At least she'd gained some useful info. Regarding the administrative fee charged to the artists, she didn't buy Felicity's reasons for implementing it. Likely Ossie and Maurice weren't even aware of this requirement. She'd follow up with the group's president when she had the chance.

Otherwise, Winnie sold a health care supplement introduced to her by Garvan Connor. Did his wife use it, or had he heard about it from someone else? Could he be the supplier?

It would be helpful to determine the extent of his involvement. This might warrant a trip to St. Augustine. While there, she could ask Garvan how well his son Hugh had gotten along with Fiona.

As for Maurice and John Beekman, they rubbed each other's elbows to get what they wanted. Pam might be able to explore this issue better through her connections.

Once on the road, she glanced into her rearview mirror to make sure no one was tailing her. The land guy had said his people were watching her. She couldn't be too careful.

Her next stop was Chef Jarek's restaurant in Hamilton Square. Huh, it must be near the cottage Fiona had left her. Too bad she didn't have the address. Diane would probably let her know the details when the time was right.

As she entered the restaurant, she dodged a deliveryman carrying a large carton. Smells of sawdust and fresh paint pervaded the air.

The main dining room had a pleasant, contemporary vibe with polished wood tables, etched glass dividers, and framed pictures of vegetables on the walls. The exposed kitchen in the back gleamed with white stone countertops and stainless-steel appliances under bright overhead lights. While it appeared the front of the restaurant was ready, there must be more work to be done in the rear.

"Excuse me, miss." A carpenter scurried past, the tools in his kit rattling.

"Wait. Where can I find Chef Jarek?" she called.

The guy jerked his thumb. "Storage area behind the kitchen."

"Thanks." She crossed the tiled floor, picturing the place filled with customers. Residents would love exploring a new restaurant in town, but how long would the buzz last? Would they keep coming here for lobster mac and cheese or fancy meatloaf?

Homestyle Cooking with a Fresh Twist was Jarek's slogan. Maybe they could link his interest in sustainable farming to his menu. Like, were any of his suppliers from local farms? That might give guests another incentive to keep coming, assuming they liked the food.

Eager to mention her idea, she hunted for Jarek and found him supervising installation of a refrigeration unit. His face split into a grin when he spotted her.

"Keri, it's good to see you."

"Likewise." She handed him the printout for his flyer. "I sent you a copy via email, but I wasn't sure if you'd seen it. If you approve, we'll have the flyers printed. I also need to review some details for your launch party, if you've a few minutes to spare."

"For you, I'll always have time. Let's go sit in that corner where it's quiet." He led her into the dining room and gestured to a booth along one wall.

Once seated, she opened her notebook and then mentioned her latest idea to him.

"I love it," he said with an answering grin. "I'll send you a list of our local suppliers."

"Great." She wrote a few notes to herself. "I like how you've decorated the place. Very modern and yet with a cozy feel at the same time. How come you're waiting until February to open? This place looks like it's almost ready."

"It takes time for the permit inspections." His eyes deepened to indigo. "Plus, I have to go home for the holidays. There's a family issue I need to settle."

"If you opened earlier, you could get the Christmas crowd."

"I know, but I'd prefer to wait. Valentine's Day works better for me. Although, you might try convincing me over dinner tomorrow." He gave her a sexy smile, making her blood warm in response.

She resisted the urge to yield, aware that it wasn't wise to mix business with pleasure. If things went sour, she'd risk losing another client. "I may be going out of town, so my schedule is up in the air for the next few days. Maybe we can do something another time."

Her excuse was valid if Garvan agreed to see her. She might have a better chance to catch him now than over the weekend, when he might have family plans.

Jarek's expression sobered. "When the restaurant opens, I'll be working evenings. My hours will be flexible only for the next few months."

"I'll keep that in mind. Meanwhile, I don't want to take up too much of your time." She proceeded to hammer out the points they needed to solidify.

Shortly thereafter, Keri felt they'd covered everything important. She closed her binder and sat back in her chair.

"According to your resume, you graduated from Orlando Culinary Academy. Has it always been your dream to open a restaurant?" she asked, hoping to learn more about him.

His posture relaxed. "I like to make people happy through my food. I'd worked at various restaurants to gain experience, including Le Jardin in New York. Then I got some investors interested in helping me open my own place. Eventually, I'd like to get into cookbooks and maybe even a cooking show."

"That's ambitious. Regarding your menu, are there any regional dishes from your hometown that you could feature?" If so, it might make his restaurant stand out from the competition.

He gazed into the distance. "The food where I grew up was

quite different. I doubt you'd care for it. Florida has enough fresh resources for people to enjoy."

"Do you have family back home? How do they feel about your career?"

"They're proud of me." He glanced at his smartwatch. "Are we done? I have an appointment with a contractor in ten minutes."

"Sure. We've covered everything on my list." It was clear he didn't like talking about himself. Perhaps he'd be more at ease after his restaurant's grand opening.

She gathered her purse and stood. "If anything changes, please let me know. I can't wait for your event. I'm sure it'll be a success."

He rose, his physique more like a football player's than a chef's. "When my kitchen is ready, I'll have you over to taste my dishes. Then you'll see how food can be the elixir of life."

I've already heard of one elixir today, thank you. And I need to see Garvan about that one.

Once outside by the curb, Keri texted Lora. *Flyer approved. Run print order. You free tomorrow during the day?*

Good. Okay. No, Lora answered.

Too bad. Having Lora's company would have made the two-hour trip to St. Augustine more enjoyable. Maybe Pam would like to go. She could interview Garvan for her article.

"I don't see how that magic tonic is relevant to Fiona's case," Pam said after Keri had updated her.

"I'm not sure it is, but I'd like to talk to Garvan about it anyway."

"You think he'd be willing to see us?"

"I'll tell him I have news about Fiona, which is true. He may not be aware of her collusion with Crogher or of her romantic interest in Tony. Either way, it would be helpful to hear his version of her past. And you can always interview him for your article."

"All right. I could use a break from the newsroom. Should we do an overnighter? I've always wanted to see the Lightner Museum."

Keri pressed her lips together, hesitant to commit the time. "Let's decide later. We can each bring a bag just in case." If they did linger, she'd have to call Purdy to reschedule her appointments. That wouldn't give her any brownie points with her clients, but she needed to clear these issues from her mind. This trip might help if they gained useful information.

After disconnecting from Pam, Keri phoned Garvan to get his approval.

"Hi, it's Keri. My friend Pam and I will be in St. Augustine tomorrow, and we're hoping we can stop by to see you."

"What for?" His tone wasn't friendly.

"I have some interesting news about Fiona. Also, Pam is doing a profile on her for the *Sunny Grove Gazette*. As one of her only surviving family members, a quote from you would elevate her article." She figured flattery might win him over.

He paused. "It'll have to be a short visit. I have a tight schedule."

"Would it be more convenient to meet at your workplace? What is it you do, anyway?" She couldn't believe she'd never asked him before.

"I'm a pharmacist. You can meet me at home, though." He gave Keri his address.

They agreed on a time, and she ended the call. Her heart thrummed with excitement. This would give her a chance to discuss the issues on her mind, and maybe she'd be able to discover why Hugh had always annoyed Fiona.

Chapter Nineteen

Thursday morning, Keri pulled up outside Pam's rental apartment complex and texted her arrival. Her friend burst out of the exit a few minutes later, looking every inch the inquisitive reporter with her auburn hair tied in a ponytail, sunglasses on her nose, and an excited grin on her face. She wore a jade top with black pants and had dressed up her outfit with gold jewelry.

Pam tossed her wheeled tote and a jacket into the rear seat. "This is so cool. I feel like Lois Lane. Maybe my article will finally attract attention."

"I'm sure it will." Keri checked the rearview and side mirrors as Pam settled into her seat. She didn't see anyone who might be tracking them but didn't dare to let down her guard.

"What time is our appointment?" Pam asked, as Keri pulled onto the road.

"Two o'clock. We'll meet at Garvan's house." She merged into traffic and soon headed toward I-4 east.

"What does Garvan do for a living that he can take off in the middle of the day?"

"He's a pharmacist. I expect they work different shifts. Maybe he came across Vivonin at his job. I have to admit Winnie looks amazing. However, it's more likely due to the cosmetic enhancements she's had rather than a miracle drug."

Pam patted her cheek. "I'll have to see if that tonic can get rid of my freckles. How did Garvan learn about it?"

"That's one question I need to ask him. Maybe he sells it as an herbal supplement."

"Does he have his own pharmacy, or does he work at a chain?"

"Good question. He could work at a hospital for all I know."

Pam wagged a finger at her. "Hey, I can do an exposé on cure-alls with false medical claims. Plenty of gullible people would try anything to look young and feel healthy."

"That's a great topic." Although she liked the idea, Keri hoped Pam would finish the profile on Fiona before going off on a tangent.

Pam grabbed her purse and rummaged inside. "I was rushing to get ready earlier and didn't eat much for breakfast. Want some trail mix or peanut butter crackers?"

"No, thanks. I'll wait for lunch." She'd eaten yogurt with fresh berries earlier. That should tide her over for the next couple of hours.

Wispy clouds drifted overhead as they sped east on the highway and then north on I-95. Soon billboard signs for Florida oranges, shelled pecans, and tropical jellies marched along the roadside as they approached the exit for St. Augustine.

"I'm hungry. We have some time before we meet Garvan. Where should we go for lunch?" Keri asked as they drove down King Street toward the historic district. She recognized the San Sebastian Winery, Flagler College, and Lightner Museum from previous visits. Founded by the Spanish in 1565, St. Augustine was the oldest city in Florida. It was a fun weekend destination with shops, museums, historic sites, and restaurants.

"How about the Ale House?" Pam suggested, studying her phone app. "It's at the end of this street at the bayfront and has a good menu."

Keri nodded. "That's an easy choice."

Parking wasn't so simple, though. She wound around the narrow streets until they found a lot with space available. It cost twenty dollars to park on a packed dirt field. Normally, it would be a small price to pay for the convenience of being near the attractions, but they were eating and leaving.

Thankfully, there wasn't any wait for a table at the upstairs level of the Ale House. They had an impressive view of the glistening water from where they were seated.

Rolling her shoulders after the long drive, Keri studied the menu and decided on a coconut shrimp platter while Pam opted for grilled grouper. They chatted about work and upcoming social events until their meals arrived.

"I should start our conversation with Garvan," Pam suggested at one point. "I'll interview him for my article to open him up, and then you can ask the questions on your mind."

"Sounds like a plan," Keri responded, hoping the large meal wouldn't make her sleepy.

After a satisfying lunch, they trekked back to the parking lot. Keri followed directions to a residential section and found Garvan's house, which had a gray Dodge Hornet parked in the driveway. She pulled up to the curb and cut the ignition.

Outside, the scent of freshly dug earth filled the air. Hugh stood on the front lawn next to a pair of flamingo garden statues, regarding them with a snarl on his scuzzy face and a shovel in his hand. A row of dwarf junipers sat in small pots in front of a hedge. *Looks like Hugh drew landscaping duty,* Keri thought. She wouldn't have figured him for a gardener, unless his father had assigned him the task.

The single-story, sand-colored house was a modest design with a white, rolled-tile roof and a covered front porch. A couple of wicker chairs vied for space on the deck, along with pots of flowering plants.

"Pop told me you'd be coming," Hugh said, as Keri and Pam approached.

"Pam is interviewing him for her profile on Fiona, and I have some new information to share," Keri explained.

"Is it about Aunt Fiona? If so, I don't understand why you still care."

"Fiona was a dear friend to me as well as a client. I care that she receives justice. You don't seem too sad that she's gone."

Hugh snorted. "She constantly criticized me about my job choices. I don't miss her nagging."

"What is it that you do?" Pam asked with a sweet smile.

"You'd like to know, wouldn't you? I don't talk to nosy reporters. Ask the cops if you want the deets."

Keri gritted her teeth at his rudeness as he turned away. His mother didn't seem too happy about their visit, either. Enid let them in with a frown, her thin mouth adding to the harshness of her features. With her straight black hair and wide forehead, she'd make a perfect witch at Halloween.

"I didn't expect to see Hugh here," Keri told Enid. "Does he live with you?"

"He has his own place not too far away. He agreed to put in the plants when Garvan asked for his help. Every now and then, he surprises us."

No kidding. Or maybe he's burying something in there that he doesn't want to be found.

She immediately berated herself for the irrational thought. Fiona's death had set her on edge and sent wild ideas into her head. If she wasn't careful, she'd end up spewing conspiracy theories like Veronica Batten.

Except, Veronica had been right about them and now she was dead.

Enid led them into a comfortable living room with worn contemporary furnishings and bright windows. Framed photographs dotted the tabletops, while a collection of Florida landscapes adorned the walls. A mouth-watering aroma drifted from the kitchen. Was Enid baking a cake?

"What smells so good?" she asked, to break the ice.

"I'm making cookies. They should be done in a few minutes. Go ahead and sit. I'll tell Garvan you're here."

Pam settled beside her on the sofa, withdrawing a notebook from her large bag. They remained silent until Garvan ambled into view, his heavyset figure filling a navy sports shirt that made his belly look like a beach ball. His round face had a hound dog look. He plopped onto a chair across from them and crossed one leg over the opposite knee.

"Enid will bring us some iced tea after she shuts off the oven. Keri said you're doing an article on Aunt Fiona?" he asked Pam.

"That's right. Fiona was a prominent member of our community. I thought you could offer a unique perspective as her relative. Had she always been a patron of the arts?"

Garvan nodded. "She owned an antique shop in Greenwich Village and collected unusual items from around the world. She made buying trips abroad at least twice a year."

Keri knew who had funded those excursions, but she remained silent on the subject and let Pam take the lead.

Pam asked several questions about Fiona's charitable activities and her community involvement before finally getting around to more personal topics. "Had Fiona already decided to retire when she moved here?"

Garvan, evidently appreciative of the attention, readily responded. "We weren't close, so she didn't share her plans with us. I did know her father's death came as a shock to her. It took the wind out of her sails. She seemed to lose enthusiasm for her business after his loss."

With a start, Keri remembered Mrs. Brody's remark that Fiona had lost her zest for life. She'd assumed it was because Tony's actions had hurt her, but maybe Fiona had missed her father's financial support more.

She folded her hands together. It was a good opportunity to jump in. "I told you I had news about Fiona. I paid a visit to Diane's Uncle Tony. He lives in Sarasota. Were you aware he and Fiona had once been in love?"

Garvan shook his head. "I wasn't familiar with Diane's family, and Aunt Fiona never mentioned a boyfriend."

"Fiona's father didn't give his consent and chased Tony off. Crogher was involved in the Irish mob, and Tony was from Italian stock. I suppose that was reason enough for Crogher to disapprove."

"I'd always suspected Grandpa's business wasn't entirely legal. Ma told me to be careful what I said around him because his enemies tended to end up in the river."

"Of course! I'd forgotten Crogher was your grandfather." She'd lost track of their connection, and from the confused look on Pam's face, so had her friend.

Garvan's mouth twisted. "My mother, Kathleen, was Fiona's younger sister. She and Fiona had little in common. They were only two years apart but had completely different interests."

Fiona had never mentioned her sister, but then how else would Garvan be her nephew? If she'd been thinking clearly, she should have figured this out beforehand.

"So your mother got married while Fiona stayed single?" she said.

"That's right. My parents had a good marriage. I think Aunt Fiona was always jealous of Ma. She refused her invitations to join us for the holidays."

"How was your mother's relationship to Crogher?"

"She didn't care to associate with him. His friends weren't her type of people, she used to say. Our family moved to get away from his reach. She didn't want him to influence me."

"Were you aware Fiona sold things for Crogher in her shop?"

"Not really. What sort of things?"

Keri wove her hands together. "Fine jewelry and works of art. It's been brought to my attention that some of those goods might have been stolen."

A frown creased his face. "Where did you hear this?"

"Pam and I spoke to a former antique store owner in Sunny Grove. She'd sold things on consignment for Fiona when she first moved here. The shopkeeper discovered that a necklace Fiona brought in had been stolen from a collection abroad. Fiona claimed her father had given it to her. Do you believe she acted willingly as a fence for him?"

"Who knows? When they say ignorance is bliss, that might

apply in her case. She may have turned a blind eye to things where her father was concerned, especially if she knew about his unsavory connections. As for him, she must have been merely a cog in his wheel."

Keri showed him the photo on her phone. "Do you recognize this picture?"

He squinted at it. "That's Fiona and Crogher. Looks like they're at some sort of party. See that jewelry she's wearing? It's not fair that Diane inherited her personal property. Those things should have gone to us. Aunt Fiona didn't even think about leaving Enid a token remembrance."

Why would she if Enid gave her the cold shoulder whenever they met?

"Diane was like a daughter to her," Keri felt compelled to explain. "Fiona regarded her family as her own."

"Huh. If you ask me, Diane cozied up to my aunt because of Cal. He may act like a wuss but watch his eyes. That man is smarter than you think. I'd bet he's the one who put the bee in Diane's bonnet to relocate. I don't know what she sees in him, but he treats her kids real nice, so maybe that's it."

Keri gasped. "*Her* kids?"

Garvan gave her a sneer in response. "You seem to know everything. How did you miss that Cal is Diane's second husband?"

Chapter Twenty

Stunned by Garvan's revelation, Keri stared at him. "I didn't realize Diane had been married before." How come Diane hadn't mentioned this to her? But then, why would she? Happily married to Cal, she had no reason to tell people it wasn't her first marriage.

"When Diane was widowed, Cal swooped in and swept Diane off her feet," Garvan said. "They got married in Las Vegas six months later. Aunt Fiona moved to Florida the following year. Shortly afterward, Diane announced their plans to follow her here. I suspect she meant to influence my aunt into changing her will."

"Diane could have been worried about Fiona living on her own," Keri suggested.

"Aunt Fiona was quite capable of managing things herself. At least she thought of Hugh in the end and left him her car. Diane just notified us."

Keri jumped into this opening. "We saw Hugh outside putting in some new bushes. It's nice of him to help you with the gardening."

"Doing yard work is getting harder for me. Hugh can be useful at times."

"Did he do chores for Fiona? She might have needed a man to do the heavy lifting around her house." She didn't mention that Fiona had a handyman in her next-door neighbor.

"Hugh dropped by her place whenever he was in town. If she asked him to do things for her during those visits, he didn't tell us about it."

"Hugh said Fiona criticized him about his job choices. What does he do for a living?" She held her breath for the response.

"He works at a pain clinic," Enid snapped. She breezed inside the room carrying a tray with glasses of iced tea and a plate of freshly baked chocolate chip cookies, which she set on the coffee table before taking a seat next to Garvan.

A pain clinic? What a perfect place for a drug dealer, Keri thought before chastising herself. She had no idea of his role there and shouldn't jump to conclusions.

"Doing what?" Pam asked, after which Keri cast her an approving glance. Pam must be thinking along the same lines.

"He's a certified medical assistant." Enid sounded defensive, as though she thought he could have done better for a career choice.

"He could probably get a job anywhere in that field," Keri said. Unable to help herself, she lifted a cookie and took a bite. The chocolate chips melted in her mouth. "This is delicious. Will Hugh join us when he's done outside?"

"He's not staying," Garvan replied, snatching two cookies. "He plays the guitar and is getting together with friends from his former band."

"That's cool. I didn't realize he was a musician." Keri tilted her head. "How about you, Enid? Do you work outside the home, or are you retired?"

This garnered a smile that melted Enid's frosty exterior. "I own a gift shop on St. George Street. We get good traffic from the tourist crowd."

"Really? That's awesome." She wouldn't have guessed Enid to be a businesswoman. Maybe she was shrewder than she let on.

"I took off this afternoon so I could be here for your visit."

"That was kind of you. I'd love to see the place. What's the name? Maybe Pam and I can stop by there later."

"It's The Green Parrot." Enid got up and retrieved a couple of business cards to give them.

"Does Hugh ever assist you in the store?" Keri asked,

hoping to learn more about his activities. "I'd expect he would be helpful in unboxing inventory and such."

Enid reclaimed her seat. "He'd have been more useful had he taken some business courses like Fiona suggested."

"Perhaps he prefers working with patients." Keri wanted to broach the subject of Winnie's miracle drug but wasn't sure how to proceed. A glance at Pam only got her a shrug in return.

"Have you spoken to that police detective lately?" Garvan asked, breaking the silence. "He called to tell us that the neighbor across the street from Aunt Fiona had died in some freak accident."

"Yes, I heard the news. What a horrible thing to happen."

"He wanted to know when I'd last come to town. Did you put him up to that?"

No, but I did tell him to check up on Hugh.

"I'm sure he's looking into everyone's alibis," Keri replied.

"Why would he care if the woman's death was accidental?"

"Because it happened so soon after Fiona died," Pam offered. "Veronica had been friends with Fiona. Perhaps they both knew something that got them killed."

Garvan's gaze sharpened. "If you're right, anyone closely associated with my aunt had better keep their heads down."

Was that a subtle warning? "That would include the staff members from PHEADA," Keri said, venturing into this topic. "I stopped by their office yesterday. Winnie looked fabulous. She told me about a health tonic called Vivonin that's made by Nutrious Industries. Apparently, she's a sales rep for them. She told me you'd introduced her to the product. How did you come across it?"

Garvan's face turned red as a radish, making Keri wonder what nerve she'd touched. "It's a compound I devised on my own. Customers at the pharmacy are always asking me about supplements. Vivonin provides nutrients needed for healthy tissues and strong bones. It also helps to remove toxins from the body produced by bad living habits."

You could use some yourself, Keri thought, surveying his rotund figure.

"Isn't it a conflict of interest for you to sell a product you manufacture?" Pam asked.

"Not if it helps people." He rose and plucked at his pants, as though pruning imaginary threads. "At any rate, I'm afraid we have to cut this interview short. I'm working the late shift today and I need to get moving."

Keri took a last sip of her iced tea and stood alongside Pam. "Thanks so much for seeing us and for the snacks. Enid, we'll stop by your store when we're downtown."

"And I'll send you a copy of the *Gazette* when my profile on Fiona is published," Pam promised on their way out. "This has been really helpful."

Once outside, Keri noticed the new plants were neatly aligned in the ground with fresh mulch surrounding them. Apparently, Hugh had already left, since his car was gone.

"Now what?" Keri asked after she and Pam were inside her vehicle with the A/C turned on. "Garvan seemed to get upset when I mentioned Vivonin. You'd think he would have offered us a free sample instead of chasing us out."

Pam nodded. "I agree. He must be hiding something. Do you have an address for the manufacturing plant? If I do an article on false cure-alls, I'll need accurate sources."

"I did a search on Google Maps and didn't find anything at the location given on the website."

"That's odd." Pam glanced into the sideview mirror. "Hold on. Garvan is pulling out of his garage. We should follow him."

"Why? He's going to work."

"Humor me. He's leaving awfully quick. Maybe he's going somewhere else first."

"Okay." Keri put the car in gear and merged onto the road some distance behind Garvan's older model Buick.

"I need to do more research, but healthcare products that make false or misleading claims are subject to the law," Pam said.

"This also applies if they contain undisclosed ingredients that could be harmful."

"Winnie said resveratrol is one of the ingredients in Vivonin. I looked it up. It's a natural substance with antioxidant properties that can normally be found in red wine."

"Oh, yeah? That's a good excuse for a glass of cabernet at happy hour. It would be helpful to have a sample of this miracle drug."

"I can always buy a bottle from Winnie." Keri paid attention to the road as they approached an intersection with a couple of drugstores catty-corner to each other, but Garvan didn't stop there. He turned left and headed west.

Stores with barred windows, tattoo parlors, and pawn shops told her this wasn't the best part of town. The terrain became more rural, with older frame houses and weed-infested lawns. Fortunately, traffic remained steady, so they could stay on Garvan's tail several cars behind.

"Looks like your instinct to follow him was correct," she told Pam, who gave her a thumbs up in response.

Garvan turned right just past an automotive place. Maybe he needed car repairs, in which case they'd guessed wrong about his intentions.

"I think he's heading for that property beyond the brick wall," Pam said.

Sure enough, Garvan drove toward a wrought-iron gate that opened at his approach. He must have a remote, Keri figured, as the barrier opened and he drove through.

"I'll have to park so we can take a closer look," Keri said. She turned down a side road and pulled up to the curb under the shade of a moss-draped oak.

Soon she and Pam were walking along a cracked sidewalk covered by fallen leaves and acorns. She regretted not wearing sturdier shoes. Her strapped sandals scrunched along, the sound adding to a dog barking in the distance and an airplane droning overhead.

They approached the brick wall, partially covered with creeping vines. A sign said *Nutrious Industries*. They'd found Vivonin's manufacturing site.

"What do you suppose Garvan is doing here?" she asked.

Pam's lip curled. "I'll bet he's warning his staff that we might show up."

"That would only matter if he has something to hide. If he does, maybe Fiona found out about it and threatened to expose his operation. How do we get inside for a better look?"

They peered through the gate's iron bars. Beyond a wide swathe of lawn sat a squat, rectangular building. No one appeared to be patrolling the grounds, but they could have other means of security.

"We could squeeze through the gate after Garvan leaves," Pam suggested, "but that grassy expanse won't provide any cover if someone is watching."

"Then what? We knock on the front door? Garvan's employees will notify him we're there. We should come back after dark when no one can see us." Keri didn't want to pass up this opportunity. If Garvan had been so alarmed by their visit that he had run over here, she decided not to leave until they learned what secrets he hid behind those walls.

"You're right. Let's see if this trips an alarm. If not, we can climb over the wall later. Maybe we'll find an open window once we're inside the property." Pam picked up a rock and tossed it high beyond the rim. It thudded to the ground on the other side.

No bells clanged or sirens rang out. Nor did Keri note any barbed wire or visible cameras. "If we're going to reach that ledge on top, we'll need a boost," she said. "Let's book a hotel room and figure out a strategy. Then we can go to Home Depot to get some tools. We need to be better prepared for our next visit."

Chapter Twenty-One

After a delicious dinner of *ropa vieja* at the Columbia Restaurant, Keri freshened up at their hotel and changed into warmer clothes plus sneakers before she and Pam headed back to Garvan's production plant.

They'd spent the rest of the afternoon viewing the exhibits at the Lightner Museum that Pam had wanted to see, then they'd stopped by Enid's gift shop on St. George Street. Keri had hoped to see what she could find out from the cashier about her boss, but too many customers had precluded a private conversation. At least they'd been able to relax for a few hours.

Her neck tensed as she parked in the same spot as before on a quiet side street. Armed with a folding stepladder and sturdy flashlights, she and Pam approached the brick wall that surrounded Nutrious Industries. Crickets chirped in the distance and a half-moon rode the sky. The cool air made Keri glad she'd dressed appropriately.

A spicy scent from a nearby plant tickled her nose as she positioned the stepstool in place. She went first, stepping onto the highest rung and hoisting herself up. After gaining the ledge, she dropped to the other side as Pam followed in her wake.

Using the length of cord they'd bought at the home superstore, they hauled the lightweight stepstool after them. At least they'd had the foresight to equip themselves earlier.

After crossing the grassy expanse, they made a stealthy inspection around the warehouse exterior and discovered a partially open window at the rear. Bingo!

Nancy J. Cohen

"I'll need the stepstool again for a boost," Keri said in a hushed voice.

Pam's eyes glowed in the moonlight as she handed it over. "It's strange we haven't seen any signs of a security system."

Keri shrugged. "Why would a manufacturing plant for an herbal tonic need one?"

"Industrial espionage is a good enough reason, especially if this magic elixir is a money- maker."

"Maybe Garvan runs a legitimate operation. He could have just been working late here. Are we being overly suspicious?"

"I don't think so," Pam said. "Best we see for ourselves if anything is off about this place. Hey, don't forget to put on your gloves."

They'd bought a box of nitrile gloves at the hardware store. Keri donned the pair she'd stuffed into a pocket. Her heart raced as she climbed onto the stepstool, raised the window and levered herself over the edge.

She plummeted to the floor in the darkened interior, freezing upon impact. No alarms clanged, and only silence met her ears, except for her panting breaths. Pam came next, tugging the stepstool up and over the windowsill so they'd have a means to escape.

Certain her friend could hear her pounding heart, Keri flicked on her powerful flashlight. She swung it in a wide arc, revealing a cavernous laboratory with beakers, tubing, and other equipment she'd seen on science shows. In one corner sat a grouping of machinery. A closer inspection showed it was a section for bottling, labeling and packaging.

"Are those wine bottles?" Pam asked, pointing to a table in the near distance.

Keri went over for a better look. "You're right. I wonder if they're using this red wine to provide the resveratrol ingredient rather than buying the extract. That's not exactly a crime, though."

Worry assaulted her. What if they were barking up the wrong

tree? She expressed her doubts to Pam. "Suppose Vivonin is just a mixture of vitamins and other harmless compounds? In that case, this lead is a dead end."

"The drug isn't harmless if gullible people believe it'll cure their diseases," Pam countered. "Relying on a health supplement can have serious consequences if patients avoid traditional medicine. Are there any scientific studies to back up the claims on their ads?"

"Winnie said there's a certificate of authenticity."

"Maybe we can find it. See that closed door? If it's an office, we can look for supporting documents inside."

"Or we could leave," Keri suggested. Sweat beaded her upper lip, and her pulse raced. At any moment, they might be caught with no excuses to offer for their behavior.

"I'm not giving up now." Pam loped ahead, while Keri followed in her wake.

They'd already crossed a moral boundary by intruding on private property. What were a few more minutes? It wouldn't diminish her guilt if they discovered something worthwhile, but it might get them a step closer to learning what had gotten Fiona killed.

Pushing aside her qualms of conscience, Keri entered the office.

"I'll search the file cabinet. You take the desk," Pam said.

They worked in silence for a few moments until Keri found an interesting item. "Look, it's an envelope from Diane addressed to Garvan."

Pam came over. "Go ahead and read what's inside. It's already unsealed."

Keri's curiosity got the better of her and she withdrew a letter. She gave an exclamation of surprise upon noting Fiona's signature. "Diane told me she had a bunch of letters to give out as executor of Fiona's estate. This must be one of them."

Keri read the letter aloud. *Dear Garvan, I want to explain why I've decided to leave everything to Diane. Due to your bad investment choices, you've weighed yourself down with debts and have taken out a home equity loan that you're struggling to repay. Then there's that medicinal formula you sell with its false claims of miracle cures. I fear it may impact your pharmacist's license if your connection is discovered.*

Oh, yes. I have my ways of finding out things. This might not have happened had you listened to my advice. As it stands, you need to learn how to live within your means. Giving you an inheritance to squander will not benefit you. I wish you the best and hope you'll understand my decision. Love, Aunt Fiona.

"How sad," Keri said. "Diane told me that according to Fiona's lawyer, Garvan had been her original beneficiary, but then she'd amended her documents once Diane's family moved to Florida. This explains her reasons."

She took a photo of the letter in case it became useful later and then replaced it in the envelope. A further search of the desk proved unfruitful. Keri moved on to the bookshelves, thinking it was odd that Garvan kept so many books at a manufacturing plant. Then again, a closer look showed most of them were chemistry texts or other reference titles.

They went back to work, rummaging silently through their individual tasks.

Pam held up a document from the file cabinet. "These files contain printouts of fulfilled customer orders, supply requisitions, and product endorsements. Nothing unusual there, but here's the certificate of authenticity Winnie had mentioned. I should do some research to see if it's genuine." She took a photo of the paper and then replaced it.

"Have you come across any scientific studies?" Keri asked.

"Not yet."

Keri ran her fingers along the books on the shelves. Most seemed legit… well, except for that big fat one. She pulled it out with a grimace at the weight and opened it.

Her heart lurched. Inside a hollowed space were sealed white packets labeled *Kratom*.

"Pam, look at these. Have you heard of this substance before? The packets feel soft, like they have crushed herbs inside."

"It's not familiar to me. We can look up the name later. We've stayed here too long already, and I don't want to press our luck."

Keri took a photo of the book's contents and then replaced it on the shelf. They left, careful to leave everything in place, and crossed the flat expanse outside without incident.

Back at Keri's car, they stashed their supplies in the trunk. Soon they were zooming away into the night.

"We've gained a few pointers tonight," Pam said, peering out the window while Keri drove.

"I'm curious about those packets. I'd ask you to look up Kratom now, but I need your help finding our hotel in the dark."

She should have felt vindicated that their excursion had proven useful but knew they'd crossed a line in obtaining information. Nor was she sure how their discovery related to Fiona.

Pam accessed her browser once they were securely back in their room. "Listen to this," she said, sitting cross-legged on her bed. "Kratom is derived from an evergreen tree grown in Southeast Asia. The leaves can be chewed, brewed for a cup of tea, or distilled into a liquid extract. Kratom is used as a pain remedy, an appetite suppressant, or a treatment for panic attacks, among other potential health benefits."

"That's a broad range. How does it work?" Keri sat on the desk chair and untied her shoes.

"The drug interacts with the brain's opioid receptors. At low doses, Kratom is a stimulant so that you feel more energetic. If you increase the dosage, it'll reduce pain and bring on euphoria."

Keri's brows arched. "No wonder people like it."

Pam read on. "Researchers who have studied Kratom believe the potential for adverse side effects outweighs the advantages. In high doses, it can cause seizures, hallucinations, and death."

"Is it illegal in Florida?"

Pam shook her head. "Not here. It's up to each state to make that decision. Other countries have restrictions against it, but Kratom appears to be unregulated in the U.S. at the federal level."

"So Garvan can use it in his tonic without repercussions?" Keri asked. The legalities confused her. Regardless of the law, this sounded like a dangerous ingredient.

"Vivonin doesn't list Kratom as an active component. That would make his tonic risky for users who aren't aware of the potential for adverse side effects or drug interactions. Plus, if he's making unsubstantiated medical claims for his product, the FDA could get after him. Either way, what he's doing is unethical."

Keri considered the implications. "It's possible his pharmacist's license would be revoked if the authorities got onto him. Or is Vivonin such a cash cow that he'd commit murder to avoid being exposed? He wouldn't want production to be shut down during an investigation."

Pam frowned. "Maybe Hugh did it to protect his father's operation. He works at a pain clinic and could easily sell the stuff on the sly to patients. He wouldn't want the plant to be closed either."

"I'd like to share this information with Detective Saunders without revealing how we learned about it. He has better resources to investigate the issues." Keri removed her shoes and socks and wiggled her toes.

"Aside from Garvan and his son, who else is left on your suspect list? Can we eliminate anyone at this point?" Pam asked, unfolding her legs and leaning against the pillow.

Keri got up to pace the carpet in her bare feet. "There's still Sarah and Bob Underwood. Or Ossie, who wouldn't want his affair with Sarah exposed."

"Oh, right. And don't forget PHEADA's vice president, who is up to something shady with the real estate developer. I'm still looking into a land deal that involves John Beekman, but I don't see the connection yet between him and Maurice."

"Maurice wins over votes on the city council that Beekman needs passed. If you keep digging, I bet you'll find a definitive link. Meanwhile, I'll speak to Ossie. He wasn't in his office the last time I went there. I need to alert him about the administrative fee Winnie charges artists. And somehow, I want to subtly suggest that he inspect their accounts to see if Felicity is fudging the numbers."

Keri felt as though they were getting closer to exposing Fiona's killer, but the truth might not be what she wanted to hear if it implicated somebody she knew.

Chapter Twenty-Two

They left St. Augustine on Friday morning and arrived back in Sunny Grove before lunchtime. Keri dropped Pam off, stopped by her condo to change clothes, and then headed out for her scheduled afternoon appointments. She didn't have time to follow up on the things they'd learned from their trip.

She finally reached her office by five o'clock. Purdy and Staz had already left for the day. After answering her more urgent email messages, Keri notified Lora that she wouldn't be home for dinner, since she had to deal with a client request that would take a while. She'd grabbed a bite to eat earlier anyway.

At seven o'clock, she gave up. Her eyes were too bleary to continue, and it was dark outside. Time to go home.

Feeling overburdened by so many things on her mind, she locked the office and strode toward the parking lot around the corner. Away from the restaurant scene, the street was quiet. Overhanging tree branches blocked the light from streetlamps and cast skeletal-like shadows on the building walls.

A car engine idled nearby, and yet none of the cars parked along the curb had their headlights on. Goose bumps rose on her arms, and her pulse rocketed. John Beekman had said she and Pam were being watched. Was this one of his people keeping tabs on her?

She picked up speed, anxious to reach her Honda, but an uneven ledge of pavement caught her shoe and made her stumble. She regained her balance and hurried on just as a roar hit her ears.

She turned to see a pair of headlights flashing in her eyes as a car headed directly toward her.

She flung herself backwards against a building. The vehicle lurched over the curb and missed swiping her by inches. It veered off and careened down the street, tires squealing as it rounded the corner.

For a few moments, Keri couldn't move. She stood frozen in place, too stunned by what had just happened to make sense of things. Then she became aware of something warm trickling down her arm and her fingers came back sticky when she probed her skin. She must have hit that piece of metal sticking out from the wall.

Afraid the dark sedan would return for a second attempt, she scurried back to her office. It wouldn't be wise to drive home right now anyway. The driver might still be out there, waiting to follow her. Or not. Perhaps they'd only meant to scare her.

Then again, if she hadn't jumped out of the way, she'd have been seriously hurt… or worse.

She didn't feel safe until she was inside her office with the door locked. Then her body reacted, shaking all the way to her toes. She forced herself to take calming breaths and headed to the storage closet to grab their first aid kit. Using a clean gauze, she pressed on the gash in her arm. Her knees wobbled, and she sank onto her desk chair.

What now? She was shaking so badly that she couldn't drive if she wanted to, plus she was afraid to go back outside. Should she summon Lora to come get her? She didn't want to alarm her roommate.

Call Detective Saunders. He'll know what to do.

She accessed his number on speed dial. Thankfully, he answered almost immediately.

"Hi, it's Keri. Someone tried to run me down just now. I'm in my office, but I'm scared to walk to the parking lot by myself."

"Are you alright? Were you hurt?"

"My arm is bleeding from a cut, but I'm okay otherwise."

"Stay there. I'll be right over."

Time slowed to a crawl as she waited for him to arrive. Her

eyes kept darting fearfully to the door. Was her attacker lingering on the side street, waiting for her to reappear?

Panic gripped her but she squashed it down. *Think about who might have done this.* John Beekman had said he'd wanted her watched, not harmed. It seemed less likely to be him. No, she had a better idea of who'd wanted to get her out of the way.

She and Pam had just broken into Garvan's production facility. If he had hidden surveillance cameras, those would have shown the intruders. Garvan could easily have driven there to silence them.

Or else he'd sent Hugh to do the job.

In sudden worry for Pam, Keri dialed her number. "Thank goodness," she said when Pam answered. "I need you to be careful. Somebody just tried to hit me with their car. I'm thinking it was a result of our excursion yesterday."

"Oh, no. Where are you?"

"I'm at my office. Detective Saunders is on his way."

"Thanks for the heads-up. Are you okay? You don't sound so good."

"I'm fine, except for a cut on my arm. My nerves are rattled more than anything."

"Do you want me to come over?"

"I don't think so. Saunders should be arriving soon. I'll talk to you more in the morning."

The detective arrived shortly thereafter. He wore a pair of jeans and a blue polo shirt, making her feel guilty about disrupting his weekend.

"Tell me what happened," he said, after inspecting her wound. She'd gone through three pieces of gauze already.

She described the incident. Her gut felt as though someone had poured a tumbler of ice water inside. She had to clench her teeth to keep from chattering. "The driver might still be out there," she ended, her voice shaky.

"You'll need stitches. I can drive you."

"I don't want to go to a hospital," she protested. Ever since her mother's sudden illness, her heart pounded whenever she entered a medical facility.

"There's a standalone emergency room not too far away. We can get you fixed up there."

"All right." She understood the necessity, even though she quailed inside at the prospect.

Once he'd led her to his vehicle, she slid in and buckled up, grateful for his presence.

After he pulled onto the road, he glanced at her. "I'll need you to file a formal statement, but that can wait until tomorrow. Did you happen to notice the make or model of the car? The license tag? See who was driving?"

"Not really. I was just trying to get out of the way."

"What were you doing at your office so late, anyway?"

"I was out of town yesterday, and I needed to get caught up on a project."

"Any ideas on who might have been responsible?"

She sighed, knowing her confession was inevitable. "I visited Garvan yesterday in St. Augustine. My friend Pam came along so she could interview him for a profile she's doing on Fiona. Are you aware he runs a side hustle selling a cure-all miracle tonic?"

"So? There are plenty of naturalist remedies on the shelves."

"His ads make false claims about purported medical benefits. Garvan does more than just sell the product. He's involved in the manufacturing process. That could be a conflict of interest for him. He's a pharmacist and could lose his license if what he's doing is unethical." Or illegal, she thought. Either way, he'd want to cover up his connection to the production plant.

"And you know all this how?" Saunders queried, raising an eyebrow.

She fidgeted. "Pam and I toured his production facility."

"Are you saying Garvan just let you inside?"

"Not exactly." A guilty flush heated her cheeks. "What matters is what we've learned. We saw packets labeled Kratom in the factory. I looked up Garvan's tonic, and there's no mention of this component in the ingredients listed."

She explained why Kratom could be dangerous to patients. A brief thought about showing him the picture she'd taken quickly got dismissed. He'd want more details on how she had obtained it. She and Pam had been impulsive in wanting to get answers, and now she regretted their methods. If she expected integrity from others, she should practice it herself.

"Do you think Garvan is the one who tried to injure you?" Saunders asked.

"Either him or his son, Hugh, who works as a medical assistant at a pain clinic. Hugh could be selling the tonic to their patients. He'd want to protect his father's interests."

"Garvan's alibi checks out for the night of Miss Sullivan's murder, but the son couldn't account for his whereabouts. Who else have you been speaking to since our last conversation?"

Keri told him about her visit to the PHEADA offices. "I have a hunch that Winnie and Felicity may be abusing their positions," she said. "Have you checked the organization's financial records?"

"I'd need a warrant to look at their books, and speculation isn't enough of a reason to request one. Meanwhile, keep in mind that it's my job to investigate crimes, not yours. You almost got yourself killed tonight."

Keri pressed her lips together and fell silent. Her anxiety grew as they neared the brightly lit emergency facility. Saunders pulled into an empty space in the parking lot that was crowded even for this hour.

"Do you want me to come with you or wait here?" he said with a sympathetic glance.

Her lower lip quivered. "I'd be grateful for the company, if you don't mind."

"No problem." He lumbered out of the vehicle and accompanied her like this was an everyday occurrence for him. Maybe it was part of his job.

"I feel like an idiot getting treatment for a little cut," she muttered as they approached the double front doors. But when her fingers came away wet from where she'd been pressing another gauze, she acknowledged that this had been a necessary trip.

Inside, she checked in at the front desk. Other seats were occupied with slumped individuals, and one person coughed at the far end. She hoped she wouldn't catch anything contagious from being there.

She took a seat to wait her turn, and Saunders sat beside her. He pulled out his cell phone and scrolled through his messages while she wrestled with unpleasant memories.

She'd waited in a similar place for her mother to get processed. It had taken hours in the hospital ER room while diagnostic tests were run before Mom was admitted. Her gut roiled as past traumas returned to haunt her.

When a nurse called her name, she leapt up. The woman had brown skin and a weary face, and she gestured for Keri to follow her through a set of doors and into a treatment room.

"Hi, my name is Rosie, and I'll be your nurse. Please have a seat on the bed."

Keri sat on the treatment table while Rosie took her vital signs and inquired about her medical history.

"Would you like me to get your husband?" Rosie asked when she'd finished.

"Oh, um, he's just a friend. He'd probably rather wait outside." Her face heated at the nurse's assumption.

"The doctor shouldn't be long." Rosie left, drawing the door closed in her wake.

Keri sat there swinging her legs until she felt her circulation being cut off. Then she stretched out on the bed, which wasn't much more comfortable. And the room was cold. She could have used a sweater. Or was it her reaction that made her shiver?

The ER doctor didn't take long to enter. He was younger than she'd expected, with a thick head of coffee-brown hair, intelligent eyes, and a clean-shaven jaw. With his looks, he could star in one of those medical dramas on TV. She would bet he didn't lack attention from the nursing staff.

His mouth quirked into a grin. "Hi, I'm Dr. Worthington. I understand you have a laceration on your arm." He paused to wash his hands at the sink, his broad shoulders filling his white lab coat.

"Yes, that's right." She quaked when he approached, suddenly apprehensive. She'd never had stitches before.

With a gentle touch, he removed her soaked gauze, cleaned the area while she gritted her teeth, and probed the surrounding skin. "Any contact with broken glass?"

"No. I fell against a piece of metal."

"When's the last time you had a tetanus shot?"

Keri shrugged. "I don't remember."

"We'll do the full DTaP then. Do you have any allergies?" She shook her head. "Can you tell me how this happened?"

Keri fumbled for a rational excuse rather than someone trying to kill her. "I was working late and didn't watch where I was going when I left the office. I tripped on an uneven edge of pavement and fell against a building."

"What kind of work do you do?"

Keri babbled on about her job, realizing he'd asked the question to distract her while he stitched her up. She winced during the procedure. When done, he applied a bandage and instructed her on wound care. Then he called for the nurse and ordered a vaccine.

"You'll need to visit your primary care physician in a week to ten days to remove the sutures or else come back here and we'll do it. In the meantime, try not to get the area wet."

"Okay. Tell me, is this where you work full-time?" she asked, to avoid the thought of a needle. She probably needed to get caught up on all her vaccines but wouldn't admit it. "I imagine the hours are better than at a hospital."

"Not really. We still have night rotations." He smiled, and the resultant dimples in his cheeks prompted a responsive coil of warmth to swirl through her veins. "I may switch to an urgent care center when I'm ready for a steady schedule. For now, I like the variety of patients that come through the doors at all hours. It's challenging and keeps me on my toes."

Keri could say the same for her job. She liked having a variety of clients with different needs. However, it was good having weekends off when she didn't have to work.

The doctor scribbled notes on a tablet device until Rosie returned with a syringe.

"I'll be back shortly," he said with a wave as he walked out the door.

Keri looked away as the nurse jabbed her arm and then applied a Band-Aid. "I'll go and get your discharge papers ready," Rosie said before stepping out and leaving Keri feeling alone and abandoned.

She messaged Detective Saunders that she was almost done. Maybe she should have let him leave after dropping her off. She could have caught a rideshare home and picked up her car the next day. Oh, well. Too late now.

She hopped off the treatment table and took a seat in one of the two hard chairs in the room as fatigue suddenly weighed her down. She folded her hands and bent her head until the door slid open.

Dr. Worthington came in and handed over her discharge instructions. "Hey, what's your agency called again? I might check it out one day," he said with a twinkle in his eye.

"I'll give you a card." She gave him one, unsure what to gather from his comment.

He chuckled as he read her slogan. "I like it. Now you need to take care of yourself same as you do for your clients."

Detective Saunders reiterated nearly those same words as he drove Keri back downtown. "I appreciate the information you've provided, but I don't want you putting yourself at risk again. Do me a favor and stay out of trouble."

Keri should have known that piece of advice was coming. Nonetheless, she wouldn't give up on things now just because someone had tried to scare her. That must mean she was getting closer to the truth of what happened to Fiona.

Chapter Twenty-Three

When Keri entered the condo, Lora leapt up from where she was reading a magazine on the couch. Dressed in her jammies, she ran a hand through her unkempt blond curls.

"Where have you been? I was ready to call the police. It's nearly ten o'clock. Didn't you get my text message?"

Keri remembered that she'd silenced her phone in the ER. "Sorry, it's been a crazy night. As for the cops, I've already seen Detective Saunders."

Lora's gaze zeroed in on Keri's bandaged arm. "You're injured? What happened?"

Keri shared her news while Lora stared at her in dismay.

"It sounds as though someone targeted you on purpose."

"I'm assuming this is connected to Fiona's case. I've been learning things about people that they'd prefer to keep quiet, same as she did." Keri put her purse down and sank into an armchair. "Hugh and Garvan top my list since I'd just seen them in St. Augustine. Otherwise, the PHEADA board members stand out as having issues they wouldn't want exposed."

"So, it appears to be true that not everyone appreciated Fiona's influence. What did you learn from your overnight trip?" Lora asked, bringing her a bottle of water.

For once, Keri was glad to let her roomie play mother hen. She related her adventures with Pam and their interview with Garvan.

"You're lucky nobody caught you trespassing in that factory. Somebody knows you've been snooping around, though, and they might try to attack you again. Please be careful."

"I will." Keri got up, her mind blanking on any further theories. "I need to get changed. How can I keep this bandage dry in the shower?"

"Put some plastic wrap around it. Tomorrow, you can order a waterproof sleeve online."

When Keri walked into her closet to get her PJs, her jaw gaped. Lora had organized her rows of shoes, handbags, and accessories. Even her clothes had been color-coordinated on their hangers. It looked like someone else's wardrobe.

"Lora, you've missed your calling," she hollered. "You should get a job as a professional organizer."

Lora wandered in after her. "It saves time on finding things when they're properly sorted. I'm glad you're not mad at me for messing with your stuff."

"This is amazing. I didn't even realize I needed it."

Lora pointed to her work clothes. "You know, you need something sexier to wear if you want to attract a man."

Keri snorted. "The right guy won't care what I wear."

"Maybe, but it doesn't hurt to dress up a bit. Casual business clothes don't always give off the *I'm available* vibe."

"Oh, so now you're an authority on romance? You always fall for the wrong men."

"I'm working on my choices," Lora said in a grudging tone. "At any rate, I'm going to bed. My friend Maxine and I are meeting up at the farmer's market tomorrow in Winter Garden, so I need to get an early start. You should get some rest."

"I know, and I do appreciate you looking out for me."

"My caring isn't the point. You need to take better care of yourself. Otherwise, your busy schedule will affect your health." With those parting words, Lora left to retire for the night.

Keri went to bed, tossing restlessly. She feared Lora was right, and she needed to slow down. Otherwise, she'd end up with palpitations again. Her goal in opening the agency had been to improve things for her clients, but she'd neglected to do the same thing for herself.

She woke up on Saturday morning with a longing to hear her sister's voice. After completing several errands, she contacted Zoey from her car in front of a luggage repair shop. She'd dropped off a leather briefcase there for a client. The strap had come loose and had to be reattached.

"Hey, it's me," she said when Zoey answered. "How's it going? I can come over early on Thursday if you need help setting the table." Thanksgiving had come quickly this year. Or maybe Keri had too many things on her mind to notice the days flying by.

"That's okay," Zoey said in her bubbly tone. "We'll be pretty much ready by then. But you can play with the kids. That would get them out of my hair so I can make the salad."

"Okay. I can't wait to see everyone."

As she hung up, she realized why she'd needed to touch base with Zoey. If Fiona were still alive, Keri would have been shopping at the farmer's market for her today. Lora's remark about going to the one in Winter Garden had reminded her of Fiona's absence in her life.

Before she realized where she was going, she found herself driving toward Fiona's neighborhood, as though her friend's ghost could provide comfort. Once on Fiona's street, she cruised along the road, which was lined by moss-draped oaks. Her eyes misted as she observed the manicured lawns, flowering bushes, and glistening lake beyond. How could a place so serene be the site for murder?

She pulled up to the curb in front of Fiona's house and glanced at Veronica's place across the street. It was sad how her life had been cut short. Did anyone mourn her passing? She knew so little about the woman and now she was gone like a specter in the night.

A movement from the side caught her eye. A stout figure dashed from the bushes bordering Fiona's property. Wait, was that Bob Underwood carrying a bulging pillowcase?

Needing to find out what he was doing, she cut the ignition, grabbed her phone, and exited. Her shoes kicked up clods of dirt as she sprinted across the lawn and caught up to Fiona's neighbor. A glance up the street told her she wasn't alone. A man was fixing his gutter a few houses over, and another neighbor was walking his dog. She hoped her gut feeling was wrong about Bob, but it paid to be prepared.

"Hey, Bob. I was cruising by and saw you outside."

His steps halted and he spun around so abruptly that the sack went flying from his hand. "What are you doing here?"

"I was missing Fiona and wanted to see her house again. Were you coming from her place?"

His skin flushed. "I was fixing a piece of fascia board on her patio. She'd hired me as her handyman, and I needed to complete the job."

"Oh, really? Then what are those?" She pointed to a couple of newspaper-wrapped items from the pillowcase that had spilled onto the grass. Before he could stop her, she snatched one up and unfolded it. A gasp escaped her lips as she recognized the porcelain figurine of a couple embracing against an ocean wave. The Royal Doulton piece belonged to Fiona's collection.

She unwrapped another item and her stomach sank. A glazed eagle with sapphire eyes spread its wings on a rock. It had sat in one of Fiona's curio cabinets.

"Oh my God, Bob. Have you been stealing from Fiona?"

If so, he might have taken the items Diane reported as missing on Keri's inventory list. Had he snuck into Fiona's bedroom the night she died, hoping to snag something more valuable? Keri's blood ran cold at her next thought. Was he the murderer?

Bob thrust his chin forward. "I've only been helping myself to a few things as compensation for my work. Fiona had so many tchotchkes in her house, I figured she wouldn't notice if some of them disappeared."

"I can't believe you took advantage of her this way."

"Please don't tell the cops. I know what you must be

thinking, but I'd never hurt her. I'd only go in during the day when she wasn't home."

His whiny voice didn't peg him as violent but that could be an act. Keri placed the delicate figurines on top of the newspaper scraps on the ground and took a step back.

"You know I'll have to tell Diane. She owns the estate now."

His expression panicked. "Why can't we keep this between us? If word gets out, Sarah will leave me."

"Huh? What does Sarah have to do with anything?" Was he afraid his wife would abandon him if he were arrested for stealing? If anything, Sarah might lay low to avoid a scandal.

"I've been pawning these things for cash, but I mean to buy them all back. I just need to pay off the debts from my last trip first."

"What trip?" Her eyes narrowed. Was he fooling around with another woman, as Sarah suspected? That would certainly give her cause to leave him.

"They're day cruises on the casino boat."

A lightbulb exploded in her head, and she gawked at him. "You're a gambler?" That would explain a lot. Sarah had it all wrong. Her husband didn't have a girlfriend. He went off on gambling jaunts.

His shoulders sagged, and he stared at the ground. "I've used my retirement fund to cover my losses, but it's not enough. If only I could get a clear win, I'd be okay."

No wonder he feared Sarah's reaction. "Your reasons don't excuse stealing from your neighbor. How did you get into her house when she wasn't home?"

"I have a key."

"If you'd like to give it to me, I'll make sure Diane gets it."

Shame-faced, he complied. "I swear I'll make things right."

"Tell me, where did you keep this key?" she asked, wondering if it would have been accessible to Ossie during his visits to Sarah. If so, he could have borrowed it or made a copy for his own purposes.

"I hung it on a hook by our garage door entrance. Why?"

"Just wondering. I'll return these items to Diane since they belong to her now. I won't tell Sarah, since that's your confession to make, but I'll have to inform Detective Saunders."

If Bob's house had an alarm system or cameras, Saunders could potentially verify his alibi for the night Fiona died. Unless he'd already done so.

Bob bowed his head. "I've let everyone down, haven't I?"

"I understand how you might feel that way, but Sarah may be supportive if you tell her the truth." At least his wife could take comfort in knowing he wasn't having an affair.

She retreated to her car and stowed the packed pillowcase in the back seat while Bob slinked to his house next door. After she was behind the wheel, Keri left a message on Detective Saunders's voicemail to call her and then she phoned Diane. She hit a wall there, too.

Hopefully, they both would get back to her sooner rather than later. While Bob might not be guilty of murder, he should be accountable for his actions. It would be up to Saunders to determine the extent of his crime.

Meanwhile, if she could discreetly discuss this latest development with her friends the next day, it would help her to talk things out. She still wasn't seeing all the connections that had led to Fiona's death, and their fresh insights might prove useful.

Chapter Twenty-Four

Keri couldn't wait to tell her friends what she'd learned during their Sunday morning power walk at Central Park. However, Pam brought up another subject first.

"Listen to this," Pam said, as they veered around the rose garden. "I spoke to a contact who works at the *Orlando Sentinel*. He gave me an interesting scoop on Hugh Conner."

Keri's ears perked up. "What's that?"

From beneath her wide-brimmed hat and sunglasses, Pam skewed a glance her way. "Have you seen the recent news reports about pill mills? They're clinics where people go to get pain meds that are liberally prescribed. Dispensing these pills is a big business in Florida. People cross state borders to come here. The state government is trying to crack down on them, but the clinics are too widespread."

"Hugh works at one of these pill mills?"

Pam nodded. "His name was mentioned in an article with a local slant. He gave a quote claiming his facility successfully treated patients who hadn't found relief elsewhere. They offer a wide variety of treatments in addition to prescription medications."

"Why would they interview him rather than one of the doctors?" Keri asked.

"The reporter spoke to a range of employees."

"Here's a theory," Lora said, keeping pace. "People come to Hugh's clinic where the doctor prescribes pain meds. Garvan fills the orders at his pharmacy. They both benefit."

Keri's brow wrinkled. "Then how does Hugh fit into the picture?"

"As a medical assistant, he may take patient histories, listen to complaints, and carry out treatments prescribed by the doctor. I could see him recommending his dad's tonic. He might even claim the pain meds and the tonic work in conjunction with each other. One drug relieves the pain while the other one restores the body to a healthy state. His dad probably gives him a cut from each sale."

Keri's mouth twisted as she thought this through. "Remember that Vivonin may contain Kratom, which has opioid properties. A double whammy could be dangerous to patients."

"Nonetheless," Lora said. "Hugh would want to protect his extra source of income. It can't be a coincidence that someone took a swipe at you right after your visit to St. Augustine."

Keri glanced at her friends, glad they could hash this out together. "Let's assume Fiona learned about Garvan's production plant and threatened to shut him down. According to Detective Saunders, he had a solid alibi for the night she died. Hugh, on the other hand, couldn't account for his whereabouts."

"Hugh seems the most likely culprit to me," Lora said. "Who else is left?"

"Several people. Yesterday, I was driving by Fiona's house when I spotted her neighbor, Bob Underwood, sneaking across her lawn holding a stuffed pillowcase. Inside were some wrapped figurines belonging to Fiona's collection. He admitted to stealing them to pay off his gambling debts. He seemed very contrite and promised to make things right. Please keep this confidential."

Pam snorted. "I wouldn't trust anything he says if I were you. Veronica could have seen him entering Fiona's house from across the street, and now she's dead."

Keri acknowledged that it looked bad for Bob. "Or, Veronica might have seen someone else. Saunders should be able to confirm Bob's alibi for those nights if he has a home security system."

"True, and let's not forget the PHEADA group," Pam reminded them as they skirted around two mothers pushing baby strollers. "I may have something soon that ties their vice president to John Beekman the developer, but I need to verify my source."

"Something more than those two greasing each other's palms and swaying city council votes in their favor?" Keri asked.

"Yes, it goes deeper."

Keri knew Pam wouldn't say what it was until she'd confirmed the info. "Winnie and Felicity might be embezzling money from the group," she said, to add to their list of possibilities. "Or, at the very least, they're overcharging the artists who participate in PHEADA's fundraisers. And Ossie is having an affair with Sarah that could undermine his political career. Fiona could have learned about any of these issues and used her knowledge to control them."

Pam adjusted her sunglasses. "We need to crack this case soon. My profile piece on Fiona comes out on Tuesday in the *Gazette*. A follow-up headliner on her murder would be perfect."

Keri would give Pam an exclusive if she had anything to say about it. She'd have to convince Saunders that Pam deserved one for helping her dig out the details.

As they went to breakfast, she was hoping for a callback from either the detective or Diane, but since it was Sunday, they might be busy with their families.

Nonetheless, the case nagged at her throughout the afternoon, which she spent catching up on personal chores. Maybe Staz or Purdy would offer some sage advice when she brought them up to speed tomorrow.

****

Monday morning, Keri arrived at work a few minutes late and greeted her colleagues with a wave as she swept into the office. They'd already gone to work at their desks.

"Morning, Keryn." Purdy regarded her from behind his wire-rimmed glasses. He looked spiffy in a navy sport coat, crisp white shirt, and tie. "How was your weekend?"

Keri stashed her purse in a desk drawer. "It was eventful, to say the least. You?"

Purdy grinned. "I saw Kitty again. That cat knows how to play."

"Sounds like you had a good time. How about you, Staz?"

Staz's eyes sparkled. "I went to a pressed flower class at Leu Gardens and then worked out at the gym on Saturday. Yesterday was the craft fair at Cranes Roost. I bought this necklace there." She lifted a long set of colorful beads off her peach sweater dress to show them.

"I wish I had time to go to the fall festivals this year," Keri said. She didn't feel very festive, not with Fiona's death still so fresh. She needed to put her friend to rest before she'd feel ready to move on.

"Why did you say your weekend was eventful?" Purdy inquired. He scrutinized her from head to toe but missed the bandage on her arm, since she'd covered it with a long-sleeved top.

She brought her colleagues up to date. Astonishment mixed with disapproval on Purdy's face while Staz stared at her in dismay.

"You could have been killed by that car," Staz said. "Don't you think you should back off and let Detective Saunders do his job?"

"I can't. I had another development happen this weekend, too." She told them about Bob Underwood and made them promise not to reveal a word of his secret to anyone else. "He sounded so remorseful that I want to believe him."

Purdy snorted. "He could be a sociopath. They always sound convincing."

"That's for the detective to determine. Meanwhile, I need to make an appointment with Ossie." She reiterated her suspicions regarding the group's officers.

"If you're right," Purdy said, "it could be dangerous for you to go there alone."

Keri appreciated his concern. "They're still our clients, Purdy. I'll be fine."

"Is there anything I can do to help?" Staz asked.

"Actually, there is one thing on my list. Randy Wyatt is going away next week and needs someone to watch his Doberman. He's asked me to hire a dog sitter. Can you handle it?"

"Sure, no problem."

Keri picked up her phone as Staz and Purdy turned back to their computer screens. The PHEADA offices should be open by now.

Winnie answered. "Hello, luv. What can I do for you?"

"I need an appointment with Ossie so he can sign the contract for our children's art event." That was the excuse she'd come up with for a visit.

"You can have him DocuSign via email."

"Nuh-uh. I still need to hammer out some details with him in person."

"He's a busy man. You and I could deal with it on the phone."

Winnie had never been this recalcitrant before. Did she not want Keri to talk to Ossie for some reason?

Perhaps she suspected Keri wanted to bring up the artist participation fee and meant to head her off. She'd have to make it clear that she wouldn't take *no* for an answer.

"I'm requesting an appointment, Winnie. You don't want me storming through your doors and making a fuss. Ossie wouldn't be happy to hear you're obstructing our work together."

Winnie sighed. "He has an opening this afternoon at three."

"Great, I'll take it. See you then."

With a grunt of annoyance, Keri disconnected. Then she phoned Pam to tell her she'd scored an appointment with Ossie.

"Be careful. You don't know who you can trust," Pam said. "None of those people have clean slates."

"I know. I'll text Purdy when I'm done. He can act as backup."

Pam's warning echoed in her head as she completed arrangements for a toddler's birthday party, scheduled a roofer to inspect a client's shingle roof for a leak and ordered a cake for an anniversary celebration.

After a few more calls, she left to do some small jobs for clients. She rushed around, anxious to finish so she could direct her thoughts toward her upcoming chat with Ossie.

Two hours later, she made it back to the office. She had to write up her log for the day before heading out again. Otherwise, Purdy would hound her about it.

Staz gave her a big grin as she walked in. "Wait until you hear this one," she said, inclining her head in Purdy's direction.

"What's the matter?" Keri asked, noting his hangdog expression.

He was so flustered that he sputtered. "I-I made dates for Friday night with both Svetlana and Kitty. What am I going to do? They'll both bail on me."

She gazed at him askance. Seriously, this is what bothered him? "Just call them and reschedule. Say something came up and you have to work."

"What if one of them comes by the office to check up on me?"

Keri accessed her calendar. "I made a dinner reservation at a restaurant for a Mah Jongg group that evening. You could stop by to see if they're happy with the arrangements. That would validate your excuse."

His face brightened. "Thanks, I'll do it. I knew I could count on you to save me."

She suppressed a smile. Only Purdy could come up with a romantic entanglement that rattled his normally calm personality. "If you don't mind, I need to finish up here before my appointment with Ossie."

Staz pointed a finger at her. "That reminds me. Tatiana, your artist friend, left a message for you to contact her."

"Oh? I wonder what she wants. I'll call her right now."

"Keri, thanks for getting back to me so quickly," Tatiana responded, her voice tense. "Listen, you have to intervene with Winnie for me."

"Why, what's happened?"

"She's badgering me for the participation fee I owe and has started charging interest. It's not fair. I've recommended other artists for PHEADA events and have paid on time before."

Outrage nearly stole Keri's breath. "It seems unreasonable for Winnie to charge you more money," she said, keeping her voice level.

"Maybe you can ask if she'll waive these charges. Otherwise, it's becoming too complicated to work with them."

Keri's heart quickened at the possibility that other artists would feel the same way. "I have a meeting with their president this afternoon. I'll see what Ossie has to say about it. He may not be aware this added fee exists."

Keri ended the call, anxious about her upcoming discussion with Ossie. Just in case it turned unpleasant, she instructed Purdy to notify Detective Saunders if he didn't hear from her by a certain time. Then she grabbed her purse and headed out.

Chapter Twenty-Five

Winnie was waiting at the reception desk when Keri arrived. Her hair, freshly styled, implied a recent visit to the salon, as did her burnt orange manicured nails. She'd certainly been spending money on herself lately. Money that wasn't rightfully hers?

Winnie mumbled a greeting and waved her toward Ossie's office. He rose from his desk at her entrance, and Keri shut the door after debating if it were wise to be alone with him. She'd take that chance if it meant they wouldn't be overheard.

"It's good to see you again, Keri," he said in his deep baritone as they shook hands.

"Thanks. I'm glad you could fit me in today." She took a seat opposite his desk.

"I've been working on the agenda for our upcoming board meeting. Winnie said you had a contract for me to sign." He lowered himself into his black leather chair and straightened the lapels on his charcoal sport coat.

"That's right." Keri took care of that business and then tucked away the signed document. She brought up a few details next that needed confirmation.

"You're always so well organized," he commented when she was finished.

"It's a pleasure to plan events for your group. Your fundraisers never fail to draw a crowd." She figured flattery might loosen him up before she approached the heavier topics on her mind.

"Thanks to your efforts." He beamed at her, no doubt

thinking she'd take her leave now that they were done. He'd half-risen from his chair before she stopped him with a hand signal.

"Before I go, there's one more thing we need to discuss."

"What's that?" he asked, as he sank back into his chair.

"One of the young artists who participates in your events mentioned a hundred-dollar application fee that Winnie requires. Winnie has even started charging interest if their payment is late. I don't feel it's fair to ask them to pay double."

His brow creased. "I'm not sure I follow you. What application fee?"

Does he truly not know about it, or is he putting one over on me? "Winnie receives the money, which I presume she turns over to Felicity for deposit. Felicity said it covers administrative costs, such as overhead and publicity."

He scowled at her. "It's the first time I've heard about an additional charge. I agree with you that it's not right. Thank you for bringing this to my attention."

"That's not all." How could she put this tactfully? "I also got the impression that Winnie and Felicity may be taking advantage of their positions in ways that could damage your group's reputation. I may be totally off base, but if your donors sniff even a hint of misconduct, they'll take their generosity elsewhere. It might be a good idea for you to examine the group's financial records more closely."

Ossie regarded her with slitted eyes. "I trust our officers to fulfill their duties properly, but I'll take a look as you suggest." *If for no other reason than to disprove your allegations*, she interpreted from his tight-lipped expression.

"I only want what's best for your organization. PHEADA has a sterling reputation in town, and we wouldn't want it to be tarnished." Besides, if their group went down, so did a big chunk of her business.

"I get your points. Are we done here?"

"Not quite yet." She shifted in her seat, glad he was still listening. "I ran into Maurice the other day at Ivy Morrison's soiree. He seemed very cozy with John Beekman, the developer. Is Mr. Beekman one of your benefactors? If so, I'll be happy to add him to our invite list for upcoming events."

"John is always happy to support our cause. Maurice keeps him informed about our fundraisers. He's been very generous."

"I see. And how about the Underwoods? They like to attend our events."

"Where are you going with this, Keri?" he asked with a frown.

She gave him a level glance. "I'm aware that you and Sarah are very close."

His face reddened. "We're working on a project together. It takes a lot of time. Sarah is a meticulous planner."

"Is that right? I've gotten the impression that things are a lot more intimate between you than a working relationship. Sarah very nearly admitted it during our last chat."

His mouth flattened into a thin line. "She did, did she? I warned her to keep her mouth shut. I'd encourage you not to breathe a word of this to anyone. It wouldn't be in your best interest to spread rumors."

She wouldn't call it a rumor when he'd almost admitted to having an affair. And did Ossie just threaten her? Even if he were willing to commit murder to avoid exposure, wouldn't he be more likely to silence Sarah? Perhaps he meant instead that someone in Keri's position shouldn't gossip, or it would negatively impact her reputation.

"I'm not out to hurt anyone," she explained. "I just want the truth about what happened to Fiona."

"I realize that, but you need to be more respectful of people's privacy." Ossie fiddled with a ballpoint pen on his desk. "Just between us, Sarah understands me a lot better than my wife ever will. Still, Hope and I need each other in our own ways, and I've no wish to leave her."

"Sarah might have different expectations," Keri pointed out.

"That's her problem. I've been clear in my intentions from the start."

Sarah might be unhappy in her marriage—more so when she learned about Bob's gambling habit—but she cared about her social standing. Keri could see her wanting to avoid a scandal to preserve her status.

"I appreciate your honesty, Ossie. I won't bring up this subject again."

"Good. As for the rest, I'll look into those issues you've raised. Now if you'll excuse me, I have another appointment."

Relieved that he hadn't fired her, Keri rose. At least they'd cleared the air regarding his personal life. And hopefully, he'd turn a more watchful eye thereafter on his fellow officers.

Before leaving, she noticed Felicity's office door was open. The redhead wasn't present when Keri peeked inside. Unable to resist the opportunity, she wandered in and glanced at the neatly sorted papers on Felicity's desktop. If she happened to spot anything out of the ordinary, it might give Detective Saunders a reason to get a warrant to examine their books.

With a flush of guilt, she realized she was once again snooping where she didn't belong. She'd just decided to leave when footsteps sounded from behind.

"What are you doing in here?" Felicity demanded in a high-pitched voice.

Her heart hammering, Keri spun around and plastered a sheepish grin on her face. "Oh, um, I was looking for a printout of your latest newsletter. I didn't receive the November issue, and my agency had an ad in it."

Felicity's gaze chilled. "You could have emailed me. Winnie said you had an appointment with Ossie today."

"That's right. I had a complaint from one of our artists that Winnie was charging interest as a late fee for your administrative charge. I asked Ossie about it, but he said he'd never heard about this requirement. I'm hoping he'll eliminate it, so our talent isn't charged double."

"We've been over this before. It's the cost of doing business with us. As for Ossie, he doesn't involve himself in our daily activities. Winnie and I handle the mundane tasks so that he isn't bothered by them."

"If we lose the artists, it'll hurt your organization's fund-raising efforts."

"It'll be their loss, not ours. We can find other talent to participate."

Keri's blood boiled but she forced herself to respond in a rational voice. "That may be true, but your group's reputation could be damaged in the process. Imagine if word got out that you're overcharging these young people who are donating their time to the cause. The board of trustees may decide this policy isn't justified. They might even want to examine the group's accounts, and then where would that lead?"

Felicity's face infused with color, which Keri read as guilt. If she and Winnie were misusing their positions as she suspected, how would they do it? Perhaps Winnie ordered supplies that were never received. Or Felicity might collect donations that failed to be recorded. They could split the proceeds between them and cover for each other.

"What's going on?" Winnie asked as she joined them.

"Keri is intruding where she isn't wanted," Felicity snapped.

Regardless of the consequences, Keri needed to know where they stood. "Look, Felicity, I'm aware your mother lives at an assisted living facility. It must be awfully expensive with their high monthly fees."

Felicity gaped at her. "How do you know that? Have you been spying on me?"

"I was there visiting a client the day you admitted her. Your mom is fortunate to have you looking after her welfare. And Winnie, I'd guess neither your salary nor your sales of Vivonin can begin to cover your costly makeovers."

Winnie put her hands on her hips. "I don't see how that's any of your business."

"I'm only concerned for your group's reputation. If you truly care about your organization, you might want to rethink some of your… more creative financial arrangements." She couldn't accuse them outright of anything without proof.

Winnie gave her a startled glance, poked Felicity's arm and spoke in a diffident tone. "She's right, Felicity. We should fix things while we still can."

Felicity gave her a reluctant nod, which made Keri wonder if she'd comply. The treasurer seemed the harder nut to crack. Meanwhile, she addressed the other issue on her mind.

"I'd hoped to speak to Maurice while I was here. He seems to be tight with John Beekman, the developer. I understand he's one of your larger donors."

Felicity snorted. "That's because Maurice has a financial interest in Beekman's company. No doubt he's responsible for their generosity."

"Oh? I didn't realize their connection went that deep."

"They like to keep Maurice's involvement under wraps."

"I see." She gave them a polite smile. "Thank you for listening to my concerns. I've a phone conference in a few minutes, so I have to go." With a last wave, she hustled outside.

From the parking lot, she notified Purdy that she was in the clear. Overall, she felt none of their officers were squeaky clean, but they didn't appear to be guilty of murder. Of course, she could be wrong and wouldn't eliminate them entirely, but the group's executive board took a step down on her list.

She'd just put her car in gear when a message came through from Detective Saunders.

Sorry I didn't get back to you sooner. Would you mind stopping by the station? We need to talk.

Okay, I'm nearby. I'll see you soon, she wrote, curious to hear what he had to say.

Saunders greeted her once she'd obtained her visitor's pass at the station, then escorted her upstairs to his private office. She claimed the chair opposite his desk while he sat facing her.

"I thought you'd like to know we lifted a clean set of prints from your office door after the break-in. They match a man in the national database named Carl Franklin. He's a jewel thief from up north who vanished years ago."

That information was so far from what she'd expected that Keri stared at him. She'd thought he might have news about Hugh Connor.

"Why would a jewel thief break into my office?"

"I'm not sure. This guy doesn't fit the puzzle. And why show up here when no one's been able to find him for years?"

Obviously, he'd slipped up if he'd left a set of clean prints. Could he somehow be connected to Fiona? The only way she could fathom would be through Fiona's father. Did his mobster gang still exist? If so, perhaps they'd wanted to eliminate people who'd known about their activities. But then, why wait until now to track his daughter down? Also, wouldn't their hitman be too old if he were one of their cronies?

"What age would this person be?" she asked, trying to put together the timelines.

"Franklin was in his early thirties when he disappeared. He would be middle-aged by now."

"Did you recover any prints from Fiona's bedroom?" Maybe Franklin had left evidence of his presence there, although she still didn't understand how he fit into the picture.

"We got a clean set, but they don't match Franklin's prints or anyone else in the database."

The jewel thief could still have murdered Fiona and worn gloves to cover his tracks. Otherwise, another likely culprit for an unknown set of prints came to mind.

"I can think of somebody else who might have been rummaging through Fiona's things. She'd employed her neighbor, Bob Underwood, as her handyman. He had a key to her house and has been stealing her collectibles. Bob confessed when I caught him in the act."

Saunders's brows drew together like thunderclouds. "*You* caught him? When did this happen? And why didn't you tell me about this sooner?"

Keri winced at his reaction. She explained how she'd been driving by and saw Bob sneaking away from Fiona's house. Then the contents of his sack spilled out, and she'd recognized the items. "Bob promised to buy back the things he'd pawned. He seemed remorseful rather than violent," she concluded.

"Killers don't telegraph their intent. You were foolish to confront him alone."

"You're right, but there were other neighbors around. And I had to see what he was doing."

"Speaking of neighbors, the autopsy report on Ms. Batten indicated her head injury was consistent with a blow from a blunt object. It was no accident but made to look that way. She could easily have seen Mr. Underwood slipping inside Miss Sullivan's house."

Keri swallowed, disturbed to have Veronica's cause of death confirmed. "Bob isn't the only suspect," she reminded him, hoping she wasn't misjudging Bob's character. Nonetheless, she didn't want Saunders to overlook other possibilities.

"Is that right?" the detective said, his assessing gaze drilling into her. "Do you have something more you'd like to share?"

She related her latest findings regarding the PHEADA officers.

Saunders listened patiently and then shook his head. "This is all circumstantial. I can have another talk with them, though." He riffled through his notes. "Do you still believe it might have been Hugh Connor who tried to run you down after your visit to his dad's factory? If that was the reason for this attack, why hasn't he gone after your reporter friend?"

"Good question." He had a valid point. Her office had been trashed, her person endangered, and her reputation smeared. She did appear to be the target, but why? Because she'd been close to Fiona? Did the killer fear what Fiona might have told her?

"Hugh may not have a clear alibi for the night his great-aunt died, but we have no evidence against him," Saunders stated.

"What about Veronica's friends and relatives? Have you

spoken to them? She might have mentioned something important among her rhymes and ravings."

"I need to do more digging in that regard. And I want to look further into this Carl Franklin fellow. Meanwhile, stay out of trouble, you hear?"

Keri took her leave, disturbed by their conversation. A clear suspect still hadn't materialized. If she eliminated the Connors, the PHEADA people, and the Underwoods, who was left? The unknown jewel thief? What could he have possibly wanted in her office?

Maybe he hadn't been searching for anything. He could have meant to unnerve her instead, although she couldn't conceive of a motive unless it was connected to Fiona.

She shoved aside her thoughts as she drove to the grocery store to pick up a quick meal for dinner, since she thought Lora had plans. As she browsed the prepared seafood selections, a man addressed her from behind.

"Hey, Keri. How's the arm feeling?"

Startled, she whirled around and took stock of the cute doctor from the E.R. Away from work, Dr. Worthington looked hot in jeans and a polo shirt. Judging from his muscled arms, he exercised in his off hours. His thick dark brown hair brushed his brow, making her want to feel its texture. She couldn't help the swell of warmth that suffused her veins.

"Good to see you again, Dr. Worthington. My arm is doing well, thanks."

"Call me Matt. Are you coming from work? I should stop by your agency sometime to check it out." His cocoa eyes regarded her with a glimmer of interest.

"That would be great." She gave him an inane smile. "I'm here to pick up a quick dinner. This salmon looks good." She grabbed a container with a salmon fillet and braised Brussel sprouts for roasting in the oven. "Do you like to cook, or are you here for fast food like me?" That was a dumb thing to ask but it just popped out of her mouth.

He grinned, showing his even white teeth. "With my erratic hours, I need food that's easy to prepare. Maybe we should get dinner out together one night."

"Yes, I'd like that." Blushing like a schoolgirl, she uttered a few awkward words before exchanging phone numbers with him and moving on.

What was wrong with her? She'd turned into a total teenager in his presence. Even saying his name in her head made her blood surge.

Unwilling to acknowledge her reaction, she headed home to relax and get comfortable. Since Lora was out, she had the place to herself. Grateful for the privacy, she put her meal in the oven and entered her bedroom to get changed. A legal-sized manila envelope lay on top of her bedspread, along with a note from Lora.

I picked this up at the front desk the other day and left it in your home office, but you may not have seen it. I'd forgotten about it until I went in there for some paper clips. Sorry; I hope it's not too important.

Her heart lurched when she noticed the return address came from a lawyer. Hopefully, none of her clients were suing her. She tore open the seal with shaky fingers, and a leather-bound book slid out along with a scribbled note from the attorney.

Fiona Sullivan requested this item be mailed to you in the event of her death.

Her eyes widened as she recognized Fiona's ledger. Fiona must have given it to the lawyer for safekeeping. But why had she made him wait until after her death to send it out?

Sinking onto the bed, Keri smoothed her hands over the worn cover. With bated breath, she opened the book and thumbed through its pages.

She scanned the entries, noting the sources that said *Dad*. Perhaps Fiona hadn't wanted Keri to learn about her past. This would make it a lot easier to separate out the goods Crogher had given his daughter. Those needed further research into their provenance.

Another question begged an answer. How come Fiona had sent this to her instead of Diane? Fiona couldn't have known Diane would hire Keri to help dispose of things.

Unless… Fiona had sent it to Keri because she didn't trust Diane.

No, she'd treated Diane like her own daughter. A more logical explanation came to mind that stunned her. Could it be that Fiona had reason to mistrust Cal, Diane's husband? If she recalled properly, both Tony and Garvan had mentioned Cal and not in a good way.

A sense of unease gripped her when she realized two days had passed since she'd left Diane a message. Diane might have been busy with her kids over the weekend, but now her silence took on a new urgency. A quick phone call didn't garner a response, either. Nor did a text message.

That didn't mean Diane had come to any harm. She might be too occupied to reply, or she could have set her phone on silent mode and forgotten to reverse it.

Nonetheless, first thing in the morning, she would track Diane down to ensure her safety. The possibility of Cal being involved now seemed very real. It brought home Fiona's last words to her—*You're the only one I can trust*. It made sense if Fiona had reason to doubt Cal's motives. Now it was up to Keri to determine what she might have discovered about him.

Chapter Twenty-Six

Keri arrived at work on Tuesday morning before her colleagues. She'd just set down her bag, intending to give Diane a call, when Hugh barged into the agency.

"You," he said, jabbing a finger in her direction. "We need to talk."

Her pulse rocketed before she even knew what he had to say. Aware that they were alone together, she cast a glance out the front window. Purdy or Staz might walk in at any moment. And passersby could see them through the glass if Hugh meant her any harm.

"What is it? Has something happened?"

"Yeah, I'll tell you what's happened. You and your nosy reporter friend broke into my dad's factory."

Surprise stole her breath. How did he find out she and Pam had been there? "What makes you say that?" she asked in a squeaky voice.

"Video surveillance. What did you think you were doing?"

"I'm looking into all the possibilities regarding Fiona's death. She meant a lot to me, and to Diane. We both want to learn the truth."

Something flickered in Hugh's eyes. Was that reluctant understanding?

"You wanted to know more about Vivonin, right?" he snapped. "Dad's product helps patients with health issues. You bring him down, and it'll hurt people. Conventional medicine doesn't always provide the relief they need."

"What about the harm Vivonin causes sick people if they rely on it for a miraculous cure and don't see a doctor?" she countered. "Did you know this tonic contains Kratom, which has opioid properties?"

"Does that make it a bad thing if it works?"

"Yes, if the ingredient isn't disclosed. People who don't know about it could have adverse drug interactions or dangerous side effects." She had no idea if this omission would be considered a crime or not, but Pam seemed to think so.

Hugh sneered at her. "It doesn't matter. You had no business snooping inside Dad's plant. He could charge you with trespassing or breaking and entering."

An icy sensation seeped through her veins. Would Garvan go that far? Or had he already retaliated by sending his son to sideswipe her with his vehicle? Since Hugh had come here to yell at her, that theory seemed less likely.

"Somebody tried to run me down with their car the other day," she said, figuring her best defense was offense at this point. "You wouldn't happen to know anything about that, would you? It happened right after my visit to your family."

"What, you think it was me?" He gave a harsh laugh. "You're totally offtrack. A murderer is loose out there, but it's not us. It's someone who must have slipped past Aunt Fiona's guard to get close to her. If you're smart, you'll watch your back."

She examined his expression for any hint of deceit but found none. Was he truly concerned about her welfare? If so, this might be the real reason he'd come there. Perhaps she'd do him a favor in return.

"I understand you want to protect your father. You might suggest that he disclose all the ingredients for Vivonin and be truthful about its medical benefits. Then he won't jeopardize his professional license."

"I'll mention it," Hugh replied sullenly.

She swept her arm in an arc. "He's not the only one who needs to clean up his act. You gave a quote for an article on pill mills. Federal drug agents are giving those places a closer look. Maybe it's time for you to start searching for a new workplace. I'd think as a medical assistant, you could get a job anywhere. What made you decide to pursue that field, anyway?"

He shrugged. "I tried business classes at college, but it wasn't for me. This job only requires a year or two of training, and then certification. It was a no-brainer. The healthcare sector is booming and will continue to grow."

"You could become a nurse, if you really like working with patients."

"Now you sound like Aunt Fiona. She constantly nagged me to go back to school and finish my degree. She didn't like my friends, or the way I dressed, or anything about me. I knew she'd never accept me no matter what I did. I said I'd go back to college if she left her money to me."

"I'll bet that went over big."

"She laughed in my face and said, 'Over my dead body.'"

Did you make that happen? Keri assumed Hugh wouldn't be explaining himself if he posed a threat. He seemed more concerned about defending his family.

"It sounds as though you had a difficult relationship," she said sympathetically. Maybe he'd offer some ideas on who else might have resented his great-aunt.

A pained expression entered his eyes. "I wasn't the only one she picked on. She criticized my parents, too. None of us were good enough for her, not that she was perfect. Everyone admired her but they didn't see her in the same light as we did."

Had it really been Fiona who'd pushed her family away, like she'd done to Tony? Garvan had implied much the same thing.

With his bluster gone, Hugh glanced at the floor, but not before she caught a glimpse of a vulnerable young man. The tough guy persona was now seeming more of an act. Well, except for the duck in the road, although that could have been an isolated incident. Maybe he'd thought it would waddle out of the way in time.

"Why did you really come to town, Hugh?" she asked in a soft voice. "Was it to warn me to be careful?"

"That's part of it. I'm transferring the title for the car Aunt Fiona left me. Now I'm giving you some advice. Stay out of our lives. I'll tell Dad to overlook your transgression this one time, because we know you cared about Aunt Fiona, but don't drag us down or you *will* be sorry."

He spun around and stalked out as Keri stared at his wake. Did he mean to threaten her, or was he implying a lawsuit would be instigated if she trespassed again?

He'd seemed sincere in his attempt to alert her that a killer was on the loose and it wasn't a member of his family. She'd already surmised the PHEADA officers were consumed with their own internal problems, making them less prone to violence. Nor did she believe the Underwoods would resort to murder to cover their personal indiscretions. That left family members, and Hugh had just removed his side of the equation. This only solidified her suspicions regarding Cal.

Anxious to hear from Diane, Keri called her again and gave a whoosh of relief when she answered after two rings.

"Can we meet?" Keri asked, needing to get some hard questions answered. "I have news to share."

"I was just about to return your earlier phone call. I'm free this afternoon," Diane said in a subdued voice. "Is one o'clock at Fifi's house okay?"

"Yes, I'll see you then." Relieved that Diane was safe, Keri patted her tote bag that held Fiona's ledger. She'd give it to Diane and then they had to discuss Bob's confession.

Purdy and Staz arrived, but Keri didn't tell them about Hugh's visit. She didn't want to get into a conversation about her being alone with him. After returning a series of phone calls, she ran out to do some errands and grab a bite to eat before it was time to meet Diane.

As she approached Fiona's house, her nerves tingled. She felt close to solving her mentor's murder but still had some loose ends to resolve. She pulled into the driveway beside Diane's car, parked and grabbed her handbag along with the sack she'd taken from Bob.

After greeting her with a hug, Diane led her inside and into the study. Cartons rested on the floor, some sealed and others open, while a stack of books piled into one corner.

"You've been busy," Keri said, setting her bag on a side table and the sack on the floor.

Diane regarded her with frank blue eyes. "I'll donate these books to the library for their book sale. It's been harder to go through Fifi's desk. She had notes scribbled to herself all over the place. It's sad how these small scraps of life get tossed in the trash when you're gone."

Keri's heart swelled. "I know. I had to do the same thing for my mother. It's a sad task but they'd want us to be the ones to do it." She withdrew the ledger from her tote. "This should help with our research."

Diane's eyes rounded. "You found the journal? Where was it?"

"Fiona gave it to her lawyer with instructions to mail it to me after her death."

"No way. Did you look inside?"

"I gave it a brief glance." Glad that Diane hadn't asked why Fiona had sent the record book to her, she plowed on. She'd cross that bridge later. "Now we can match the items in this ledger to the goods in the house. That will give us an idea of their original values and place of purchase."

"Great. Then we can set aside anything Fifi received from her father. If they turn out to be stolen goods, perhaps we can return them to their rightful owners." Diane indicated they should take seats in the two armchairs divided by a small accent table.

Keri complied and crossed her legs. "That's not the only reason I needed to see you. I've discovered where the missing objects in the house have gone."

"That's good news. Where are they?" Diane said with a curious glance.

Keri disliked having to relate this tale. Nonetheless, as Fiona's heir, Diane had the right to know. "Bob Underwood, who lives next door, had worked for Fiona as her handyman, and he kept a key to her house. I was driving by the other day and saw him crossing her lawn and carrying a stuffed pillowcase. When I went over to ask him what he was doing, I startled him into dropping the sack. Several pieces from Fiona's collection tumbled out."

Diane's jaw gaped. "What are you saying? He's been stealing from her?"

"Bob admitted he has gambling debts. He's been pawning the things taken from her house but plans to buy them back when he has the money. That pillowcase I brought has some of the items. They belong to you, now."

Diane's face paled as the implications must have sunk in. "Did he murder Fifi when she woke up that night and discovered him in her bedroom?"

Keri shook her head. "He said he'd only entered her house during the daytime when she wasn't home. He seemed very ashamed of his actions."

"That could have been an act for your benefit. Veronica across the street might easily have seen him. If he was lying, he could have murdered her as a witness."

Keri paused as a thought struck her. Veronica had held up a placard the day after Fiona's death that mentioned *criminals*. Plural, not singular. This could mean she'd seen someone else besides Bob entering Fiona's house.

"I think Veronica saw someone else there," she suggested, explaining her reasoning. "As for Bob's involvement, it's up to you if you want to press charges."

Diane's gaze hardened. "I need to ask for the key back. Or better yet, I'll have the locks changed. I should have done that right away after Fifi passed."

"I took the key from Bob. Here, you can have it." Keri got up to retrieve her tote bag and handed over the key, along with a copy of the *Sunny Grove Gazette*. She'd picked up several copies earlier. "My friend Pam's profile on Fiona has been published. It's a lovely tribute to her."

"Thanks. I can't wait to read it. Have you learned anything else since we last spoke?"

Keri related her visit to St. Augustine and her subsequent near-miss with a car.

Diane gazed at her in fright. "Oh, my God. You could have been seriously hurt."

"I know. I thought it might have been Garvan or his son, but then Hugh came to see me and said I was viewing things wrong." She repeated the gist of their conversation. "Even Tony suggested we look closer to home for the killer."

"I'm stymied, Keri. Who else could it be?"

"Maybe we should ask Cal for his opinion. Did he ever stop by to see Fiona on his own?" she asked in a casual tone.

"No. Why do you ask?"

"Just wondering if he ever did odd jobs for her like Bob Underwood. He might have noticed something relevant while he was at her house."

"He'd help her out when we were over with the kids. She would need a lightbulb changed in the ceiling or a dish brought down from a high shelf. Small things like that."

"I'm sure she was grateful. You know, I tried to reach you over the weekend. Did you guys go out on Friday evening?"

Diane must have read something in her expression because her shoulders went rigid. "I hope you're not thinking Cal was involved in your accident. Why would you even entertain the idea? He's been nothing but supportive to me and the children."

"I'm sorry. I'm merely concerned about your well-being. You didn't get back to me right away when I left messages, and I worried that something had happened to you."

Diane's jaw tightened. "If you must know, Cal was at his store that evening. He got home around eight and read to the kids before they went to bed."

That would have given him plenty of time to swerve at Keri in his car and then drive back to Winter Garden. "How about the night Fiona died?" she asked, hating this train of thought but needing to follow it through.

"He had a poker game and came directly home afterward. His buddies vouched for him to Detective Saunders."

Oh, yeah? The detective hadn't mentioned this to her, but he must have confirmed the timing. She'd still like to know the interval between Cal's leaving the card group and his arrival at home. If there was a gap, it would need further investigation.

"That's a relief. I just feel we both need to be more careful," she said, to mollify Diane. She didn't dare admit her suspicions aloud. Not only would that alienate her friend, but Keri wouldn't want Diane to say anything to Cal to tip him off.

Diane straightened. "Hey, I have an idea. Remember how you told me the same collector has been buying Fiona's goods on eBay? You could track him down."

"How would that help?" Was Diane trying to deflect Keri's attention away from Cal? Or was she using this as her own reason not to look too closely at him?

"The buyer and the killer might be one and the same. They could be searching for something that belonged to Fifi. That could be why her bedroom was ransacked, and your office was searched."

"You have a point. Have you ever heard of a man named Carl Franklin? Detective Saunders said his prints were found on my rear office door."

Diane shook her head. "It doesn't ring a bell. Who is he?"

Keri waved a hand. "Nobody I know. Anyway, I looked up the eBay buyer's address," she said in response to Diane's earlier remark. "It's a mailbox at a local UPS store. There's no way we could stake out the place and wait for somebody to come by to get a package."

"Could Detective Saunders obtain a warrant to see who rents the box?"

"I can ask him. I'd assumed the buyer must be a collector who either wants the goods for his own hoard or to resell them. But if you're right about the guilty party searching for something, what else could be so valuable aside from Fiona's ledger?"

"Cal asked me about the brooch Fifi had been wearing in that photo with her dad. It wasn't among her jewelry or in her safety deposit box. I figured she must have sold it, since I'd never seen her wearing the piece. But it got me wondering what she'd done with it."

Keri's interest sparked. "She may have noted its disposition in her ledger. Or maybe it's one of the items Bob stole and had pawned. Tell me, why would Cal mention this piece in particular? Fiona had lots of other jewelry that she'd worn to social events."

"He has an eye for value from his silver business. Maybe he recognized its worth."

Or maybe it was more than that. A jolt shot through Keri as she connected a couple of dots. Saunders had said Carl Franklin's prints were on the back door of her office. Why had neither of them realized Cal Foster shared the same initials as the jewel thief? Could it be mere coincidence?

Not in her book. A shiver chittered up her spine as Cal's odd personality quirks took on new meaning. He shied away from having his photograph taken. He never traveled outside the country, which would require a passport. And he seemingly had no other living relatives. Taken together, this could indicate someone who didn't want their identity questioned.

She remembered Diane had expressed her own suspicions about Cal's behavior. Perhaps she could use this angle to gain more information.

"Speaking of Cal's business, you had mentioned that he's been working late recently and that you were worried he might be seeing someone else. Have you resolved this issue?"

Lines creased Diane's face, and her shoulders sagged. "Not really. If anything, he acts more distant toward me. Something is on his mind that's eating away at him."

"Why not use the Find Me app to verify his location?"

"Cal wouldn't install it on his phone. He said he didn't want me spying on him."

That's not something a devoted husband would say. "Have you thought about swinging by his store to see if he's there when he works late? He could be burning the midnight oil to maintain his business. Some men don't like to burden their wives with work issues."

She'd rather believe this idea than her notion that Cal had something more dire to hide. However, she couldn't deny that he was looking more guilty by the minute.

Diane grimaced. "I'd have to drop the kids off at a neighbor's house first. How about this instead? Next time he's working late, I'll text you. You can run by his store to see if he's being truthful."

Keri agreed, if only because it would give her the opportunity to discount Diane's suspicions about infidelity. But she'd still need to be super careful, since he could turn out to be dangerous. She didn't care to end up in the same place as Fiona— six feet underground.

Chapter Twenty-Seven

Wednesday evening, Keri's phone rang just as she was leaving work. She'd lingered until six to complete her daily log, since tomorrow was a holiday. She wanted to go home and assemble the dish she had to make for Thanksgiving, but one glance at her caller ID showed this call didn't bode well for her plans.

"Cal is working late again," Diane said, her voice tense. "Can you run over to his shop to see if he's there?"

Keri's pulse accelerated as she calculated the distance and the traffic. The prospect of checking on his excuse for working late both unnerved and excited her. "He might be gone by the time I make it across town. Did he tell you what time he'd be home?"

"Nine-ish or so. I may drop the kids off next door and meet you there, but I don't want him to spot me. I'll wait in the parking lot by your car."

"You don't have to go to the trouble."

"Yes, I do. It's something I need to see for myself."

Keri had already thought of a valid reason to stop by Cal's store. She had stashed in her car a silver bread tray that she'd inherited from her mother. She'd ask Cal if he could fix the pitted surface and restore the tray to its former shine.

By the time she neared the exit to Winter Garden, rush hour traffic had lessened. Hopefully, this would be a quick visit to confirm Cal's story about working late. She didn't want to admit her other suspicions to Diane without talking to Detective Saunders first. He could do a more thorough background check on Cal and perhaps obtain a set of his prints for confirmation.

Meanwhile, she'd let Diane's family get through Thanksgiving before potentially disrupting their lives.

She'd followed GPS directions to Cal's store, and dusk had descended by the time she found a parking space in the nearly empty shopping center. She chose a spot near a convenience store that still had customers.

Her heart leapt with relief upon noting the Open sign in Cal's storefront window. She texted Diane that she'd arrived, and Cal appeared to be at work inside his shop.

I'm on my way, Diane wrote back. Be there in ten.

Intending to finish this quickly so she could go home, Keri grabbed her tray from the back seat and set off for Cal's store. A chemical scent hit her nose when she entered. Silver jewelry and serving pieces sparkled inside a series of lit display cases.

Cal stood behind the counter, wearing a stained leather apron over his street clothes. He was leafing through a stack of papers and glanced up at her entrance. His pasty complexion was as ashen as his gray shirt.

"Keri, what a surprise. What brings you to this part of town?" he asked with a friendly smile.

"I was in the area for a client and thought I'd stop by if your place was still open. I didn't realize you worked such late hours."

"I have a special project that's been keeping me busy. How can I help you?"

She unwrapped the tray she'd brought. "Are you able to fix this? I've used silver polish, but these pits seem to be ingrained."

"Let me take a look." Putting on a pair of special glasses, Cal examined the surface. "Have you noticed these dents? I can fix those along with the pitted spots and shine this up for you."

"That would be great." She gestured to a display case showing a gleaming silver coffee and tea service. "Did you restore this set? It's beautiful."

"Yes, that's an example of my work. I like to go to garage sales. It's amazing what people are willing to sell for a cheap price." He put down the tray in his hand, removed his glasses and peered at her. "I'll remove the imperfections, straighten uneven surfaces, and replace any missing parts. Then I'll polish the items and sell them as good as new."

"You have a definite talent. How about this pitcher on the counter? Can you restore something that is this tarnished?" she asked, hoping to loosen his tongue by getting him to talk about his work.

He pursed his lips. "In this case, I'll buff it down to its base metal, then I'll polish it to remove those pits and scratches. After the surface is smooth, it'll go through several rinses and pre-plating steps. Finally, I'll apply a heavy layer of silver plate using high-grade pure silver. That's what I'll be doing to your tray as well."

"What's the difference between sterling silver and silver plate?" she asked, having a vague notion. She knew sterling was more valuable.

Cal stroked the pitcher. "Pure silver is soft, so it's usually mixed with copper to make a stronger alloy. Silver plate, on the other hand, is made by coating base metals with either pure silver or a silver alloy via electrolysis. It doesn't last as long as sterling because the base metal will show through as the plate wears off."

"Is there much demand for your services? People my age aren't into this stuff like my grandparents were," she said, trying to get a sense of his success.

He shrugged. "I have a steady customer base. They either want to preserve their family heirlooms or fix them up to sell. I can help either way. Here, look at these other pieces I've done."

Cal opened an album and showed her before-and-after pictures. She was impressed by the difference between the dented, lopsided soup tureen in the "before" picture and the sparkling piece he created afterward.

"You're an artist. I'm impressed. Where did you learn to do this?"

"I went to a school in Manhattan."

"Oh? Was that where you met Diane?"

He gave her a thoughtful glance. "Yes. I was working at the

gym she'd joined after her first husband died. Her positive attitude and determination impressed me. We started dating, and the rest is history."

"What made you move to Florida?" she asked, meaning to find any inconsistencies in his story that would lend credence to her theory about him.

"Diane was close to Fiona, especially after her mother died. She didn't have any other relatives up north, and neither did I. It seemed the right thing to do."

"So you opened this shop after you'd moved here?"

"That's right. It was a good decision on my part. I was tired of the snow and ice and had finished my training. With so many retirees in Florida, I knew my business would thrive." He tapped her tray. "Anyway, how fast do you want this done? I can have it ready in two weeks if that works for you."

"Sure. There's no rush."

He stowed her tray with a ticket and handed her the other half. "Tell me, have you heard anything more from Detective Saunders? This case is hanging over Diane's head. The sooner we get back to normal, the better."

"He hasn't shared much with me."

"Haven't you been interviewing people on your own? What's your opinion?"

"I can't begin to guess," she said, as the hairs on her nape prickled. This turn in their conversation was making her edgy. To cover her unease, she moved further along to examine a tarnished lidded bowl with decorative trim that sat on the counter. As she touched the metal, she accidentally brushed a wrapped package beside it. Her eye caught on a red label.

Wait a minute. That tag looked familiar. She used a similar one to mark the packages she sold on eBay as fragile.

A glance at the printed address label sent a shockwave through her core. More dots connected in her brain, but she still couldn't see the whole picture.

Cal snatched the bundle off the counter and stashed it out of sight. "People often send me things for restoration through the mail," he explained. "I'll take care of this later."

His gaze met hers with unexpected enmity.

The walls suddenly felt as though they were closing in on her. Time to leave.

She tapped her watch. "Oh gosh, it's getting late. I have to go, or my roommate will wonder what's happened to me."

"I'll call you when your tray is ready for pickup," he said, his expression impassive.

"Thanks. I'll be anxious to see how it turns out." She exited to a tinkle of bells and fled to her car.

Diane stood waiting for her, arms crossed against her jacket. Sunset had arrived along with a cool breeze. "Thanks for doing this, Keri. What did Cal say? Did he give a reason for staying late?"

"Let's get in the car. I don't want him to spot us."

Keri unlocked the doors, and Diane slipped into the front passenger seat.

"He has a special project that's been keeping him busy," she said once they were secure. "I gave him the silver tray I'd inherited from my mother as an excuse to visit. He said he'd learned the restoration business in Manhattan."

"Yes, that's where we met. He'd already had schooling in metalsmithing and went for additional training after we started dating."

"It must have been a whirlwind romance if you married him six months later."

Diane sighed. "He was so kind to the kids and shared many of the same interests as me. It all happened so fast."

Keri pressed her lips together, thinking that Diane had met Cal when she was especially vulnerable. She must have thrown caution to the winds in marrying him.

She was about to pose more questions when Cal exited his shop. He glanced first one way and then the other, while they both ducked their heads. Then he strode toward his car. She'd noticed he had the irregular package tucked under his arm.

"See that bundle he's carrying? I thought the red sticker looked familiar. I got a closer look, and the label is mine. It's one of the items I've sold for Fiona on eBay. Cal must have picked it up at the mailbox."

Diane gasped. "Are you saying he's the buyer?"

"It looks that way, although I can't understand why he'd want those things."

"Let's follow him. If he's heading home, you can circle back and drop me off at my car. I'll buy some milk and say I ran out to get groceries."

Keri merged into traffic a few car lengths behind their quarry. They headed north toward a commercial district on Hiawassee.

"He's definitely not going home," Diane said shortly. "What could have brought him out here?"

"We'll soon find out. Let's hope he doesn't go too far."

Ten more minutes up the road, Cal turned into the driveway of a self-storage facility. She couldn't follow him through the gate, or he'd see them. Cruising slowly past, she saw him enter and veer left toward a series of units facing the fenced perimeter.

She drove around the block, angled back, and pulled into the visitor lot. Maybe Diane could think of some way to get inside.

"This could be where he works on his special project," Diane suggested, a hopeful note in her voice. "He might need the extra space. But then, why would he keep it a secret from me? I've searched through our checkbook and credit card statements and haven't noticed any strange entries."

Keri lifted her brows. She was surprised Diane had the gumption to act that way. Perhaps she was more attuned to things than Keri had thought. If so, it was sad how their relationship had devolved due to lack of trust.

"He might be paying for the facility through his business account," she said.

"That's true. I don't have access to those records. He keeps them at the store."

"How can we get in?" Keri asked. The single-story buildings had garage-like bay doors. Surrounding the complex was a wire fence. She didn't relish another break-and-enter scenario.

Diane gestured. "Let's go into the office. I'll say I was supposed to follow my husband inside, but he got ahead of me."

"Then why couldn't you call him to meet you?"

"I'll think of some excuse."

Keri shut off the engine. A sign out front said the office was open until eight.

Inside, a bearded fellow wearing jeans and a plaid shirt sat peering at a computer screen behind a counter. Keri noted packing boxes, sealing tape, shipping labels, and bubble wrap for sale in a corner display. Pine scent permeated the air, probably coming from that open box of Christmas decorations on the floor.

"Hello, how may I help you?" the man asked in a polite voice.

Diane gave him a loopy grin. "This is embarrassing, but I was supposed to follow my husband inside. I wasn't fast enough. and the gate closed. Can you please let us in?"

"Why don't you just call him to come and get you?"

"I tried, but his phone went straight to voicemail. He's not responding to my text, either."

"What's his name?"

"Cal Foster." Diane spelled them for him.

The guy typed it in and peered at his monitor. "You're right. He's the last entry. May I see your driver's license?"

"Of course." Diane handed it over.

The man nodded upon confirming her identity, then swiped the card and handed it back.

Keri held her breath that he wouldn't insist on trying Cal's phone for himself. But apparently, he was satisfied because a few moments later, they were inside. She drove around until they spotted his car outside an open bay door.

Keri slammed on the brakes and then backed up. She didn't want to park where he'd notice them. Hopefully, the guy in the office wasn't observing their movements either on any surveillance cameras.

"I'm going to notify Detective Saunders that we're here," she said. If her instincts were correct, this could go sideways. She didn't want to be caught unaware.

"Why?" Diane asked, giving her a perplexed glance.

"We have no idea what Cal is doing in there. It might be something we don't expect."

"Like what? This has to be where he's working on his pet project." Diane's expression brightened. "My birthday is next month. Maybe he's making me a surprise gift."

Are you really that naïve or are you denying the truth that's in front of your eyes? "Do you think?" she said aloud. "Regardless, it's better to be safe than sorry."

She left Saunders a message, then put her phone on silent mode and tucked it in her pants pocket. She'd lock her purse in the car so she could move around without hindrance.

Diane opened the door and swung her legs out.

Keri's pulse quickened. "Wait. Let me take a look first. Cal will be upset if he realizes you followed him."

"I don't care. He's been hiding things from me, and I won't stand for it any longer."

Bile rose in Keri's throat. This could be a bad idea. At least the office manager knew where they'd gone if they disappeared.

Outside, she locked the car and signaled for Diane to halt by the wall. She crept forward, her heart thumping so hard, she thought it must be audible. Finally, she paused and peeked around the corner of the bay door.

Astonishment made her gasp. The inside of the bay looked like an antique shop. All manner of goods and furniture crammed the large storage space to capacity.

Cal had unwrapped the package he'd brought along. Sure enough, it was the mother and child figurine she'd recently sold for Fiona on eBay. As she watched, Cal tapped the base and shook it upside-down. Then he stuck his finger inside the bottom hole.

A frown lit his face as he placed the object on a nearby table next to a set of jeweled porcelain eggs.

Other items looked familiar, too, like that Marcel Bouraine bronze sculpture, the Karl Springer lamp, and the walking stick with a hidden flask. They'd been listed in her inventory, along with that Hildegard Gunzel doll with blond pigtails and a fluffy taffeta dress. She'd wondered who would pay over two thousand dollars for it.

When Cal plucked a teapot from a carton, she cried out. That had been one of Fiona's favorites. His head jerked up, and he spotted her.

"You!" he yelled. He put the item down and plunged in her direction.

Diane stepped into view. "I'm here, too, Cal. You can't avoid me any longer. What is it you're doing here, and why have you been collecting all this stuff?"

A scowl marred his face as he regarded his wife. "Step inside, and I'll show you both what I've been working on."

Diane complied before Keri could yank her back.

"You, too," he told Keri, catching her by the arm and tugging her into the cavernous space. Then he thrust her aside, bounded forward, and slammed the button to lower the heavy door. It rattled closed, sealing them inside.

Chapter Twenty-Eight

Keri's fingers drifted to the cell phone in her pocket. Maybe she could send an emergency signal. Would she even get service in this place?

Before she could touch the buttons, Cal grasped her arm and jerked it upright. "What are you hiding in there? Oh, no. I don't think so." He snatched the phone from her hand and tossed it onto the concrete floor. "Why are you here? Were you tailing me?"

Diane stepped forward. "Leave Keri alone, Cal. I asked her to help me learn why you were working late so many nights. I was afraid you might be having an affair. We met at the parking lot for your store. We were about to leave when you came out and headed this way. Why haven't you told me about this storage unit?"

"You didn't need to know. It's a business matter."

"No, it's not. These are the things Keri sold for Fifi on eBay. Why would you want them?"

His eyes gleamed. "I'm looking for a piece of jewelry. Fiona couldn't remember where she'd put it, so I've been buying her knickknacks to see if she'd stuffed it inside one of them. It wasn't in any of her drawers that I'd looked through."

Diane stared at him. "What jewelry? Do you mean that brooch you'd mentioned?"

Cal gave his wife a derisive glance. "It's a priceless royal heirloom called the Sisi Star. Ten points of a star surround a large pearl, and each point is studded with diamonds. Two of these stars were stolen from a museum in Vienna."

"How did Fifi get one?"

"I figure Crogher must have bought it through his black-market connections and given it to her to sell. Either she couldn't get rid of it because the piece was too hot, or she decided to keep it for herself."

Diane shook her head. "I still find it hard to believe she acted as a fence for her father."

"Fiona was far from the lily-white image you had of her, Diane."

More jigsaw pieces fit together in Keri's head. Cal must have been searching for this jewel the night Fiona died. Her theory about him gelled into a horrifying conclusion.

"How did you discover Fiona still had the brooch?" she asked.

He switched his beady gaze to her. "She came into my store one day and showed me a copy of that photo. She admitted to having the jewel and asked if I could remove the diamonds to sell for her. However, if left intact, I knew the piece would be worth millions to the right buyer."

"You would recognize its value, wouldn't you? I assume your real name is Carl Franklin," Keri said brazenly, hoping to coax him to confess. "Detective Saunders lifted your prints from my rear office door. You must have slipped up then, didn't you?" She turned to Diane. "The detective told me Carl Franklin is a jewel thief from up north who's never gotten caught."

Diane made a strangled sound while Cal stepped between Keri and the bay door.

"I'd forgotten to wear gloves. That was my bad, but I figured nobody would connect me to some random crook. You're clever to have caught on. I assume Saunders doesn't know or he would have brought me in by now. Unfortunately, I can't let you share your conclusions with him."

A shiver chased up her spine. Did that threat include his wife? Or did he assume Diane would overlook his crimes?

"Were you looking for the jewel or the ledger at my office?" Keri asked, to keep him talking. She hoped Diane would realize their danger and attempt to reach the door.

"Both. I thought Fiona might have given you the brooch for

safekeeping. Or, if I found her record book, she might have made a note as to where she'd hidden it. When I said she could bring me the jewel, she had forgotten where she'd put it."

"Fiona did tend to have memory lapses in recent times," Keri said. She could very well imagine Fiona squirreling away a valuable jewel and forgetting where she'd hidden it.

Diane recovered her voice. "No wonder you wanted to look through the pieces I'd inherited. Are you… It couldn't be, but I have to ask. Did you break into Fifi's house that night?"

Keri cast her a relieved glance. At last, Diane was realizing she didn't know the man she'd married. They'd both need to use their wits to reach safety. Cal hadn't made any aggressive moves yet, but he wouldn't let them leave with this knowledge.

A frown creased Cal's brow. "I wasn't expecting Fiona to be home. *You* told me she was going out that evening. She must have changed her mind because she was asleep when I entered her bedroom. She woke up and screamed, and I panicked."

"Omigod. You murdered her in her bed!" Diane's pitch rose in hysteria. "All you cared about was your precious jewel. Was that why you married me? You knew about it even then?"

He shook his head. "I had no idea until she came to me to sell the stones."

"And then your greed took over. You meant to steal it from her. You're a monster," Diane said with a horrified expression.

He spread his hands in supplication. "I did it for us, babe. I would have used the money to buy prepaid college tuition for the kids and to pay off our mortgage. I wanted you to be secure. You're what I care about the most."

Good Lord, he seemed to truly believe his wife would ignore his actions. Her heart went out to Diane, who'd just learned the man she married was a criminal. Even worse, he had committed the ultimate sin and murdered someone dear to her.

He reached for his wife, but Diane backed away as though he had the plague. Cal still blocked the exit. Keri hoped he'd keep talking so she or Diane could reach the door.

"How did you get inside Fifi's house without a key?" Diane asked. "I assume you damaged the back door to make the cops think a robber had been there."

"I made a copy of the key she'd given you. It was easy for me to slip inside after dark. Once I silenced her, I staged it to look like a drug addict had broken in through the rear. I even emptied her bottle of sleeping pills to distract the cops. Keri's detective friend took the bait very nicely."

"Why did Fiona want you to sell the stones?" Keri asked, curious about that one point. Maybe she'd gone through her funds and needed a quick infusion of cash. She hadn't said anything to Keri about financial troubles, though.

He glowered at her. "She said she needed the money, and I didn't ask why."

"No wonder you offered to help me clean out the house," Diane said, staring at him as though he'd sprouted horns. "I can't believe you deceived me all these years. How did you avoid discovery? I assume you could still be convicted for your past crimes."

He smirked. "No one had an accurate likeness of me. My partner, Susie, was a makeup artist for the theater. She made sure I never looked the same when we did our heists."

"Is that why you were so good at making the kids up for Halloween? You must have picked up some of your partner's skills."

Cal's chest swelled with pride. "We made a good team. We would target small stores that had lax security. Susie and I pretended to be engaged and asked to look at diamonds."

"Did she distract the clerk while you stole the gems?"

He chuckled. "I used to love magicians as a kid and learned some sleight-of-hand moves. Susie would chat with the saleslady while I stuck a few diamonds up my sleeve. I'd substitute fake ones in their place. Then we'd thank the person and leave."

"That explains how you learned magic tricks to entertain the kids at birthday parties." Diane rubbed her hand over her face. "Was this how you could afford the down payment on our house?

It wasn't from investments, like you said, but from selling stolen diamonds. I'm such an idiot. I should have realized the mortgage was in my name only for a reason."

"I couldn't risk applying for a loan. The deed is yours, too. I've always looked out for you and the children."

"Did you quit the business before or after you met me?"

"I'd already retired and changed my identity when we connected at the gym. That's where I fell in love with you. You've made me a better man."

"Is that so? And yet, you lied to me all along." Diane wavered like palm fronds in a summer storm. A slight push would topple her.

"I never lied about my feelings for you. I'd do anything to keep what we have. You'll see. I'll change my name again. We'll take the kids and move away. No one will find us."

He was fooling himself if he thought Diane would agree. Keri stepped toward an accent table that held a set of onyx bookends shaped like pyramids. She could use one to bean Cal if he became aggressive. Keeping her hands behind her back, she gripped one in her palm.

Diane went mute, and Keri understood this must be a terrible shock to her. Would she be able to act against Cal if their lives depended on it? He probably hadn't attacked them yet because he was still hoping to sway Diane to his side.

She picked up the conversation. "When did Fiona catch onto you? She told me I was the only person she could trust. I assume that's because she'd become suspicious of you."

Cal glowered at her. "Her nutty neighbor, Veronica Batten, clued her in. She was into true crime shows and saw a feature about jewel thieves who'd never been caught. She and Fiona were friends, and Fiona must have told her enough about me that made Veronica put things together."

"Then Veronica shared her suspicions with Fiona?"

"I figured she must have gotten Fiona thinking about why I didn't appear in family photos and how I'd become so skilled at magic tricks. At first, I deflected her questions easily enough. But it made me more compelled to find the jewel myself. Afterward, I had to get rid of the nosy neighbor."

Diane made a choked sound. "No! You killed Veronica, too?"

He gave her an imploring look. "I had no choice. She would have ruined the life we'd built together. Veronica threatened to tell the press that I had murdered her friend. She wanted ten thousand dollars in return for her silence. Apparently, she needed the money for a hip replacement because her doctor wouldn't take insurance."

"What did you do to her?"

"I snuck over one morning and waited for her to come outside at dawn and do her yard work. Then I bashed her with a shovel. I loosened the wire on the overhead lamp to make it appear to fall on her head."

Diane had no rejoinder, and Cal's shoulders tensed. He looked as though he might be getting ready to make his move.

"Did you try to run me down in your car?" Keri asked as a last-ditch stalling tactic. Frustrated that she couldn't reach the door, she was careful to keep some furniture between them.

"I did. Too bad I missed. This might be messier. You don't have to watch, babe."

He lifted a sharp-edged letter opener from a nearby chest. It had a bone handle and a silver blade that gleamed in the harsh florescent lighting. His eyes hardened as he tapped the sharp blade against his palm.

Diane held out her hand. "Please don't hurt Keri. It doesn't have to end this way."

With a growl, he grabbed her arm and flung her against a tall bookcase. Diane hit it with a startled cry and fell to the ground. The bookcase toppled, pinning her in place. Keri didn't have time to see if she was hurt before Cal lunged at her.

She parried the thrust with her forearm, feeling a stinging pain slicing into her skin. Her breath came short as she hurled the bookend at him and missed.

With a sweep of his foot, he tripped her behind the ankles. She crashed to the ground with a grunt of surprise. Cal stood over her and plunged his blade downward.

She rolled sideways, bumping into a table. Items clattered to the floor, including a brass candlestick with a square base. She grabbed it by the stem and leapt to her feet. Her only chance was to disable him.

She swung the piece at his head with all her might. He turned at the last minute, and a corner connected with his cheek. It cut a gash into his flesh that dripped blood. Muttering a curse, he clapped a hand to his skin, looking dazed.

Keri rushed to pry Diane loose from the bookcase. "Can you slide out if I lift this corner?"

"I think so. Hurry, before he attacks you again."

"Get ready," she told Diane, grunting with effort as she barely managed to raise one edge.

Diane slipped her legs out from under the furniture and then Keri let it drop. Diane appeared intact but shaken as she stood.

Pounding sounded on the bay door. "Keri, are you in there?" Saunders's voice called.

"Yes. Help!" she shouted in return. Just then a roar of rage sounded from behind. She whipped around to see Cal coming at her with his hands outstretched.

He'd strangle the life out of her in seconds if she didn't do something.

Her glance fell on an antique desk lamp with a weighted bottom. This might work better than the candlestick. She grasped its column with both hands and swung the base at Cal as he neared.

The heavy metal impacted his skull. He staggered but didn't stop. With a murderous gleam in his eyes, he lurched at her once again.

Before he got her in a stranglehold, Diane reached the exit and punched the door's release button. Saunders and the site manager rushed inside as soon as the bay door opened. The detective's gun was out and aimed.

"Stop where you are and put your hands where I can see them," Saunders yelled.

Cal's rage deflated, replaced by a look of defeat. He glanced at his wife as he raised his hands in compliance.

Diane looked away, refusing to meet his gaze. She folded her arms across her chest and rocked herself, making little keening noises, like a child lost in the woods.

Keri's heart went out to her. She knew that feeling of being shattered, but Diane didn't have to struggle alone. She had Tony and her cousins a few hours away. Maybe now she'd be more open to approaching them. Their support could help her to heal from this trauma.

Saunders cuffed Cal and read him his rights while the manager addressed her.

"Are you ladies all right? Did he hurt you?"

"No. We're okay. Thanks for getting here in time." Keri's knees wobbled, and she leaned against a sturdy chest of drawers. "Cal is Carl Franklin, the jewel thief," she informed Saunders. "He's confessed to murdering Fiona and her neighbor."

A police car squealed to a halt outside. Saunders handed the prisoner over to the pair of uniformed officers who entered the bay, but not before Cal cast Diane a final glance.

"I love you, babe. I did it all for you."

Diane didn't respond. She appeared so frail that Keri moved to put an arm around her.

"I'm so sorry," she said as Cal was led away. "You couldn't have foreseen any of this." She hoped Diane didn't blame herself for not noticing the signs earlier, but why would she? Cal had been a devoted father until his past caught up to him.

"Fifi saw through him, and he killed her," Diane croaked.

"That's only because Veronica clued her in. She'd trusted him enough beforehand to tell him about the jewel. He fooled everyone, Diane."

Keri knew words wouldn't provide the balm to Diane's soul that she needed right now. Only time could provide that comfort.

They stood together in numb silence until Detective Saunders approached.

Keri separated from Diane and gave him a weak grin. "I assume you got my message. Thank you for coming so quickly."

He gave her an assessing glance. "I was on my way to bring Foster in for questioning when I saw your text. Did he harm either one of you?"

Keri lifted her arm. "I'm bleeding where he cut me, but it isn't bad." At least this wound appeared to be a surface cut that wouldn't require stitches. She found a linen napkin nearby and pressed it to her skin.

"I don't know what I'll tell the kids," Diane murmured.

Her remark triggered a surge of anger in Keri. Cal's actions would scar their lives forever. He didn't think of the effect on his family when he murdered two people and covered up his crimes, not to mention lying to Diane about his past. Nonetheless, she stifled her fury for Diane's sake.

"Maybe just say Cal loves them, but he wasn't the man you thought him to be. It won't be easy, but you'll get through it. And I'm here to support you in whatever way I can."

Diane regarded her with misty eyes. "I know, and I'm deeply grateful to you for being there for me. I couldn't face this alone."

"Ladies, I'll need statements from you both," Saunders said in his gruff tone. "It's late, and tomorrow is a holiday, so let's wait until Friday. Shall we meet at the station around ten o'clock? Right now, I'm more concerned about you getting home safely. Do either of you need a ride?"

Diane gave him a wan smile. "I'd appreciate a lift. My neighbor can drive me to get my car at Cal's shop tomorrow."

"Do you want me to come along?" Keri asked, worried about Diane being on her own.

"Tomorrow is Thanksgiving. I'm sure you have your own plans. And I'll need to break the news to the kids." Her voice ended on a sob. She yanked a tissue from her pocket and dabbed at her eyes. This would be a sad holiday at their house.

Keri felt helpless in knowing how to reassure her. "Please don't hesitate to call if you need me or just want to talk," she offered, feeling it wasn't enough but the best she could do.

Saunders returned with a first-aid kit from his car and applied a bandage to her arm. "Will you be okay driving home?" he asked her.

"I'll be fine. I'm just glad this is over." In a tremulous voice, she gave him a quick summary of Cal's confession. She couldn't believe they'd caught Fiona's killer. Tony had been right after all that the killer was someone close to them.

He gave her an appreciative glance. "I must admit that you've been helpful in solving the case. I hope now you'll be able to relax and enjoy your holiday."

"You, too," she said, grateful for his recognition and support.

She turned away, yearning to be with Zoey and her family. After this horrible evening, she appreciated her relatives even more. Tomorrow, she'd spend the day with them without worrying about what came next.

Her goal in opening the agency had been to give her clients more time to spend with loved ones. She finally realized that she needed to do the same thing for herself.

Chapter Twenty-Nine

"How was your Thanksgiving?" Pam asked when Keri and Lora met her at Central Park on Sunday for a stroll prior to brunch.

It wasn't their regular bimonthly meetup day, but Saunders had given permission for Pam to get an exclusive on the murder case. Her friend had been too excited to wait for the scoop and insisted they get together this weekend.

"I enjoyed being with my sister's family after the Wednesday from hell," Keri replied, finally able to relax with Fiona's murderer behind bars. She felt bad for Diane, though. She'd seen her at the police station on Friday when they'd both come in to sign their statements. Diane had looked exhausted, but her eyes held a determined glint. She was a survivor, and no doubt she'd recover from her husband's deceit in due time.

Keri realized Lora was speaking. "I went to my cousin's house on Thursday," Lora said. "Uncle Edgar told his off-color jokes as usual. What about you, Pam?"

She and Keri both knew that Pam chose not to go home for the holidays. Her parents always invited her, but she felt like an interloper in their lives.

"I covered the social scene," Pam said with a shrug. "It was a workday for me, like most holidays. Why don't we go to breakfast now? I need to take notes while Keri fills me in."

At the restaurant, Keri stared blankly at the menu, unsure where to start her story. She was still trying to assimilate all that had happened. She'd taken Friday off, briefly summarizing events over the phone to Purdy and Staz. They'd been stunned by her news but relieved the killer had been caught.

"Keri, are you in there?" Pam said, jolting her back to reality.

"Yes. I just have a lot to say and don't know where to begin." She waited until the server filled their coffee cups and took their orders.

"You said the detective had been on his way to question Cal when he got your message. What tipped him off?" Pam asked, poising her pen over a notepad.

"He'd interviewed Bob Underwood. Bob confessed that he had seen Cal entering Fiona's house when she was out. He'd been afraid to mention it because the cops might discover he'd been stealing from her."

Pam nodded. "I did some research after you revealed Cal's identity to me. He'd worked at the gym that Diane joined after her first husband died. He was a renowned jewel thief from Manhattan who slipped up on his last job and left behind a dry-cleaning receipt that fell from his pocket. Knowing the cops would be able to trace him, he retired and changed his name."

Keri picked up the thread. "After he met Diane, he went back to school to learn silver restoration. He'd already been trained in metalsmithing. Meanwhile, the trail for Carl Franklin had gone cold until now. The authorities have been able to link him to the jewel thefts up north. Saunders said he'd made the mistake of using his mother's maiden name for his new persona."

Lora shook her head. "It's hard to believe Diane lived with the man all these years without having a clue about his past."

"Fiona was blindsided, too," Keri reminded her. "They both thought his superstitions made him avoid social media and not want to travel. He rarely appeared in family photos, but then not everyone likes to have their picture taken. Plus, he was adept at magic tricks and he knew how to disguise people. He used these skills on his kids at Halloween."

She went on to relate the tale of the brooch. "Fiona asked Cal to remove the diamonds and sell them for her. I think that's the mistake she said she'd made. She had revealed to Cal that she had the Sisi Star, but then Veronica raised suspicions that he might be a jewel thief. Fiona got to thinking about his odd behaviors and realized her friend might be right."

Pam looked up something on her cell phone. "Listen to this. The Sisi Star was one of twenty-seven pieces commissioned in the 1800s for the Austrian Empress Elisabeth, whose nickname was Sisi. Each star could be worn as a brooch, pendant, or hair ornament. Some of them have been lost, but others are in museums or private collections."

"We still don't know what Fiona did with hers," Keri pointed out. "That might always remain a mystery."

"Nonetheless, my editor is thrilled by the prospect of an exclusive on the murder case. And she's greenlit my article on false cure-alls."

"That's great, Pam. You're heading in the direction you've always wanted." Keri truly felt happy for her. She deserved recognition for her journalistic skills.

The waitress chose that moment to deliver their meals. After she left, Lora waved her fork at Keri. "I still don't understand everything. Was Cal the one who trashed your office and tried to run you down in his car?"

"Yes, and he spread those nasty rumors about my business. I suspect that was to distract me from talking to people about Fiona. Oh, and I've realized what announcement Fiona meant to make at her birthday party. Enid had asked me about it when we visited Garvan."

"It wasn't that she planned to change her will to benefit PHEADA?" Pam asked.

"No. She did leave them a generous bequest, but Diane got the rest of the story from her lawyer. Fiona's memory issues made her decide to move into a life-care community. That's why she'd started selling off her antiques. Besides downsizing, she needed money for the facility's million-dollar buy-in fee. I gather this was the reason she'd asked Cal to sell the diamonds for her. The cash would have given her the lump-sum payment she needed. She didn't want to sell her house because she intended to leave it to Diane."

Sorrow filled her heart at the wasted lives, but at least the victims had achieved justice.

"I assume this means the PHEADA group is off the hook for her death," Pam remarked, sticking a forkful of veggie omelet into her mouth.

"That's right. However, Ossie contacted Detective Saunders after discovering that Winnie and Felicity have been embezzling money from the group. He's not only fired them, but he also eliminated the application fee for the artists."

Keri had contacted Tatiana, who reported that Ossie had cancelled her debt. She'd be willing to participate in future events now that the unjust charges had been removed.

Pam jabbed a finger at her. "That reminds me. I've confirmed that Maurice Chauvel, their vice president, is a silent partner in John Beekman's development company."

"No kidding?" Keri gave her a thoughtful glance. "Felicity had mentioned that Maurice might have an interest in Beekman's firm. It's more than an interest if he's a major shareholder. No wonder he wants to sway the city council decisions in their favor. It might be in the group's best interest for Ossie to ask him to resign."

Ossie hadn't been in touch, but neither had he terminated her contracts. She still believed in PHEADA's cause and would work with whomever was on the board after the fallout.

"What about Garvan?" Pam asked. "Is he in trouble for his conflict of interest in selling a product he manufactures? Or because of the Kratom ingredient?"

Keri ate a bite of whole wheat toast and washed it down with a gulp of orange juice. "He's revised his advertising materials to disclose the Kratom along with a warning about potential drug interactions. However, he could still have problems unless he advertises his tonic as a health supplement rather than a medical cure-all. Detective Saunders didn't admit it, but I think Garvan's operation may be under investigation by another department."

Pam tilted her head. "What about his son?"

"Hugh must have taken my advice because he quit the pain clinic. I understand he's now working at a doctor's office. And he never actually sold his dad's tonic to patients. He only handed out the flyers." She hoped he'd do well in his new position. Treated like a failure by his mother and aunt, he'd acted the part to spite them. Now he could forge a new path for himself.

Lora finished eating and rested her fork on her empty plate. "What happens next?"

Keri squared her shoulders. "I'm meeting Diane later at the cottage Fiona left me. The deed transfer is still pending but she's giving me a key."

"That's exciting," Lora said. "Can I come along? I'd love to see the place."

"Thanks, but I need time alone with Diane." She saw the disappointment in Lora's eyes. "Although, there's another way you can help me. How would you like to join my staff as our graphic designer? You'd be a great addition to the team, and your creativity would be an asset. We could use your skills as an organizer, too."

Purdy had been fielding calls from potential new clients ever since Pam's profile on Fiona had been published. She'd given their agency glowing reviews. With their increased business, Keri could easily meet the rent increase and afford another employee. Plus, Lora would have the chance to be more creative than at her current job. She held her breath waiting for a reply.

Lora's eyes glistened. "Do you mean it? You're not tired of my company?"

"I couldn't have gotten through all this without your support. What do you say?"

"I'd love to join your agency." Lora clapped her hands. "This is so exciting. But don't worry, I'll still look for my own place to live."

Keri realized she'd come to appreciate Lora's presence. It was nice having someone at home with whom to talk about her day and who cared about her.

"There's no rush on that score," she said. "Let's get through the holidays and then we'll talk about it."

Lora gave her a grateful smile and Pam grinned at them both.

Things were going to be fine.

Chapter Thirty

"I'm glad you could meet with me today," Diane said later that afternoon. She and Keri walked along a paved path leading to the cottage Fiona had bequeathed to Keri. Diane's face looked haggard, but she'd put on a blazer that gave her a professional air. Perhaps she'd renew her former real estate career.

"How are you doing?" Keri asked, concerned about her wan complexion.

"I'm good, thanks. It's strange not to have Cal at home. I can't deny that he cared about us, but in the end, he cared more about his own greed."

"Cal believed he was doing everything for you. That doesn't excuse his crimes, but he was sincere in his love for you and the kids."

"True. Anyway, today is about you and not me. Let's focus on more pleasant things."

Keri was happy to comply and swung her attention to the bungalow. Painted white on the outside, the house had a gray shingle roof and latticework on a covered front porch. Other homes crowded in on either side of the small lot. She still couldn't believe Fiona had left her this property. It exuded charm as well as a sense of history.

"I love it. It's adorable," she exclaimed.

Diane pointed ahead. "According to her lawyer, Fiona bought the place intending to reopen her business here but then changed her mind. The zoning is mixed use for commercial and residential."

Keri indicated the trimmed shrubbery and shady laurel tree gracing the front yard. "The landscaping is nicely done. I'll have to retain the lawn service."

A short flight of steps led to the porch, where she pictured adding a small table with two chairs and a potted plant for a comfy feel.

She took the key from Diane's outstretched hand. A thrill ran through her as she unlocked the door and stepped across the threshold. Inside, she faced a spacious living room. French doors at the far end opened to an adjoining dining room. Wide windows gave a street view from both vantage points.

"This is perfect," she said, charmed by the high ceilings, crown molding, and overhead fans. The living room fireplace had a mantel with built-in bookshelves on either side. They were painted eggshell white same as the walls.

Diane gestured to her. "Wait until you see the kitchen. It's been completely updated."

Passing through the archway, Keri stopped to admire the design. She ran her hand over the quartz countertop, admiring the snowy white color with gray accents. The tall white cabinetry, stainless-steel appliances, and gray tile floor also met with her approval. A window over the sink gave a side view of the yard, where a white fence bordered the neighboring properties.

"It's perfect," she said. "I couldn't have chosen better myself."

"What will you do with the place?" Diane asked with a warm smile.

Keri leaned against the counter. "I'm not sure. I could rent it out, or I could move here and rent out my condo instead. Or I could switch my agency to this location. It's not as visible as our spot downtown, but we don't rely on walk-in traffic anyway. Plus, then I wouldn't have to worry about future rent increases. Maybe I'll bring my staff here to get their opinions, but we'll have to decide fast. The deadline for renewing our current lease is next month."

She envisioned her employees occupying the living room as their workspace while she used the dining room for a private office. With glass French doors dividing the space, it was the ideal setup. But what about the rest of the house?

She peeked inside the two bedrooms that shared a bathroom with double sinks. Each room had its own walk-in closet, which was a nice feature. Near the kitchen was a narrow laundry area, but what she liked the most was the spacious Florida room in the rear with floor-to-ceiling windows. Keri felt a surge of excitement as she imagined filling it with a cozy seating arrangement and perhaps a minibar at one end.

Fortunately, the rear faced south so it wouldn't get the blazing afternoon sun. She might even add an open deck outside with a couple of lounge chairs.

"You'll need to give me a date for switching over the utilities," Diane said as they headed back to the kitchen. "I've been maintaining the basics while the estate is settled."

"Okay, will do." They discussed logistics until Keri spied some sealed boxes stacked in a corner. "What are those?"

Diane frowned. "Fifi must have dropped them off at some point. Look, your name is scribbled on the tops."

"Let's see what's inside." Curious to learn what Fiona had left her, Keri used the miniature Swiss Army knife she kept in her purse to cut one open. It held a set of dishes, while another one had glassware. A third box contained pots and pans. "Fiona thought of everything," she said with a sad shake of her head. How she wished her mentor could have been there in person.

"She was always generous that way," Diane responded with a warm smile. "You may have enough here to equip the kitchen."

Keri went to work on another box. "Look, these are teacups and saucers. Of course, Fiona would have remembered to include a tea set."

A gasp escaped her lips at the next item she uncovered. It was a ceramic teapot shaped like an English cottage. "No way. It's her favorite teapot. I thought it had gotten lost or perhaps Bob had stolen it. How kind of her to leave it for me. She used this one the most when I came over."

She lifted the lid. A black velvet pouch lay at the bottom. "Wait, there's something inside." She pulled out the tiny sack and opened the drawstring.

Her jaw dropped as she withdrew a star-shaped brooch that sparkled in the sunlight streaming through the window. Each one of its ten points had three graduated diamonds. In the center was a luminous pearl.

She could barely speak in her excitement. "Oh my God, I think we've found the missing Sisi Star."

Diane whooped. "Fifi must have hidden it here and forgotten about it."

"It belongs to you now." Keri held it out to her, but Diane waved her away.

"That's stolen property. What should we do with it?"

Keri gave her a thoughtful glance. "Cal said two of the stars were stolen from a museum in Austria. Assuming this is one of them, we could return it. If you're interested, I'll have Purdy research the recovery process."

"That would be the right thing to do. I think Fifi would be pleased to make amends."

"I agree. What about you, Diane? Do you have any plans going forward?"

Diane sighed. "I've contacted my attorney to file for a divorce. My intentions are to sell Fiona's house and mine and move out of town with the kids. It'll be better for us to get a fresh start elsewhere. Once things settle, I'll see about renewing my real estate license."

"I'm sorry you feel the need to leave, but I understand. Where will you go?" A pang hit her at the thought of losing a friend. Keri would miss their conversations.

"Sarasota is tempting." Diane's lips curved upward. "I'm told we have family there."

"That's a great idea. I'm sure Tony would appreciate having

you nearby." It would be tough resettling with two kids, but Diane was strong and resourceful. Keri had confidence she'd adjust to the change and likely even flourish on her own. And since she had relatives there, her kids could get to know their cousins.

"How about you?" Diane asked. "Are you going to slow down so you don't overwork yourself?"

Keri took a moment to respond. After her narrow escape, she'd realized life was short and that she was missing out on her future. She'd achieved her work goals. Now it was time to focus on her personal objectives.

She didn't want to be alone forever. Fiona was a prime example of that life. She'd given up her one chance at true love and presumably had always regretted it. Keri didn't want to bypass her own opportunities. She had been delaying getting back in the dating game for too long.

"I have been too much of a workaholic since I opened my agency," she admitted. "I've asked my friend Lora to join our staff as a graphic designer. With her pitching in to share the workload, I'll be able to cut back on my hours."

Diane's eyes crinkled. "Sounds like a good plan. How about your social life? Despite my bad experience with Cal, there are still some good men out there."

"I couldn't agree more."

"Oh, I see that look. Do you someone special in mind?" Diane asked with a teasing grin.

Keri smiled. "I can think of a couple of guys who might be worth the effort. Maybe I'll give one of them a call."

She was still smiling as she walked to her car after Diane left and she'd locked up the place. Then her cell phone warbled, and Purdy's face lit up on her phone's screen.

"Hey Keryn, you got a minute?" His voice sounded unduly excited.

"Sure, what's up?" She'd planned to go home and hoped this wouldn't require a detour.

"I've received a request from Gisette Emerson, the

Broadway actress who is slated to star in *A Little Night Music* at the playhouse in January. Unfortunately, her manager had an accident and will be out of commission for several months. It's too close to the holidays now for Ms. Emerson to find a replacement, and one of her media contacts mentioned you."

"Me? For what, exactly?" Keri opened her car door and slid inside.

"Ms. Emerson wants you to be her personal assistant during her stay in town. She's offered a generous fee."

Drat. Just when Keri wanted to give herself more time off, this dropped into her lap. "How generous?" she asked, thinking about the improvements to the cottage she'd like to make.

Purdy named a sum that made her eyes pop. Oh, heck. She could always reduce her hours when this job was done.

"Why not? Go ahead and book it for me. After all, how tough can it be to cater to a diva for a few weeks?"

THE END

Author's Note

If you're feeling overwhelmed, imagine how helpful it would be to have a personal concierge at your service. She could deal with your mundane tasks so you would have more free time. Or, she could help you plan a family gathering or a big party to reduce your stress. When I moved to Orlando, I could have used a professional to help me unpack and organize my house. But instead, I created Keri's agency and made her the character I'd want to hire.

As the concierge agency's owner, Keri can take on any job as long as it's legal and ethical. No task is too big or too small for her to handle. Along with the community where Keri lives and works, I also created the supporting players who may hinder or help her in subsequent books. Toss in a murder along with a distinctive setting, and there's a built-in cast of suspects.

As for Keri, she tends to be a workaholic and struggles to find the same work-life balance that she aims to give her clients. And now that she's ready to seriously date again, we'll have to see which guy she likes better—the chef or the doctor. She also needs to decide what to do with the cottage she inherited. It'll be fun to see which direction she chooses to follow next.

If you enjoyed this story, please write a REVIEW at your favorite online bookstore. Customer reviews are critically important in helping new readers find my work. It doesn't have to be lengthy. A few words on what you liked about the story will suffice, and I'd be infinitely grateful.

For updates on my new releases, giveaways, special offers and events, please join my reader list at NancyJCohen.com/ newsletter. Free Book Sampler for new subscribers.

Nancy J. Cohen

Acknowledgements

First, many thanks to my editor, Marsha Zinberg, from The Write Touch. Her expert guidance was critical to improving this story. I appreciated her honest remarks and valuable advice that set me on the right path throughout the book. She improved my sentence structure, caught repetitions, and pointed out when my protagonist acted too rashly. I learned a lot from her sage comments.

Next, I hold deep gratitude to my beta reader extraordinaire, Sally Schmidt, whose insightful observations smoothed out my story and strengthened my main character. Her viewpoint was critical in presenting this work in the best way possible for readers. She even caught typos that my editor and I had missed, proving you can never have enough eyes on a manuscript.

And finally, I wouldn't have finished this book without the input from my critique partners, Ann Meier and Janice Hardy. With their help, I shaped the story and refined it to a final polish. Belonging to a critique group is essential to my writing process, and I'm grateful to Ann and Janice for inviting me to join their partnership when I moved to Orlando.

Reader Discussion Guide

- If you could hire a personal concierge, what would you ask her to do?

- What did you think about Keri's motivation for getting involved in Fiona's murder?

- Regarding Garvan as a suspect, did you believe he was acting out of greed or resentment?

- How did you feel about Keri's interactions with the PHEADA board members?

- What did you make of Veronica's initial cryptic remarks and her subsequent death?

- Do you believe Bob Underwood should be punished for his crime? How do you think his wife will react upon hearing his problems?

- Was it wise of Pam to join Keri's incursion at Garvan's factory, or should she have dissuaded her friend from being too impulsive?

- Who did you believe might be the murderer and why? At what point did you begin to suspect the actual killer?

- What did you think of Purdy and Staz's personalities? Will Lora fit in when she joins the agency staff?

- How would you say Keri changed by the end of the story?

Nancy J. Cohen

- Which love potential do you like best for Keri—Chef Jarek or Doctor Matt?

- What do you think Keri should do with the cottage Fiona left her?

- Did the story's pacing hold your interest?

- Are there any unfinished story questions you wanted answered?

- Do you like this sleuth enough to read more stories about her?

About the Author

Nancy J. Cohen writes the Bad Hair Day Mysteries and the Keri Armstrong mystery series. Her books have been named Best Cozy Mystery by Suspense Magazine and have won the Readers' Favorite and FAPA President's Book Awards, the RONE Award, the Royal Palm Literary Award, and IAN Book of the Year. She's placed first in the Chanticleer International Book Awards and third in the Arizona Literary Awards. Her nonfiction title, *Writing the Cozy Mystery,* was also an Agatha Award Finalist. Active in the writing community, Nancy is a past president of Florida Romance Writers and Mystery Writers of America Florida Chapter. When not busy writing, she enjoys reading, fine dining, cruising, and visiting Disney World.

Follow Nancy Online
Newsletter – https://nancyjcohen.com/newsletter
Website – https://nancyjcohen.com
Twitter – https://www.twitter.com/nancyjcohen
Facebook – https://www.facebook.com/NancyJCohenAuthor
LinkedIn – https://www.linkedin.com/in/nancyjcohen
Goodreads – https://www.goodreads.com/nancyjcohen
Pinterest – https://pinterest.com/njcohen/
Instagram – https://instagram.com/nancyjcohen
BookBub – https://www.bookbub.com/authors/nancy-j-cohen

Nancy J. Cohen

Books by Nancy J. Cohen

Keri Armstrong Cozy Mysteries
Murder Pays a Call

The Bad Hair Day Mysteries
Permed to Death
Hair Raiser
Murder by Manicure
Body Wave
Highlights to Heaven
Died Blonde
Dead Roots
Perish by Pedicure
Killer Knots
Shear Murder
Hanging by a Hair
Peril by Ponytail
Haunted Hair Nights (Novella)
Facials Can Be Fatal
Hair Brained
Hairball Hijinks (Short Story)
Trimmed to Death
Easter Hair Hunt
Styled for Murder
Star Tangled Murder

The Drift Lords Series
Warrior Prince
Warrior Rogue
Warrior Lord

Science Fiction Romances
Keeper of the Rings
Silver Serenade

The Light-Years Series
Circle of Light
Moonlight Rhapsody
Starlight Child

Nonfiction
Writing the Cozy Mystery
A Bad Hair Day Cookbook (Companion to Bad Hair Day Series)

Order Now: https://books2read.com/NancyJCohen